Acknowledgements

This book is dedicated to my family.

For going from the laughing to the supportive during the process of my writing and putting this novel together.

Thank you and love you all.

I'd like to also dedicate this book to two special people. My father, Stafford Dulake, who at 87 beat Covid, and to Julie's father, David King, who was lost this year to Cancer, he will be sadly missed.

Chapters

1. Discovery of bodies
2. Party two days before
3. House investigation
4. Incident Room
5. The Shard
6. Emma Interview
7. Mick Jones
8. Scandal eight months before the party
9. Breakfast at Caroline's
10. Searching for the truth.
11. Awakening
12. Funeral
13. Play Bunny
14. Burning
15. Building renovations
16. Black ledgers
17. Confrontation
18. Arrest
19. The Visit one year on

Prologue

"I do." Caroline replied, smiling straight at Charles as he gazed into her eyes, a smile beaming across his face like never before.

Charles asked Caroline to marry him not that long ago. Now less than three months later they stood before the registrar in this wonderful Tudor mansion. Both sets of parents had been present, along with a few friends from both sides of the family. Caroline's parents struggled but managed to put together this magical event with an autumn theme extremely quickly. Ice sculptures were set on each individual table with extravagant red and gold arrangements filling the reception ballroom.

Caroline and Charles had enjoyed a whirlwind romance, ending in the inevitable conclusion, marriage. They first met at a symphonic metal Nightwish concert in The O2, having been allocated seats next to each other that night when Caroline was out with her friend Louise. Charles had chatted to them throughout the evening and ended up insisting he take Caroline along with her friend Louise home. It had been a late night after he'd treated them to VIP lounge passes after the show.

So here was Louise, now standing beside Caroline as her Maid of Honour along with Sophie and Olivia, her best University friends, as bridesmaids. All the girls back together having the time of their lives.

They'd already discussed wanting lots of children, and the sooner the better. Alas, that wasn't to be. Charles's fertility problems had become apparent to them within months after an operation which should have been a routine procedure. Leaving them both distraught and frustrated.

Having thrown everything into the business to take their minds off the situation, they became extremely wealthy, but were never blessed in the way they both desperately wanted.

Until now…

TRIANGLES

Chapter 1.

Discovery of bodies

Detective Chief Inspector Mac Savage sat at his desk. It was another hot summer's morning. The sun was already shining through the massive large windows. His office was immersed in rays of sun all around the room, making it too bright to concentrate and distracting him. He'd already got up and adjusted the blinds to stop the light from interrupting his thoughts and work. Still, the temperature in the room was beginning to rise steadily as it had done in the early mornings for many weeks now. It was already warm enough for him to need to turn on the air conditioning, and it was whirring away in the background as he worked. The hot summer days over the past weeks were starting to cause vast problems with water supplies throughout the country. Many cases of heat exhaustion being reported daily as vulnerable people were exposed to the extreme heat.

Having made his way into the office early. He'd just finished the paperwork from the recent case his team had solved. Mac wanted a quiet day and hoped that it might be, giving his team a well-deserved long weekend off. They had worked tirelessly on the case, without an actual break for weeks. The case long and strenuous and also frustrating at times. Eventually, through sheer hard work and determination and meticulously sifting through endless evidence, they consequently got their man.

There was a knock on the office door, startling Mac out of his thoughts. He looked up as the door slowly opened and Jim came in carrying two large cups of coffee.

"Morning, Guv, bought you a latte just as you like it." Jim said.

"Thanks, mate, good to know someone around here takes a bit of notice." replied Mac, with a grin on his face.

He knew that everyone on his team appreciated how he liked his coffee. It still never surprised him at the level of detail they took, not only in their daily detective work but little things like that.

"Thought you'd be here, Guv, your wife on earlies this week, right?"

Bloody hell, how does he know that, Mac thought to himself before replying.

"Yes, of course, I forgot you've got an excellent memory, or just a clever bastard?" he grinned, knowing Jim was the clever type.

"Just an excellent memory and I've been told I'm really clever as well, Guv." Jim smirked, as he handed over the coffee.

Jim was part of the team that Mac had been culturing now for nearly four years, and he'd admired Jim's attitude and honesty from day one. Jim kept him on his toes a lot and questioned choices he'd made on numerous occasions. Some he appreciated and others he didn't, but they made him think about his decisions and subsequently his actions.

Mac had joined the force not long after leaving school at eighteen. He hadn't gone through the full rigmarole of the officers starting out nowadays, volunteering and becoming a special officer. He was old School taught. He'd worked his way up from a constable to where he was now over the last twenty years. An imposing man with thinning grey hair, he was just under six foot and now in his early fifties. He'd been married to his childhood sweetheart Cara for thirty-two years and continued to think the world of her. Cara still looked beautiful in his eyes, despite the advancing years.

They had two grown-up children, Lizzie, who was now twenty-six and Ronnie twenty-nine. They both left home and now working in jobs well below their capabilities unfortunately. Their University debts alone would take them years to pay off, but both seemed happy, confident and doing their own thing.

Mac had a difficult and sometimes painful childhood. His father had been beaten by him occasionally, and he'd been associated with the notorious Kray twins back in the sixties, when Mac was a mere boy and consequently, had been in and out of prison for money laundering and GBH. His mother had a hard and worrying life bringing him up, trying to make ends meet. Mac as he entered his teenage years he was determined not to follow his father's footsteps, but instead try to make the world a better and safer place. Subsequently joining the force when he could.

Detective Jim Wilson on the other hand was much younger than Mac. He still needed to learn a lot but possessed the energy and enthusiasm to be able to do it. He was good looking, kept fit and regularly worked out in the gym as and when schedules allowed him the time. He lived in a rented flat along with his fiancé Jackie; they'd been engaged eighteen months and had been organising a wedding for the following summer. The preparations were well under way and it was getting excitingly closer to that special day for them both.

"Hopefully it'll be a quiet one, Guv," Jim added.

Mac laughed. "Bet you by lunchtime we're on another case. So we better make the most of it."

"You're probably right," Jim replied, "but that's why we love this job."

Sure enough, less than half hour later the phone buzzed.

"Morning, Mac."

"Morning, Sir" Chief Superintendent Willis was on the other end of the phone.

"Excellent result on that Benson case, Mac. Well done."

"Not an easy one. Sir, but the team worked hard, and we got the right result."

"Glad to hear that. You'll be needing them on top form for the case I've just been contacted about. Just got a call concerning an incident out on the estate at St George's Hill."

"Okay, what do we have, then? I've given the team a few days off as a recompense, but I'm sure that they are willing to cancel any plans so we can deal with it Sir."

Mac glanced at Jim, who already had his phone in his hand and messaging the team via a 'What's app' group set up for everyone's convenience. Jim nodded back to Mac while waving the phone to let him know he was on to it.

"That's sorted, Sir, what are we looking at?"

"They've described this as a double murder, one female and one male simultaneously. So, here's the interesting part. Dr Banks thinks at the moment that both murders were committed with just the one bullet. Also, Mac, I must warn you this could be tricky. The female victim we believe to be Caroline Stone, wife of the multi-millionaire, Charles Stone. They own a company that's just signed a contract with MI6. He also has a contract with the government to supply all the security systems for the refurbishment of the Houses of Parliament. Their house is in a secluded area out in the Surrey countryside and full of high-tech equipment. So let's hope you'll be able to sort this one out quickly and quietly. I'll text you over the address."

"Thank you, Sir," replied Mac as he ended the call.

"Ok Jim, we've got an interesting one. I take it you've informed the team?"

"Yes, Guv, I've managed to get hold of them all and they're on standby waiting for address confirmation."

"Good, I've just got the text from Willis, so forward it on to the others. "

"Ok, got it boss, thanks."

They left the office and headed down to the garage. Quickly getting into Jim's Ford Hybrid, they drove quickly along the river through to the A3. Traffic was as heavy as normal for the time of the day, Mac gave permission for Jim to use the emergency system when necessary as they sped along the crowded streets of South London and into the green of the Surrey countryside.

Approaching the estate's entrance, the security barriers were maned today by two officers, unlike normal uneventful days, when they were left unattended. The two officers patrolled the entrance barrier, stopping every car going in and also coming out. Mac wound down the window as they approached the office's, warrant card already in his hand.

"Morning Sir," the female officer greeted Mac. "The house is straight up the road ahead and the road you're looking for is the fourth on the right."

"Thank you, officer." Mac replied.

They drove past several substantial and expensive mansions, each one an impressively designed individual and a statement of wealth and stature in its own right. Mac thought to himself, what did people do for money in this neck of the woods? Finally, on reaching the address, a marked police vehicle was partially blocking across part of the driveway that lead up to a modern contemporary building. They drove slowly up to the open large electrified wooden gates which were connected to large substantial and imposing brick pillars. Two officers were positioned on either side, waving them down. Both Mac and Jim showed their ID cards and were waved through. The drive was long and tarmacked, with pine trees and rhododendrons running along both sides. Mac and Jim somehow weren't surprised when they saw the house, its size and architectural design was astonishing. Someone had gone to a lot of trouble to get this looking so appealing and individual. Being mainly built of glass It captured the sunlight with sheer perfection from every angle. The early morning sun gave an impression of a laser light show on it, glittering light bouncing off the glass in every direction. Mac's first thought though as they approached was how much their window cleaning bill must be!

The gardens looked vast, but they were well manicured. Someone loved this garden and had taken great pride in keeping it this beautiful. Several large oak trees sat on lawns leading off to a large lake in the distance. Rhododendrons seemed to enclose the entire garden, except where a summerhouse was prominent, a large wooden structure that looked as though it had been there for years. Beyond the summerhouse they could just about see a wooden jetty extending from the veranda into the lake. A small rowing boat was tethered secured alongside it, bobbing and swaying gently in the water.

At the main house entrance, there were already half a dozen police cars, along with an ambulance and three forensic vans, and people were busy. Everyone being dressed in their hazmat suits carrying on like a fine turned Swiss watch. The scene preservation well-coordinated and underway, insuring, that no potential evidence could become contaminated.

Detective Baker had been notified of Mac's arrival by the officers from the front gates. He'd been the first detective to arrive at the house an hour or so earlier along with two other squad cars. But also well aware that Mac and his team had been notified about the incident, and he'd been expecting them.

"Morning, Sir." He greeted Mac, before turning to acknowledge Jim with a glancing nod and smile. "Good to meet you both again."

"Morning, detective, what have we got?"

"Well sir, the cleaners arrived here around eight and were clearing up after a party this weekend. They were apparently hired to come in early today as the client who was due to leave early this morning on holiday. We believe a young cleaner went into the main bedroom and came across the two bodies on the bed. She ran out screaming and her boss heard her and called us. What she'd witnessed horrified her obviously. Two bodies slumped on the bed, one on top of the other and both covered in dried blood."

"Ok," Replied Mac, turning round to check that Jim was taking notes as they spoke.

"First signs are they were having sex when the trigger was fired, possibly kissing at the time of the killing. We also think at this point that one bullet continued through both the female and the male victim's heads, fired at point blank. There's no sign of more than one shot. Forensics turned up half hour ago and have been upstairs for a few minutes. We also believe there was a party here on Saturday afternoon and evening containing numerous guests. The catering boss was here cleaning up the last of his company's equipment and he informed us that there were approximately two hundred and twenty guests plus his staff of twenty here."

"That's going to make life more difficult for the forensics." Mac replied, not envying the task ahead of them. "Well, better let me and my team take a look. We can start sorting out this mess then and find who done this." Mac realised his team were now arriving parking up in the driveway.

Putting on their usual white forensic hazmat suits, Mac and Jim walked over to the large front door.

The entrance itself was a two metre wide door, made from English oak, with a solid steel core, pivoted in the centre like a revolving hotel entrance, though it moved with far more grace and style. Large stainless-steel handles allowed the door to rotate open smoothly on its hydraulics. Although today it was being kept open by a colossal marble statue in the hallway. Normally the Stones would have used a face recognition panel, pre-programmed and set into the large oak frame of the doorway. This would activate the door, opening it without the need for keys. The white epoxy resin floor reflected the sun as it radiated through the large glass panes either side of the entrance. Some eight metres in front of them was the bottom of a formidable staircase, made from oak and glass, a wide contemporary and impressive feature as you entered the ultra-modern house.

Standing at the bottom like guards on parade were two uniformed police officers. With orders from Dr Banks allowing only the forensic technicians up at present, so they urged the detectives to wait for permission to go upstairs. Mac knew they wouldn't wait long.

Mac and Jim both took the few moments to observe the white hallway. Modern works of art were mounted all around on the walls. Some contemporary pieces by a local artist, exotic plants and fruit trees in stunning chrome pots stood about. Just beyond the staircase was a lounge area where they could see white coated forensic pathology team working methodically, dusting and photographing everything. Turning back towards the stairs. Mac noticed him standing on the first landing. He noticed Jim was glancing down through a two inch thick pane of glass into a large tropical fish aquarium. The tank itself was the size of the stair landing area and the glass walls giving the illusion it was floating completely in mid-air. And an impression they supported the whole staircase. The treads of the staircase were also solid glass, making the fish tank visible from every side. There were several exotic species of fish swimming amongst coral and plants, a stunning collection that any tropical fish enthusiast would envy of. From the landing you could go left or right, up onto the balcony or straight across, which took you back down into the lounge area. You could also see across to the kitchen on the right and the pool area around to the left. The entire area was completely open, light and yet seemingly homely and inviting. Towards the far end of the lounge and to the poolside were extensive sets of bi- folding glass doors, opening out onto the patio area outside and the immaculate garden. The pool was long but narrow obviously designed for swimming lengths rather than as a family pool for children; it stretched along one side from almost the front of the house to the back.

"Some people have too much blooming money," Mac commented to Jim as he walked up the first flight.

"You're telling me, Guv, any chance of a pay rise?"

Mac just looked at him with a smile. "You wish."

"Up to your right, sir." came the voice at the bottom of the stairs. Turning , they noticed a member of the forensic team coming out of one of the bedrooms and was beckon them to follow him.

"Ok, on our way," Mac responded.

The glass treads felt and looked odd to Mac, as if he was walking on the air. Reaching the top, with its glass balustrade wrapping the balcony, Mac and Jim took in the scene. The landing was spacious as it wound its way in a horseshoe form. It allowed you to walk around to the far side, where two further bedrooms and bathrooms were situated. They could see down into the lounge, kitchen and pool areas from the balcony. The plush cream carpet it felt like walking on cotton wool, with its long pile, so thick it left footprints behind in it. The main bedroom door was open, the thick frosted glass doors slid back totally into a pocket in the wall, therefore disappearing completely from view. Where the doors had been, there was now a large opening as though the bedroom instantly turned into a spacious extension of the hallway.

Mac stopped at the doorway to capture his first impressions, getting his thoughts together about the room and what could have happened in those tragic moments. He noticed the complete silence before he stepped fully into the room, but as he entered he could clearly hear Doctor Banks talking to her assistant in a normal voice.

"Hi, Mac, please, come in, but be careful." River hadn't even glanced up from her work as she spoke to Mac.

"Thanks, hi River, how are you? What do we have? I assume you know Jim," Mac turned and nodded towards Jim who now entered slowly behind Mac.

"Hi Jim, we should stop meeting in these circumstances."

Jim was a little taken back at that, even though he'd been ribbed at work for some time about how Dr Banks, had a soft spot for him. Jim might well have asked her out if he wasn't already engaged to Jackie. They had to cancel their wedding last May because of the Covid 19 outbreak and would have already should be married to the lovely lady couple of years.

Mac really didn't need to ask River. He could see in front of him the bloodstained bed. On the near side of the bed lay two bodies. From where he stood he could make out their heads, both covered in blood, and that they were both completely naked. The sheets stripped back.

Pathologist Dr River Banks had been friends with Mac for the past twenty-odd years. Now in her early forties, she was still single, despite one long standing affair. Her olive skin, with long black natural hair and amazing figure made her a popular lady. She'd had been introduced to Mac on a case back in the early years of her career, a murder case that became her first assignment after leaving university and joining the force. She had excelled in her first case, Mac knew at that point she would become one of the best in her profession. It was ten years later that River was promoted to the lead role, above her male colleagues, who to be fair, seemed to take the appointment very well. No one questioned the decision, and she lived up to her reputation as a fantastic and diligent lead forensic scientist. They continued to work to together, resolving many cases throughout the years. It had been quite a while before Mac realised River wasn't her actual name. It's a nickname given to her at school by the other pupils when she was young. Her given name was in fact Anahita, a Persian word meaning River, and her school friends picked up on this and thought it funny. So River became her name.

The male victim was lying beneath the female. Both faces looked badly disfigured from where the bullet had penetrated through both their skulls. Leaving a hole in the back of the female's head along with the traces of recall splashes of blood from her skull. The silk bed sheets were splattered with blood, consistent with a close, fired bullet. The blood staining continued through to the pillows, which were now completely soaked through after the past few hours.

It's been quite a while since the murders, thought Mac, looking around inspecting the room while also taking in the bodies in front of him.

"What can you tell us at this stage, River?"

"Well, as you can see, the female body, who we believe to be that of Caroline Stone, was approximately mid-thirties. We believe the male was approximately in his early twenties. We have yet to identify him, but there's no distinguishing marks on the body other than a small tattoo on his right upper arm, that of a scorpion. The female's head we suspect would have been on top of his, so they were probably kissing as they were murdered. Her head, we believe, slid down after the shooting to where it is now. The blood draining out of her face and penetrating the bed. There would have been a fraction of a second where she might have felt the gun. But the killer didn't hesitate at that point, otherwise it would have got far more complicated for them. The head, as well you know, is a heavy part of the body, so it ended up sliding down to this point. This would also explain the amount of blood everywhere, his face, the sheets, pillows and then soaking through to the carpet.

"His face is completely unrecognisable. I think the only way to identify them both from the Coroner's point of view would be though DNA testing and dental records. But having said that, I'm almost certain the female was Caroline Stone.

As you can also see, the entrance wound is through his nose area and we believe the exit wound is through the back of his skull. Which would imply that they fired the bullet from a slight angle, not straight down. We must wait until we can move the bodies back to where they were initially before I can give you more details on that one. I'm glad you're here, Mac, to see the scene first. We were just going to move the female's head back to where she would have been as the gun fired. I'll then be able to work out the exact angle of the bullet entry. Which, in turn will give us a more accurate trajectory of the bullet and where to look for it. Before we do that though, just in case, please note the genitals of both victims. There're signs of male semen on the sheets as well as female ejaculation fluid. They both climaxed almost simultaneously, her possibly seconds before being shot or even as she was doing so. One of her legs, as you see, is still on top of him. So it's obvious she was on top and could well have been leaning forward kissing him as both of them climaxed." She paused for a brief second.

"Neither victim would have been aware of the presence of anyone else approaching. It also seems to imply to me why that precise moment was waited for, or why did the perpetrator choose that instant, maybe to let them have their final pleasure before killing them both, who knows? One shot, two victims, quick and easy as far as they were concerned," River explained in her usual professional manner.

"So, you think this could be someone who knew them both? Not just a grudge against one of them?" Mac was beginning to wonder which one was the actual intended victim or if they were both meant to die.

"Probably suggests that to me, but that's your job, Mac, not mine."

Jim listened to everything that was said, taking in the bedroom scene while they talked. Opposite the bed was a long glass wall which Mac walked over to with Jim. Standing, looking through the glass, they could easily see the ground floor space, the lounge area and kitchen, everything except the pool. The ground floor still looked a complete mess from the party, glasses left half full of wine and beer littered all over the place. Everything was being carefully photographed, emptied, and bagged up, then numbered and packed in plastic boxes. All would be thoroughly tested and with luck would be of use later for evidence.

Jim shifted his attention back to the room where he was standing. Above the glass was a row of blinds which could only be seen from where he stood, close to the windows. When he stepped back, he could see that they were set into a recess across the entire width of the glass and the entire wall. He then noticed that beside the usual cupboards and dresser there was a very large Television on the wall to his right. It must have been at least 85 inches, and a dominant feature of the room. Walking further around past the television, he came across a recessed area which was almost invisible when you stood in the room. Jim turned and noticed an opening and a small chrome door, at the top of a staircase leading down to the ground floor. Again, a pocket door was left open and drawn back into the wall unseen unless you looked especially for it. Next to that was another chrome door that became more apparent as he took a couple more steps. It was the lift to the lower levels.

"Over here, boss, there's a lift and a staircase down to the lower floor." He called loudly to Mac, standing a few metres away from him now and out of his sight.

"Ah, yes," said River. They both travel down to the lounge, also into the garage in the basement. I've got two guys taking fingerprints off the lift as we speak, so please don't push the button to call it. It's on the ground floor in the garage, and believe it was when we got here. Knowing both of you, you'll appreciate the garage area."

"Why's that?" asked Jim.

"Expensive cars," River gave a sarcastic chuckle. "Boys and their toys." she whispered under her breath and carried on with what she was doing.

Jim continued to stroll round the room, moving through another door to the right of the bed which led to the en-suite bathroom. It was a vast wet room with yet another glass panel going across most of the rear wall with entrances at each end. A state-of-the-art power shower lay beyond the glass, the controls being set into volcanic lava rock, which then continued all the way around the sides of the room. Jet black, they looked spectacular, with inconspicuous lighting set amongst the uneven textured wall. There were the usual Jack and Jill basins. Along the far wall along were his and her toilets, something Jim hadn't encountered before. The lighting came on automatically, making the room look amazing with the shadows from the rocks and the reflection from the glass. Jim felt as if he'd entered Aladdin's cave.

"Far too much money," he said to himself under his breath.

He returned through the other bathroom door at the far end, round the back to the other side of the bedroom. Mac and River were there still, they were discussing how someone could have entered and yet not have been noticed. Along with assessing the bodies positions and the plausible scenarios that could have occurred, River's camera was constantly clicking away as they spoke.

"You know what I'm going to ask next," Mac said.

"Yes, the time of death. Well, I'm assuming at the moment that it would have been probably between 11pm and 3pm, give or take an hour on Saturday. But we will narrow that down later with further tests."

"Thanks, River. Call me when you're done. I'd like my team up here as soon as possible to look round, to be able to get a good feel for this one."

"No problem, Mac. I'll call you soon."

Mac and Jim left River and her team working while they continued round the rest of the upstairs rooms. The landing was fascinating, a large horseshoe around the other bedrooms, from the other side you could see down to the pool area and the lounge. They encountered person working in practically every room as they walked round. Dusting and photographing all the evidence, no matter how insignificant it seemed to them at this point. There was surprisingly only three bedrooms in this magnificent house. Although it had been designed with such love and care, each with an en-suite similar to the master bedroom, but nowhere near as large, all containing the dramatic volcanic rock on one wall and the glass features.

Jim's phone rang, interrupting Mac's line of thought for a moment.

"Boss, the team are standing by to see the murder scene. They're all outside waiting,"

They went down the stairs and outside to where Mac's team had gathered, waiting patiently to be briefed before entering the house.

Chapter 2.

Two days earlier.

Caroline Stone had been preparing and organising a surprise fiftieth birthday party for Charles for a few weeks now. She'd been thorough working out every little detail exactly and a lot of thought about how important it was to get everything just perfect. She needed it just right for her loving husband, today of all days, especially with her news.

On the day of the party, she couldn't have hoped for better weather. The sun was out yet again, as it had been for the past couple of weeks. According to reports, it was going to be one of the hottest summers of recent years. Yet the temperature was now ideal for what she'd organised. The caterers arrived early to set up the hog roast on the spit. A large BBQ had also been set up alongside the hog roast, a fridge full of steak, sausages, and burgers, all handmade waiting to be cooked and eaten. The best joints of meat fresh from the market had been brought in to satisfy the numerous guests. Round tables and white chairs were being unloaded from lorries and set out around the patio area. Some on the grass to help cater for the vast number of guests. Bright white table cloths were spread across them and silver cutlery and crystal cut wine glasses were placed around each table setting.

The chairs were set up, complete with brightly coloured rainbow covers, making the setting vibrant and welcoming. The band had arrived and were setting up on the makeshift stage, doing sound checks and getting the microphones set to get the best volume and acoustics. The band was a four-piece band that played a wonderful variety of rock and other popular songs, including a playlist that Caroline had specially asked for. Lydia, Caroline's hair stylist, recommended the band to Caroline when she was cutting her hair one afternoon a few months back, after seeing them at a charity ball.

Champagne and wine were being loaded into the chillers ready for later when the guests started to arrive, beer and spirts all being carefully arranged on a makeshift bar. The whole place was a hive of activity, and things were all coming together as she'd planned.

Caroline decided it was time to prepare herself, so left them to it for a couple of hours. She'd only distract them if she stayed, and she was fully confident that the manager was well on top of things. She went down to where she'd parked her Tesla in the underground garage, then driving down the long driveway and into town for her manicure and massage, part of the process of getting ready, and something she really enjoyed before a party or any other occasion.

She arrived back at the house three hours later and was very pleased with the way things had progressed. A professional drone pilot, Sophie, arrived and was setting up a racecourse for the boys to enjoy and show off their control and racing talents. Caroline promised Sophie that whatever the guests smashed up, she'd pay for. Which was the only way to persuade Sophie to bring the drones along. Especially with all the new laws that had been introduced about the use of these types of racing drones. Sophie had set up four Go Pro Karma race drones fully charged and was testing them round a quite easy course. Which went off into the distance, round the oak tree and boathouse, outlining the lake as they buzzed and flashed round the grounds. Caroline watched her for a moment, admiring her skill and precision as they flew around at such high speed, just feet off the ground. She even thought she'd like to have a go, but then thought better of it as she turned and walked away.

Now I had better get myself ready, she thought, so went inside and up in the lift straight to her bedroom. Laid out across the bed was her dress and underwear. All designer and matching in a deep crimson red, something she knew Charles would go crazy for. He'd always got so turned on by her wearing red.

She showered and applied her makeup, although in this heat she didn't want too much on, just a nice deep red lipstick and blusher and foundation. Slipping on the red thong, adjusting it to make sure it concealed herself after her waxing earlier, Caroline slid into her dress especially designed and made for tonight. It felt cool as the lining was made from a material that helped with the heat. Caroline not only looked a million dollars, but sexy as hell. The dress hugged her body perfectly, giving just the right amount of support for her ample breasts leaving a low cleavage. It was a full-length dress, but with the splits on either side, it gave the impression that she wanted, showing her toned legs and thighs to perfection. Any man with a wife dressed like that would be proud to have her on his arm, she thought, seeing her reflection in the full-length mirror.

Caroline wasn't expecting Charles home for another hour, and the guests were now starting to arrive, being greeted at the front entrance by two smartly dressed men in black suits and ties. Glancing at their invitations, the parking attendants directed the chauffeurs to where they could park. Taking the keys to cars that arrived driven by other guests in order to valet park them. Caroline had arranged for a marquee for the chauffeurs to rest in and where they waited till the party finished. They also had supplied with a very generous amount of refreshments of non-alcoholic drinks and sandwiches, along with a TV showing the latest blockbuster films and programmes on Netflix and Prime.

Two traditionally uniformed waitresses were handing out champagne to the guests as they mingled and made small talk. Canapes had been scattered throughout the house, along with nuts and crisps. Charles had sent a text, saying he was on his way and would be there in forty-five mins, earlier than expected because traffic wasn't as heavy as he anticipated. This increased the pressure on Caroline, so she hurried over to the band, whose singer announced the update to the now increasing number of waiting guests. She then walked precariously on her high stilettos down to the garage via the outside steps. Past the cascading water feature and standing just outside the garage door to wait for Charles to appear. Caroline text back telling him to go round the back because a surprise was waiting for him there. The rear drive was longer, but the only way in and out of the garage. The front entrance drive led only to the front door for normal everyday visitors. This was mainly because of a problem with the planning, when they tried to get the entrance for the garage. The architects had rerouted the drive round the back of the lake and between the rhododendrons and trees.

She knew when Charles was approaching. The garage doors slowly started to slide back, which meant only one thing, his car was within a few hundred yards. The gates were automated and would pick up the transmitted signal from his car when it passed a certain point along the drive. The number plates would be recognised, initiating the doors. Caroline saw his car come into view from quite a way away because of the gap in the bushes. He'd driven his new Tesla Roadster, the alternative model of electric sports car that was capable of getting to sixty mph in under three seconds. Charles had pre-ordered one and liked to drive around and show it off when he could. Several times risking speeding tickets but having been lucky to avoid one until now, to her knowledge. He pulled into the garage and onto the vehicle turning circle, jumping out to look at this stunning wife now standing waiting for him, Charles was excited and happy. After walking away from the car, it started to automatically rotate. A charging platform also began to move up under the car until it connected to the terminals located under the vehicle, turning it around fully charged and ready for the next time he wanted to take it for a spin. The charging unit was one of Charles's latest inventions and is the first proto type that Tesla and other companies have taken a great interest in.

"Happy birthday, darling!" she called out as Charles was getting out of the car.

"Thanks, love, My, God you look so sexy, it must be my birthday!" He replied ironically, though delighted with what he could see in front of him.

"Why, thank you sweetie, I feel sexy too. I've arranged a few guests to help us celebrate your birthday, sweetheart. We can play later; I've got a really pleasant surprise for you."

Caroline put her arms around Charles' neck and gave him a long deep kiss. His hands began to wander down over her bum, giving her a gentle squeeze on both cheeks before she broke the kiss off. Then Charles turned his gaze directly towards her, and her ample and partially exposed breasts, he'd always found them extremely tempting and was beginning to feel horny.

"Mmm, looking forward to my present later. This dress looks bloody amazing and something also tells me it cost me a fortune. Something you're worth every penny of.

"It sure did. I had it designed and fitted to get just that reaction from you. By the feel of it, I'm right. so let's get the most out of it." Caroline could sense the arousal in Charles when they stood this close together.

"I hope you're going to be thrilled at what I've planned for you later. So enjoy the evening first and have some fun with our friends." Caroline looked at Charles, who was now standing with a big grin across his face.

Together, hand in hand, they walked back up the granite steps leading to the patio, Charles' hand continually on her bum caressing her as they walked. When they got to the top of the steps, they found all the guests standing quietly waiting for them, all their glasses fully charged with champagne. The band instantly burst into, Happy Birthday, with everyone happily joining in, many were in tune, others not so harmonious, but it was loud and well appreciated by Charles. Looking genuinely surprised and also shocked by the number of people who had gathered together for his birthday. So many of their friends and colleagues were present which was amazing. Old friends he'd known for many years not only through his success with Stones PLC, but his golf and country club friends too.

The party got under way, with the food going down a real treat, the hog roast being a big hit, some guests even asking about the company's services for their own future events. The meat was going down a storm, as it always did at a barbeque, the salmon and other fish tasted superb and so satisfying for the hot sticky weather. The drink, of course was the most welcome, and consumption was going extremely fast as the hot weather took its toll. Guests who remembered to bring along their swimsuits were enjoying a great time in the pool. Even though some costumes were, to say the least, skimpy, some less embarrassed girls went topless. The dancing continued in full flow, many of the more older guests dancing as though performing in the latest Strictly Come Dancing programme. Trying to show that they learnt the Waltz many years ago, Others ridiculously funny the more the drink flowed.

Caroline and Charles mingled with friends and family throughout the evening, speaking to all their guests and particularly pleased to see them not talking shop. Some prominent and influential people had come along, which pleased them, as they appeared to enjoy the relaxing and stress-free atmosphere. MP's were laughing and joking along with each other, something that Charles found ironic as they were on completely different sides of the political scale and come Monday would be arguing and contradicting each other as they stood on opposite sides in the House of Commons.

The drones in the garden were fewer in number. One crashed straight into the oak tree on the other side of the lake and one drowned in the middle of the water. This led to one guest was ridiculed for his extremely poor control of a piece of technology that he was allegedly an expert in, especially being as he worked for the company that had created the craft in the first place. The drone was supposed to be uncrushable. Sophie, however just got out another one from her bag and rigged it up resignedly.

At ten, the firework display got under way. Caroline didn't have any input towards the sequence of the fireworks but had given instructions to the company to use the red, white and blue of the company's logo if they could. And to be imaginative in the display. So, with great appreciation they watched as it started colouring the evening sky. The fireworks were set to music so they sparkled and detonated with fine timing, the track ThunderStruck roared from the loud speakers, it exploded across the night sky, continuing a full fifteen minutes lighting up the sky, and would have rivalled any New Year's Eve display in any city across the world.

The hog roast by this time was almost gone, only the carcass turning slowly on the spit over the red hot embers. The pig was dripping fat over a traditional wood fire had looked amazing and was being continually covered in sea salt during that time, causing the crackling to taste as good as you'd hope for, the chef obviously having done this many times and got the art down to perfection. The dessert tables were getting low, only a couple of partially eaten gateau's remained. Long gone were the profiteroles, and the trifle, even though most of the guests were now full and people had eaten enough anyway. The catering staff continually cleared away most of the plates and cutlery, discreetly making sure guests were also topped up with drink as and when they needed it.

The band kept things moving while performed an impressive set. Playing a variety of music to please all the age groups present and managing to get some of the guests dancing and fooling around to the music. There were of course some more traditional dances thrown in along the way. The birdie song and YMCA went down extremely well. Unfortunately, they had finished their allocated time and had packed up during the firework display. Much to the disappointment of the guests still sober enough to put a dance routine together. However, the Sonos took over from them simultaneously and was playing a random selection of music from rock, pop, dance and disco. Most were still singing along, or more like shouting out the old classic songs as the enjoyment continued into the evening warmth.

Charles and Caroline had been chatting with lots of heavy drinking for the past hour with Henry and Emma Thorburn. The scotch and brandy were taking there toll on both men.

Henry had always been a fit man. He was average height with now silvering hair, still long and thick enough to make him look younger than his forty-one years. He was one of those men who always presented himself well, having natural charm and manners that made you think he might be a member of the royal family. He possessed the mathematical mind of a genius that left people perplexed when it came down to figures. He had become the main accountant manager for Stones' PLC when Charles needed a cash injection to expand the company's production. Henry had heard about Charles's expansion plans through a bank connection while at a charity banquet to raise money for under-privileged children. So, having done a lot of background research on the company and the prospects of it, he approached Charles with a proposition to invest the necessary funding and invested several million into the Stones' company. Something Charles had dreamed of and could only have hoped for.

Henry wasn't the type to put money where it wouldn't benefit him, he only invested in companies that he would get back profits over the coming years, but he used his money with expertise and extensive knowhow.

Henry was the only son of a very wealthy family, so raising that sort of money from his late father's estate had been easy. He'd had now been with Stones PLC company for the last six years as chief accountant and a director of finance. Charles, on the other hand, was the creative brains behind the technical and innovation side. His mind always seemed to be creating newer and more advanced technology, ideas that just seemed to come out of nowhere with him. They made a perfect team.

Emma was in her late twenties now, somewhat younger than Henry, but that didn't seem to matter to either of them. She was average height, blonde with a slim, attractive body. She'd been brought up as an only child after being adopted by a middle-class couple in Taunton. Emma was told of her adoption when she entered into her early teens by her adoption parents, Jenny and Joe. Something she always had an inkling about being adopted, but didn't know why she felt that, she just did, being actually told late one evening over a birthday dinner. What she didn't know according to them was that her birth parents had died two years after having her. They'd been out one evening and been knocked over by a drunk driver. The driver, however, never came forward and never was caught. Her upbringing consisted of a run of the mill secondary education in a lovely Taunton school.

Emma excelled in all her subjects, and she was considered by her teachers to be an inspiration to other pupils. Her favourite subject at school, though, had been technical drawing, considered a somewhat strange subject for a girl back then, but Emma always enjoyed designing and creating new things. She managed to get into university at Bath with straight A's in her A levels and a scholarship from a local architect firm. Her first encounter with Caroline was through FineDesigns Architects, the firm she'd worked for back then. Caroline liked her design ideas for her new home and insisted that Emma be the lead architect of the project for them. With lots of hard work over the eighteen months the house became even better than the Stones could have imagined. Consequently, Caroline found Emma enough work through her recommendations for Emma to decide it was time to move to London and start her own company. She'd been busy ever since.

Henry had met Emma two years before at another one of Caroline's impromptus small parties. They seemed to have been attracted from the first time they met. So Caroline and Charles weren't at all surprised when they married so quickly the following year. A full Catholic wedding along with the full religious service, and a great reception nonetheless afterwards at the local country house near their home. After a wonderful and exhausting time, Henry and Emma decided it was time to leave. Henry needed to catch a following afternoon to Berlin, an important meeting with the financial directors of a project of offices and luxury apartments in Dubai.

Henry had done everything he could to get out of it, but to no avail, so still business always came first with Henry.

Emma had driven to Charles's party. She hadn't felt particularly good that morning. So had decided that she'd be better off driving and not drink on this occasion. Drinking was something that she rarely did, anyway, especially when out with Henry. She drank mainly at home, when she knew that people couldn't judge her and criticise her for it. So was always the designated driver whenever they went out. She felt safer when driving or in a cab. She asked for their car to be brought around to the front entrance however, as the car approached Caroline appeared and insisted that a driver should take them home. She realised Emma looked exhausted. She was, though she tried to persuade Caroline she was ok, but to no avail. Caroline kept on insisting, so with great hesitation Emma decided to accept the situation. She told Caroline that she'd pick up her car first thing, as she needed to drive Henry to the airport after lunch. Caroline gave her a friendly kiss on the cheek and hugged her before waving them off for the night.

Caroline returned to Charles, who had now come in from the garden and was getting some water in the kitchen. He still, however, held a whisky glass in one hand as he moved towards Caroline and kissed her passionately on the lips, slipping his hand under her dress. Caressing her and slowly moving his hand up her inner thigh and her pussy. Trying to ease her legs open gently, he found some resistance as she told him to behave and wait just a little longer.

"Now, I think it's time we gave you your special birthday treat. I've a couple of very exciting things for you to enjoy," she whispered in his ear. "So why don't you go up and get ready. My sweet. You know what you have to do to please me, don't you? I'll be up when I've locked up and checked all the caterers have gone, so we are completely alone."

"Oh yes, I do!" he replied, grinning.

Charles immediately turned away from her and headed towards the stairs, picking up the whisky glass and bottle before reaching them. Whisky in one hand and a bottle in the other, he gradually climbed the clear glass stairs. Looking pleased and excited.

Caroline gave him a few minutes while she walked around the ground floor of the house, closing the bifold doors, turning out the lights and locking up the house as she went. She spoke to the manager of the cleaning company, making sure he had a full set of instructions on what needed to be done on Monday when they came back to finish the clearing up. Thanking the remaining couple of staff members who were still outside tiding up, she insisted they could leave, promising them a good tip in their wages for all their hard work.

She slowly climbed the stairs after her husband, as her anticipation grew along with her excitement about what was now going to take place and what she was going to tell Charles on his birthday.

Chapter 3.

House investigation.

Mac spoke to the team assembled on the front drive. They were waiting for instructions and to start their inspection of the ransacked and soulful house for themselves.

"Ok, guys. You will be cautious and thoughtful, and be fully aware of the situation in there, so let's not contaminate evidence, please. I want you all to see the victims first. The main bedroom is at the top of stairs on the right. Dr Banks wants to remove the bodies shortly, therefore we need to be thorough and precise, recording everything quickly. I also want to know everything about the house, full layout etc, there must be plans submitted at the council offices. Danny, you're on the grounds. Go and have a chat with the officers searching the gardens let me know if you've found anything relevant. Also arrange for a diver team as soon as we can, we've yet to find any weapon and over there's a fucking enormous lake. Hunter, you're on your usual assignment, get the footage of the security cameras and also the door sensors. Together we must go through that frame by frame. I want to know when people arrived and when they left. Kara, you're on the caterers, and the staff employed here over the last few days. For a party of this magnitude, there would have been days of preparation and planning. Eli and Jude, inside there's a lot of evidence being bagged. Have a word with the forensic guys, see what they have. We need to try establishing exactly what went on here. Check for drugs, amphetamines, and anything unusual. Were there any disagreements during the night? Were people arguing or such like? Find out."

Mac gave them a briefing on the scene in the main bedroom and a basic assessment of his thoughts up to that point, but also not wanting them to feel they couldn't contradict him. The more he made them think about the possibilities, the better they functioned as a team, which was only a good thing. Mac knew full well that he didn't really need to brief them. But it was part of his routine, and he always went through it despite that.

"We'll be meeting back at the office at four. We'll set up the incident room then. That only gives you four hours, guys. So let's use it to our advantage, so let's get going."

Mac's phone rang, it was River. to let him know his team had only an hour to inspect the bodies before she would move them back to her lab stressing the obvious to Mac, as she normally did, not to touch anything and tell her when they'd finished. He thanked her and hung up the phone.

"Ok, people, River has given us a brief window to see the victims. So, I suggest we go there first. Also, let me know if there's anything River could answer before she removes the bodies."

Mac followed the team through to the hall, but instead of going upstairs again he went through to the lounge. Gazing around the room before him, he saw a white soft leather Italian looking sofa's in a sunken seating area. In front of the sofas stood an open gas and marble fireplace, with an elegant and warming appearance even before it was lit. In the centre of the sofas was a wooden oak tree stump table between the lush seats. The table was a complete contrast of design but stood out as an authentic piece of architectural design. It was highly polished and looked amazing, as the roots and trunk twisted around, making it an eye catching feature, years of growth giving character in the roots. He looked across to the right. The kitchen had high gloss, white units, an island section with the latest hob and gadgets fitted. Fitted with a black galaxy star speckled worktop, it was like looking into the depths of space. The resin floor from the hall continued into the kitchen, there seemed to be no breaks or joint lines as it flowed continually and cleanly from one room to the next. Mac saw the pool off to his left, an extensive garden with the patio beyond. In front of him, there were impressive bi-folding doors with seamless glass that bought the garden into the house, making it look as one with nature. The entire house seemed to blend into becoming part of the garden and vice versa. Large plants in discreet pots were placed in corners and alcoves throughout the total area. Mac then realised that the house was far cooler and more comfortable than the heat presently outside. Someone had gone to extreme lengths in designing and making this house a special and peaceful place to live and relax, and it worked.

    He walked out of the house through the patio doors onto the granite stones of the patio. The tablecloths were all bundled up with most of the containers still inside, presumably to be sorted when they were elsewhere. The diving team had arrived and Danny was giving them full instructions as to what Mac wanted. Finding the murder weapon was always top priority, so Danny was pleased to be in charge of this operation. Mac stood and watched as they suited up with air tanks and wetsuits, they moved slowly, but methodically into the lake, starting at the most likely place the weapon would have been thrown in, if at all. He knew it would take a while, so Mac left them to get on. He knew that if there was anything to report Danny would let him know soon enough.

Continuing his walk round the patio he saw fire pits, all with burnt-out ashes almost to their rims. The black rattan furniture had their plump cream cushions spread around, they'd been on the night of the murders. Members of the forensic team were working their way towards them, but they were still busy with other items. Glasses and cigarette trays were spread all over the place, Mac wondered what sort of cigarettes had been smoked. River would at some point certainly inform him, knowing they would come across the usual, more easily obtained drugs.

Continuing round the side of the house and down the same garden steps that Caroline and Charles used a couple of days before. He came across the garage, situated directly beneath the house swimming pool. The garage door was open and three white suited figures were busy dusting for fingerprints on the two Tesla cars and a Lexus 4x4, all with a personal number plate and all polished to perfection. It seemed like a car showroom just for them. Jim appeared from behind the Lexus UX Hybrid.

"Hi, Guv. The lift is just over there, it goes to the pool area and then up to the main bedroom, as River explained. That would have been really handy for our murderer and also for the Stones if they were late for work or needed to go without disturbing the rest of the house." Jim was smiling because he knew that Mac to his knowledge had never been late for work in his entire career.

"Forensics are still working on the inside of the lift. They say the garage door was open when they arrived, but we're not sure yet if it was the case when the cleaners came. I'm going to speak to their boss shortly."

Mac went to check the lift, round the corner at the end of the garage, out of sight from the main floor area where the cars were parked on their respective turning pads, with timers so that ten minutes rotated automatically ready to be driven straight out.

"Find out if the lift was on this floor when the bodies were found by the cleaners, please Jim," Mac said.

The two of them left the forensic team to do their job for now, there were a lot of things that needed their attention elsewhere. Jim stopped, turned back and looked into the garage as if he'd just noticed that something seemed missing and rather odd.

"Guv, I think there's something missing from the garage. The end bay over there beyond the Lexus." Jim was now pointing as he started walking back to a space with what looked like a bike support framework bolted to the wall.

"What are we looking for?" Mac was also now walking back.

"You see over here, guv, on the wall there's a jacket, right? It looks like a Harley Davidson leather jacket with that crest on it. Well, where's the bike? If the bike's not here, which it certainly isn't, then where is it and more to the point, who has it? Also, there's another hanger here for an additional suit. Most bikers would usually have more than one suit, in case theirs gets damaged or the weather is bad. Plus, there seems to be no helmets anywhere in sight."

"Yeah, excellent. So let's find out where the bike went. What the bike is to start with. Find the make, model, and what other clothing there should be in the garage. Ask Eli to sort that out.

Think we really need to talk to Mr Stone, don't you?" Mac knew that Charles Stone was their prime suspect, but then thought that could also be too obvious. This guy seemed to have everything except a faithful wife, it seemed.

"Yes, guv," Jim responded.

"Let's get the team working and incident room set up back at the offices as soon as," Mac's voice now had become more authoritative and firmer.

Kara had found the contact details of the caterers, left in the kitchen drawer along with a list of suppliers, and was now on her phone talking to the boss of Munch and Stuff Ltd, the upmarket catering firm Caroline had hired for the occasion. She arranged a meeting with Bobby Guy, the director, at nine am the following morning at his offices on an industrial estate in Epsom. For now Kara just informed Robby that they needed to speak regarding a piece of jewellery.

Hunter came across the hard drives for the security cameras while he investigated the house. He always carried wire, and heat, detecting equipment on jobs like this. Knowing from experience that some cameras are difficult and awkward to locate. Then he found a small discreet vault room on the landing, behind an exquisite abstract painting by Anselm Keifer, brightly coloured and a bit weird. Hunter though had actually stood and admired it for a couple of minutes before he realised it was distinctly mounted on a separate frame, standing off the wall, making it look as if it was a raise and fill panel, something he'd often seen on cupboards, doors, and panelling. On one side next to the art work stood a large yucca plant, behind that a small pad that just looked like a doorbell. Putting his finger up to it, a small red light appeared at the top of it. He'd had seen this type of activation panel before and realised what it was instantly. To open it, he needed a fingerprint of the person who could activate it. Hoping that would be Caroline, now lying dead on the bed in the other room, he called River on the phone to explain his difficulty and shortly she emerged from the main bedroom.

The print from Caroline did not work, but she also had a print she'd lifted from a whisky glass on the side table in the bedroom. As the print made the pad beep a couple of times and turn to flashing green, the painting slowly started to move. A small door moved effortlessly and slowly in complete silence until it reached a full 100 degrees. As the door came to a halt, there was a flash of light and the room before them transformed into a brightly lit and cool room. Red laser beams flashed across the opening in front of them and Hunter instinctively put the print back onto the pad. The beams stopped, giving a full green light on the pad.

The servers stacked neatly behind the door were large HPE Store Easy 1860 rack system, two in line and stacked together fitted with 10TB of storage capability to each one. A cooling system had been installed, as would be mandatory for such impressive equipment. The room gave out a gush of cold air when the doors swung open, it made Hunter shiver and step back for a brief moment. The extractor outlet went up through the ceiling, and Hunter assumed, outside through the roof. The room also had a smaller vault to one side. This one Hunter would have to work on, and it might take some time as the panel on the outside was completely different, from that of the first door. It needed an algorithm combination of twelve letters and numbers. He knew full well that this could be practically insoluble without prior information on the sequence and half hoped that Mr Stone would shed some light on to its combination, when they found him, that was, otherwise he might be trying to solve an unsolvable problem. Only time would tell.

The detectives re-emerged from the house three hours after entering, though Danny was still wandering round the lake in the gardens overseeing the dredging, he'd been surprised by the number of golf balls they were dragging out. Watching as the search went on, he realised that he'd be there a while longer yet. Mac called him to let him know he wanted him to stay, wait until they finished and keep him informed if anything turned up.

"Ok, you guys let's head back to the offices in a moment, but first tell me what we know so far. Make sure on the way back you grab a bite, it's going to be a long day."

He wasn't sure that the team had had enough time to do a proper search and to go thoroughly through what was required at this stage. But with Charles Stone being the prime suspect, he decided to put together the evidence they had so far, to get a picture of the night events at the house. He's main train of thought was to find Charles Stone, to question him about the murders at his home and to find out why his wife Caroline was naked and dead in their bedroom with another man.

"Ok. Until we have a full list of guests, let's start by interviewing the people we know were there. Eliminate as many people as possible, and quickly. We need obviously to find Charles Stone, get him in for questioning. Check airports, docks etc, he could be on that motor bike missing from the garage. Jim and I will go to interview Henry and Emma Thorburn when we've had a debrief later. We think they were the last people to see Caroline and Charles together and might know something we don't." Mac looked at Kara, expecting an address to be given him. He wasn't disappointed.

"Right, guv. They live at the address I've just texted you and Jim." It wasn't far, which was a good thing as traffic started to build up in the rush hour. Kara had got hold of the address from a book in the coffee machine drawer, along with what looked like a complete list of names, and contact numbers of all their guests attended the party. So her main job was, as far as she thought, complete. Usually there would quite a lot of work for her, running around trying to sort through a list this long. But, to her surprise, it was all here in black and white. She found out later that it was the emergency list for the caterer's manager. He'd left it behind by mistake, so someone had been kind enough to put into the draw for safety.

"We need to contact and interview as many of the guests as we can, before this incident gets out on social media and the news channels. We are at some point going to have to deal with them, so I'll get Willis to arrange a press conference, the old bugger has got to do something. The press will start sniffing around soon enough, so keep this as low key as we can for now," Mac smiled.

"Eli, Jude, you're both helping Kara get through sorting the list, priorities the VIP's, first and the work employees. We need to get officers to interview and get statements from them. The Commissioner has arranged for us to use some officers from the murder squad, that usually covers North London for a couple of days, so let's make the most of them. Get them doing some of our leg work, we've helped them before so it's their turn now. We need to move fast on this, as we've got lots of distinguished and busy people to get statements from."

"Kara, you're on caterers now as well, grab a couple of plain clothed detectives from downstairs to help you out if you need them. Eli, you're on other companies that were present, entertainers, band, etc. Again, get some help from the squad downstairs." Mac spoke quickly and with meaningful purpose to the group.

"Hunter, I know there's a lot to go through, so let me know if anything comes up. We need to know about the motorbike, make it a priority."

Hunter knew his assignment was going to be a tough one. All the hours of video footage captured by the security cameras, not only internal ones but also the external cameras as well. Throughout the day there must have been hours and of a different camera from all angles and maybe some cameras he hadn't even come across as yet.

"Back at the station for four, guys." Mac left them to it.

The team left the house and the murder scene, knowing full well their roles in the next few hours. Time was precious and while heading back to the station all were excited and yet apprehensive about what lay ahead.

Chapter 4.

Incident Room.

Mac had organised the incident room while he waited for the team to return. He'd wanted them to take some thinking time, he needed them refreshed and conversant about the case in front of them. There was still really another twenty minutes before he expected them, so he wasn't concerned that he was the only one in the room at the moment. He had time to think and felt confident they were discussing the case. It also gave him time to make some necessary calls, one of which was to pathologist Dr Bank. He felt concerned about the use of only one bullet and wanted to check she was confident about her theory. He put together what he imagined went on in the bedroom over the weekend and why. Surely there was a logical and proper explanation to the extraordinary way the bodies were found and how Caroline was with someone else rather than her husband.

Mac had recently asked that the incident room be redecorated and redesigned. It felt drab and uninspiring for the team. He'd purposely organised the room into a horseshoe configuration, thinking that it would make it more conversable, more focussed. Mac wanted them all to be comfortable and fully included when discussing a case, helping them concentrate better on any case and be more interactive with each other. Last thing he needed was them moaning about how uncomfortable the seats were, and that they missed any important evidence that he gave out because of bad Feng Shui.

He started looking through the images that he'd been emailed by Dr Banks. They showed the gruesome and disfigured faces of the victims, with photos of how the bodies had been found, detailed photos of the bullet entry point and exit wounds, with graphic details of the victims. She'd also supplied pictures taken from around the bedroom, showing the items in the room along with the layout. While deep in his thought process, there was a knock on the door. Without pause, the door flew open and Superintendent Willis came in, followed by a young female officer, who seemed to look interested as well as inappropriately dressed for a police detective, or for any type of office work in the force.

Superintendent Carmichael Willis had been with the force for what seemed to him an eternity. His thoughts nowadays were more concerned with his impending retirement and the days he could spend in the sunshine at his holiday home in the Canaries. He was a slender man but was starting to show his age, and over the last couple of years his face had become far more wrinkled and withdrawn, his hair almost completely white. The thick-rimmed glasses he wore told many a story. He'd been unlucky enough to lose his wife a year before when the covid-19 outbreak started. She had been due to retire from working in the NHS as a senior doctor and been working at London's St Thomas's Hospital in the Covid ward when she died, leaving him alone and depressed. He'd tried to throw himself into his work, but that hadn't helped, and Mac saw the man he'd known for so long crumble into a state of uneasiness and withdraw. Carmichael had no children of his own with his wife, but they had adopted a lovely girl when she was four years old from a rundown orphanage in Mexico. They only wished they could have helped more of the unfortunate children. Fifi was now fully grown, married, with three children of her own, living happily and in a good stable relationship. Carmichael adored and was devoted to his grandchildren and spoiled them rotten whenever he could.

"Afternoon, Mac, how's the scene down at St George's Hill?" he asked as he shook Mac's hand, something he'd always done every time they met.

"Looks as if the husband might be our prime suspect, guv, only we've got no idea at present where he could be. Doesn't look as if he's taken his clothing or anything valuable, which seems odd if it was him."

"Ok, well let's hope it's as straightforward as finding him, then. By the way I've brought along someone I'd like you to meet, this is Detective Zephyra Kostopoulos." Willis turned and encouraged the young lady to step forward.

"I know that she'll be an asset to your team, Mac. Although she's just out of Hendon, she's good at her job, especially as you've many witnesses to interview and video to wade through. You'll find her useful while dealing with a few of your suspects, so let her tag along with you Mac."

Zephyra stepped forward, offering her hand to Mac.

"Please call me Zodiac, sir, it's much easier and also what I've been called since police training college." Her English was perfect and flawless as she introduced herself to Mac.

Zodiac was in her early twenties, average height for a woman and physically fit, that's perhaps why she looked younger than her years. She had what Mac could only call a gothic dress sense. Her hair was long, down below her shoulders and was jet black. It hung straight down at the sides and back, but with a spiky thing going on at the top, tied in a red tie. Her nails were dark black. Her eyes, though, beamed through, and gave the impression of a warm person as they glowed through the pale makeup. Her dress hugged her slender upper body, but it then spread out to form a calf, length skirt, which looked as if it comprised several layers. Underneath she wore black tights and big black ankle boots with small chains attached to them. Her appearance didn't offend Mac. It brought back memories of when his daughter went through a similar gothic stage in her teens. But she hadn't kept it up. Mac just had never seen a police officer dressed like this before as.

"Ms Kostopoulos has some excellent skills that you and Hunter will very much appreciate. So will the rest of your team, I'm sure you'll all get along well." Willis raised an eyebrow and grinned at Mac as he turned and walked towards the door. Stopping briefly, he said, "Keep me informed, Mac." walking out pulling the door closed behind him.

"Welcome to the team, Zodiac. The squad members will be here any moment." Mac looked directly at her eyes as he spoke. He was watching her response, trying to gauge her reaction and understand her more. Nothing, it would take time. "What do you consider are your strong points that would help us with this investigation?" he asked.

Before she could answer, the door opened, and the team all started to enter the room, talking about the case. Some were still carrying coffee and sandwiches of some kind or other. Kara went over to Mac, passed him a large coffee and a Big Mac, smiled and went to sit in her chair. He nodded his appreciation.

"Okay, Listen up, guys. All take a seat, please, we've a lot to get on with," Mac started, in his loud and better take notice or else voice.

"First of all, I'd like to introduce you all to Zephyra Kostopoulos. Or, as she wishes to be called, Zodiac. Our bosses seem to think we could do with her assistance on this one, and the more hands we have the better I say." Mac gave Zodiac a friendly welcoming grin and beckoned her to sit. "So let's all welcome her and get her up to speed as soon as we can. Hunter, please take her with you back to the crime scene after our meeting. Fill her in and let her have a good look round."

"Jim pointed out while we were at the Stones' house, that there was probably a Harley Davidson that belonged to the Charles Stone, which at present is unaccounted for so it needs to be found. It's an expensive bike, purpose made and only made to special order nowadays, from early reports and photos on the wall in the downstairs cloakroom. Jude, get onto traffic. Get hold of any footage around the time of the murders start with a couple of hours before, and up to the morning after. Also ask the guests if anyone remembers seeing it during the day."

"It's probably got a tracker attached, I'll look into that guv." Hunter added.

"Okay, let's move on. We have two victims found lying together, as we have all witnessed. Both killed by the same gun and probably, we think the same bullet. Both seemingly there by mutual consent, and unaware that they were being watched and sneaked up on, otherwise either of them might have tried to stop or escape, and there's no indication of that happening."

"The female body we are positive, is that of Caroline Stone, thirty- four years old and married to Charles Stone CEO of Stones' PLC. As for the male, we have no identification for him, but I'm hoping that Dr Banks will shed some light on that for us shortly. He had bank cards in his trouser pockets, which were on the floor in the bedroom and do suggest that he was called Reece Taylor. So let's hope we get confirmation shortly from Dr Banks.

"Stones PLC are a high-end security and home automation company. All the gadgets and tech you came across in the house was installed and supplied by them. This is really a futuristic showcase home, something's in the house aren't even in full-time production yet."

His own phone interrupted Mac, vibrating on the desk in front of him. It was a text message from Dr Banks, saying that she was on her way over with her primary reports, not only on the two bodies, but her investigations because it might well be relevant to the case and how they approach their thinking.

Mac continued.

"We need to find and apprehend Mr Charles Stone as soon as possible, apparently no one has heard of or seen him since the party late Saturday night. The last people to see him were Henry and Emma Thorburn. He is our prime suspect right now, and really our only suspect at this time. Let's get a warrant out for his arrest. Jude, you can check to see if he's got property elsewhere, friends or even girlfriend he might well be hiding with. How do we stand with contacting the guests from Saturday?"

Kara spoke first. This was her department. Her speciality was finding these things out fast.

"I have the list I found at the property, guv, as you're aware, and I'm going to call the rest on the list as soon as we've finished here. But to recap. We have 296 people invited, 242 attended, according to the log on the door, which is a good turnout. I've yet, though, to see any footage from the front door camera to verify that count. However, on site prior to the party there were twenty employees of the catering company, Munch and Stuff Ltd, which included, four chefs, six wine waiters, two valet parking attendants and eight female waiters. I've arranged a meeting in the morning with the caterers as I texted I, guv," Kara reminded Mac. He responded with a nod.

"The other guests on the list are basically a comprehensive list of politicians, celebrities and high-powered business entrepreneurs, some of whom we might not get to interview easily, and we'll have to make appointments or even get special permission to approach them due to their status." Kara added.

Mac took over.

"Okay, let's get in touch with everyone on that list get them interviewed, there's only so long we are going to keep this from social media and the press. We need to know times, when they arrived and times they left and also where possible who they chatted to and about what at the party.

"Hunter, can you get the CCTV footage onto everyone's laptops, let's cross reference what they say to what actually happened. That way we can reduce our suspect list vastly. Spilt that up between yourselves in time sections.

"According to Dr Banks, the murders took place between 11 pm and 3 am, so that should help eliminate some of the suspects, who would have left for other reasons prior to that time. I saw signs of drug use upstairs, both in the main bathroom and the en-suites. Let's get that checked out and tested too. Have a word with the drugs squad, see if they know anything. These celebrities are usually known to the drug department. So check that out, also who bought the stuff into the house or was it already there. Eli, that's up to you also," Mac pointed at Eli with the marker he'd been using on the whiteboard to make notes as he went along and got a nod in return.

The door opened and Dr Banks came in carrying a box file and laptop with her. She didn't need an invitation to join him at the front of the room, she just walked over and started setting her computer up next to his own.

Looking at Mac as if to say, I'm ready. He nodded to her as if to say carry on.

"This one is a first for me. We do actually have three murders with this incident, the woman murdered was defiantly Caroline Stone and she was eight to ten weeks pregnant. Her blood tests came back quickly and confirmed this beyond any doubt, and for those interested it was a male embryo. This we were lucky to find out, as the foetus rarely decides on its gender until this sort of time in the pregnancy. We are cross-referencing DNA as we speak to determine who the father was.

During the identification we usually run these routine blood tests first, so that we know what else we could look for in the post-mortem process later. We test for various toxics and other factors, as again you all know. Well, this time we've also carried out a blood test as normal first, only to find there's no sign of alcohol present in her bloodstream. Given that this was a birthday party for her husband, we thought this was perhaps a mistake. So we ran a pregnancy check and found out that she was in fact pregnant. We then also decided to run the DNA tests on the foetus and we are still waiting for results for that. Oh, also just as a reference, she had Covid antibodies in other tests we ran, so at one point she had had Covid 19.

We haven't identified the male as yet. But we think he's a 24-year-old male called Reece Taylor, who recently started work at Stone's PLC. That's according to their company records on their website where there's a profile on him and a picture."

River had loaded the pictures that she and her team had taken at the murder scene onto the screen. There was a picture of Reece with his face completely covered in blood, just a hole through where his nose used to be, the blood from Caroline and some of his own mixed together completely covering his face from chin to hairline and dripping down his face onto the bed. River had also downloaded a picture from the Stones' PLC website to compare the facial structure of the body. A handsome, well-manicured man with designer stubble and a big bright smile stared at them from the screen. He didn't look like that anymore.

Next, River brought up images on the screen of Caroline's face, not a pretty sight, not the beautiful woman that she had been hours before, but a face that had been completely demolished and blown away. Her beautiful features no longer there, taken away with the exit wound of the bullet. Her skull at the point of entry of the bullet, only showed a minor wound and a few blood splatters around her hair and skin. Just the amount of blood that had splattered from the recoil of a weapon fired at very close range.

"The bullet was a 45mm shot at point blank in the victim's skull. Caroline Stone would have felt the barrel on the back of her head a split second before it was fired. There was no time for the assailant to hesitate, otherwise Caroline might well have had time, albeit a faction of a second, to move. If she had done, then the weapon would need to be used twice and risk the chance of failure in killing them both. The angle of entry meant that they fired it from almost ninety degrees into her head, the bullet passing through the base of the skull, taking the lower section of her brain along with it. This is shown in this slide here. To do this, the assailant would have partially climbed onto the bed, meaning that the couple were certainly making a lot of noise and very intense in lovemaking while the attacker went about their business. Fortunately for the attacker the mattress was a highly expensive pocket sprung bed, a very good one at that, although given the circumstances they probably didn't even notice anyone until it was too late, anyway.

The bullet then exited through Caroline's proboscis and through into the male's. By this we can state for sure that they were passionately embraced. Both would have then lost a lot of blood quickly, soaking through to the silk bedcovers, pillows and eventually into the carpet over the next few hours. The blood arrays on the rest of the bed are minimal and consistent with there being just the one shot. The bullet managed to penetrate the mattress and we found it embedded in the floor, fortunately for us not too far, as you can imagine the force of the bullet going through two skulls, a bed and a thick carpet meant it had lost velocity. We are currently doing tests on the bullet for significant fire barrel markings and trying to identify the manufacturer. Any questions? River asked, as she continued talking and had barely taken a breath.

"The male is obviously covered with Caroline's blood and DNA. Along with his own, he also had Caroline's DNA under his nails and of course around his genitals, suggesting that at the time of death both victims were at the peak of climax or just beyond it. Now there's one other thing that is puzzling. We have traces of a second male semen on the bed clothes and it's not Charles

Stone's either. So, we need to establish where that came from and who it belongs to. We also have traces of cocaine and cannabis in a couple of places in the house, excellent quality and pure. So, Mac, that's about all we have for now, but as things develop, I'll keep you informed. Oh, just to let you know, a full post mortem will take place first thing in the morning, so if anyone is interested in attending please be my guest."

"Ok, Thanks, River." Mac said.

"Any more questions for River?" Mac addressed his captive audience, not expecting a response from any of them at this stage. However, Jude did pipe up. "Were there any other signs of sexual activity in other bedrooms? Perhaps that might coincide with the third sample you found? We all noticed the second bedroom looked as if it might also have been used for sexual activity."

"Yes, you're right, they used the second bedroom for both sex and drugs. And we do have a few samples of DNA to identify, along with a pair of black silk knickers that were found in a bin in the second bedroom's bathroom. We're trying to cross reference DNA samples taken from the bedroom with those on glasses, worktops, etc. We can then determine events more logically and hope to eliminate some suspects quicker. Also, without causing too much embarrassment to those who were not involved and to save time on these people. It would be great when interviewing you could also collect DNA samples of those willing to give them. If they don't want to give samples, then get one somehow. We can then cross reference quicker, so the more samples we have the easier we will start eliminating people and know who was in the second bedroom." River paused, to allow anyone else to ask questions.

"Please, could you show us the pictures of Caroline's legs and feet again and then get a closeup of her ankle?" Zodiac spoke abruptly from across the room as she moved forward towards the video screen.

"Ok," River replied, as Zodiac was approaching her. The office seemed surprised by her question.

"Show me more of this area, please," Zodiac was pointing directly at Caroline's ankle where they could clearly see a bracelet around her left foot. River focussed onto the ankle, zooming in on the area Zodiac had indicated. It showed a fine gold anklet with small diamond studs embedded around it. At one point there was a small gold key, no more than 6mm in length, attached to the chain.

"This key on her ankle indicates that she wore this chain as a suggestion that within her relationship she's the dominant partner and that her husband is the submissive one. In different cultures over the centuries, whores wore these on their right foot, married ladies on the left. This showed that she was in an open relationship because the key symbolises her dominance, so men could approach her without the husband or partner being offended." Zodiac felt as if she was lecturing so finished abruptly.

"So, basically. You're saying that this is a sign or indication for men to approach her, chat her up and hoped to have sex with her?" Mac looked at Zodiac with a look of surprise and some confusion.

"Yes, more or less. It's not usually that simple, because in a cuckold relationship we would expect the submissive partner to participate in one form or another. This might be in the form of just knowing that their partner is seeing someone else, or even joining in with them both to a certain extent. The cuckold could be female or male, depending on the relationship parameters. This might shed some light on why she's sleeping with someone else. But could also explain why there's no sign of Mr Stone. He might well have been watching or in another room, listening. Mr Stone might also have been told to disappear, or knew he wasn't involved in this particular encounter. I think it could be relevant to the investigation and well worth looking into, especially if as you say the father of the baby might not be him but Caroline's lover."

Zodiac now had the full attention of the entire room. Mac was quiet for a moment, you could almost see his brain working round this scenario and what it could mean for the investigation, giving them a line of inquiry that needed to be followed up, and not dismissed.

"Okay, that makes some sense, and it's certainly worth pursuing. Anyone else got any comments at this stage? Okay, you've got an hour left today to get some calls done. Then all get off home. We'll reconvene here tomorrow at 9 am so let's have some answers ready, guys."

"I'll take Zodiac back to the murder scene now, guv. I want to go through and see if I can find the tracker for the bike, and I also think Zodiac needs to see the place." Hunter got a glance and nod from Zodiac from across the room as he spoke. They seemed on the same wavelength already.

Mac brought the meeting to a close. Instructing in detail to follow up on what they had discussed. He liked to send all the team to visit the crime scene at least twice. So tomorrow he would send them back anyway, especially after they had had a good period of thinking time. This would normally remind them of why they do detective work, but make them far more focused on the task, giving them determination to find new ideas and inspiration on the second visit.

Hunter and Zodiac returned to the Stones' ultra-modern high-tech eco house after Mac brought the meeting to an end. When they arrived, there were still a good half a dozen forensic workers going through the rooms in pairs, working as a team within the team, bagging up evidence and categorising it methodically before loading it into plastic numbered boxes. When the boxes were full, they were carried out to the waiting transit van, ready to return to the labs and further scrutiny.

On the way Zodiac had received her first official call from Jim, asking her to inquire about the pair of pants disposed of in the bedroom toilet bin. Jim wanted them examined quickly. The DNA that was on the gusset could well give a positive ID to Reece, if they both matched.

Both Hunter and Zodiac decided that they should start by doing a full inspection of the bedroom before starting on the outside camera and security system. Hunter had already done this previously, but he knew that Zodiac would want to get up to speed quickly and this was the best way. He had explained the layout of the property in detail as they had driven to the house. Zodiac, though, still seemed impressed and somewhat taken aback when she saw the complexity of the property. Hunter had already established in the car that Zodiac wasn't really one for talking, but, he'd still felt they would work well together, as they seemed to be on the same wavelength. Time would tell.

"So why do you think they assigned you on this one?" Hunter had asked, as they started walking around the main bedroom.

"I remember everything that I see and everything that I'm told, too. A fucking curse, but for work it's brilliant, I don't need to take notes, I just remember." Hunter was taken aback a bit as she swore but liked the fact that she felt comfortable to do so. That told him lots about her.

The blood-stained sheets were still on the bed, despite the bodies having been removed four of hours ago. Zodiac strolled round the room, taking in everything she saw without speaking. Looking closely at the sheets, she took her time, making sure she missed nothing.

"The killer would have got in and out without being seen, right? You say that we haven't any footage from this bedroom from the hall cameras or the stairwell and lift?" She seemed to be deep in thought when she was speaking.

"I've not been able to establish anything so far," Hunter replied.

"There're no cameras covering this bedroom, the first ones after that are at the bottom of the stairs going into the garage, and the landing outside. So, we can assume that the killer either went out into the main part of the house, missing the camera, or out by the pool. Or possibly got past the cameras by going down into the garage." All the time Zodiac was speaking, she'd been walking slowly down the stairs, with Hunter following while listening intently.

"If you were trying to be discreet and unseen, how would you do that when cameras are coving the entire area? You could simply adjust the camera angle to give you a blind spot. That would then allow you to get in and out with no trouble as long as you had your wits about you. Or you could dismantle it completely for a period."

"Have you seen that camera's footage yet? My bet is it will show a camera that has been tampered with and adjusted ever so slightly. So we will need to compare old footage of that of the one the other night. Or, perhaps the camera wasn't set up properly to start with. We need to find the blind spots, it'll give us an idea of how and who might be responsible, and capable of managing that."

"We'll have to check the video when we're back in the office." Hunter had already thought of this, but he didn't want to get on the wrong side of Zodiac after only meeting her a few hours ago. He was getting more confident that they would work well together, which pleased him. Two individuals like that probably would be considered weird, as eccentric as each other, both working on the same team. He was looking forward to getting to know her better.

Moving methodically round the entire house, they came across the extensive network of 4K cameras covering almost every part of the house. From the large oak and glass front door to the garage entrance, every angle seemed to be covered. Taking a walk across the grass to the boathouse, they came to one looking out over the lake as well from the summerhouse. There were no cameras set inside the pool changing area and none in the bathrooms, which didn't surprise either of them, though they found one camera in each of the second and third bedrooms, something they both felt a bit unusual and quite intrusive to anyone's privacy while staying overnight. Having someone able to watch you during the night felt creepy, even to both of them.

Time was getting on, so after nearly two hours of being on the murder scene they decided that they should head back to the office. They agreed the hard drives Doctor Banks had released were enough to get on with for now. It would be a long night.

Setting up the half a dozen screens on the computers, Zodiac and Hunter settled down with a pizza delivery, a couple of bottles of coke and crisps, ready for the night's work. Starting by organising the files they needed into time relevance sections for ease of logging the timeline, they started looking at footage two hours prior to the time that Dr Banks had indicated was the probable time of death. As they went on, one file bought up the images of

Reece laying on the bed in the second bedroom. He was on his phone, laughing and texting, looking relaxed and comfortable, whisky in one hand and his mobile in the other. Reece had entered the room at 10.46pm after making a point of saying goodbye to Charles and Caroline a couple of minutes earlier downstairs. It showed him going into the downstairs bathroom for five minutes before making sure that no one was watching, and then he sneaked back up the stairs and into the second bedroom, shutting the door behind him.

At 11.17 pm the bedroom door opened and Caroline entered telling Reece to give her thirty minutes before coming to her bedroom. The instructions were clear and unmistakable from her, giving him a kiss on the cheek as he tried to slide his hand under her dress to caress her scantily dressed bum. Caroline told him to behave and wait for the right time. So instead he slapped her across the arse, telling her how nice it was as he did so. Caroline then left, readjusting her dress.

Reece did as he was told. He literally watched his phone and waited thirty minutes before leaving the bedroom, but first went into the bathroom to freshen up. He was then caught on the camera covering the hallway, the last images they saw were of him going through the sliding pocket door into the main bedroom. Time on the image read 11.48pm. Caroline was standing in the door entrance and stretched out her hand to him as he entered the room.

Time was now late, they had watched the two hours up to the murders and nearly an hour afterwards. Nothing had come up on the screens after 11.48pm. The only image that had materialised was an image driving away on the motorbike from the pictures they retrieved. They established that the bike was a Harley Davidson from images they got from the internet and spent the next half-hour finding the tracking device information. It had last been on the property until 12.24am. Mac had called them twenty minutes earlier, telling them to go home and get some sleep. He'd know full well that they would be still working, but he needed them fit and alert the next day. They eventually decided that actually they both were really done in and went their separate ways.

Chapter 5.

The Shard

Mac was sitting at his desk when Superintendent Willis came in to suggest it would be good experience for her and also to his advantage to take Zodiac with them to interview Mr Zaman in London. Mac hadn't ever questioned his commander's recommendations before, but felt that he was pushing her in at the deep end with the responsibility, especially as this was an important man and the wrong thing said could cause problems at the interview. But he knew Willis probably had his reasons, so reluctantly agreed.

Mac held debrief in the incident room at nine, expecting the team to get in up to speed with how they were progressing, particularly with finding Mr Stone. Mac had spoken to Jim about taking Zodiac with them and asked him to give keep an eye on her and give guidance if he thought it necessary. It was now Day 2 of the murder investigation, and things were progressing well, although not as well as Mac had hoped. The team had eliminated over half the guests on the list, mostly because they had left earlier in the evening and with their dates for the evening, or a group of friends giving them a cast-iron alibi. Mac's phone began to vibrate while he was speaking to the group.

"A word, Mac, please, in my office." It was Willis.

Mac turned off his computer and completed the meeting, picking up his coffee as he went to Willis' room.

"I've just received a call from Mr Zaman's personal secretary. She's stating that you've requested he remain in the country, and you've also asked for a warrant to search his private jet? I've been informed he's got an important meeting in Dubai tomorrow and needs to leave this afternoon. I think you need to get there soon. This man has money and friends with government officials, so don't ruffle his feathers too much at this stage."

"Yes, guv, I'm waiting on the search warrant. I just wanted to make sure that no one leaves on that plane that we need to interview, including Mr Zaman or Charles Stone."

"Ok, I agree. I'll get the paperwork together, we leave in half an hour. Bring Zodiac too."

"What, you're coming, Sir?" Mac looked puzzled.

"The reason for that call I received was that Mr Zaman insists that a senior officer accompanies you. I don't know why. But also, we need to be diplomatic for all our sakes." Willis looked up at Mac over his glasses.

"Okay, Guv, I'll get an unmarked car to take us. Where are we meeting Mr Zaman?"

"His apartment on the 68th floor of The Shard," Willis replied. "Half-hour."

Mac closed the door behind him and wondered why the CS had asked Zodiac to join them. Mac was still trying to work out Zodiac in his own mind, a distraction he really didn't need at the moment, but he thought she was a bit of an oddball. Perhaps that was being unkind to her, and it was far too early to deciding things like that. He would find out more about her and her attributes to his team and the investigation, when he can sit and have a chat with her later.

Jim drove them through London, the traffic the usual nightmare, he wished he could use the siren on the car a couple of times, but resisted. Zodiac had sat beside him without saying a word throughout the journey. She seemed preoccupied with the scenery, the buildings and roads, what was going on in every shop front or bus stop. He got the impression that she was in fact quite shy, and felt uneasy.

He drove straight into the underground parking facility for the Shard apartments. The hotel was integral to the Shard, along with business outlets. The parking was clearly marked and divided into large spaces and occupied by expensive cars and SUV's filling most of the allocated parking bays. Jim pulled into the allotted parking space for Zaman's apartment as he'd been instructed, which been left for them especially. As they got out of the car, they were greeted by Zaman's personal assistant, a tall blonde female, dressed in a business suit. Her short skirt barely covered her bottom, while her top was tight and showed off her figure to its fullest, and she walked towards them as though she'd just got off the catwalk in Paris. She introduced herself as Liz Harper, personal assistant to Mr Zaman, and asked them to follow her, through to the lobby area, where they were asked to sign in as visitors before being allowed to the main lift and up to the apartment. The big security guard also asked if they wouldn't mind going through the airport type scanner, just to making sure they weren't carrying weapons or anything that wasn't permitted in the building for security reasons. Having done as they were asked, Zodiac was the only one who made the alarm beep as she went through. She apologised, explaining that she had a couple of very discreet piercings that would set off the machine and quickly offered to let Liz frisk her down instead. Liz duly did, making sure she was harsher than she needed to be, which bought a smirky look across Zodiac's face, who seemed to enjoy the experience.

Eventually they all entered the lift. Zodiac, however, was the last to enter and Liz just looked and stared at her as though she was the weird, or was it that Zodiac knew full well that Liz wasn't really who or what she claimed to be? She'd met many people within the Non Binary community over the past few years, and her open mind meant she always had good relations with them. Yes, Zodiac was a goth and dressed differently, but her presence made Liz feel uneasy and awkward, well aware that Zodiac had sussed her out. The lift was quick and silent, it rose to the 68th floor in what seemed only a few seconds, the only indication that it was moving at all was the lift's floor indicator as it sped through the numbers. When it slowed and stopped, the doors opened and they walked into a very plush wide hallway. There was a leather reclining chair on either side of the lifts and a couple of Arabic men in pristine black suits who moved aside before Liz led her entourage out and along the passage to Sabil Zaman's apartment. The two Arab men got into the lift and Liz stopped, making sure the lift closed before it descended quickly again to the ground floor. Security seemed of paramount importance throughout the building on all levels.

Leading them down the hallway, Liz became very conscious of Mac and his team watching the way she walked and looked. Opening and knocking simultaneously, Liz opened a door directly at the end of the corridor. She entered with confidence and held the door open politely for the others to enter. Chief Superintendent Willis went through first, he felt he should, being the highest ranking officer among them, and the others followed in rank with Zodiac last.

The door opened up on to a large, bright and airy apartment. A large lush expensive, looking desk and chair sat in the far corner, overlooking a panoramic view across the London skyline and out into the distance. A picture every professional in the city would like and could only hope for. In the centre of the room were two plush black leather sofas along with a matching single seat at the far end. Between them sat, a large marble table with a very ornate bowl full of fruit, that looked fresh and inviting. Gigantic statues and figurines made from various metals and marble were placed around the space, and paintings from various urban artists on the walls opposite the picture glass windows.

Liz quietly shut the door behind her and walked directly across to a bar area at the far end, as she did so asking if anyone would like refreshments.

"Water all round, I think." Willis quickly and loudly responded, while turning to face the others. He had become a health freak over the past couple of months and was trying to get everyone in the department into his way of thinking. The rest agreed, disappointedly.

"Please be seated."

Sabil Zaman gestured with an arm to the sofas as he walked across the room, from a reclining chair facing out overlooking the Thames. He sat down on the single seater, spreading his arms either side of the chair and crossing his legs, trying to appear calm but showing his authoritive side.

Willis and Mac both did so cautiously. They were now facing each other, and at ninety degrees on either side of Zaman. Jim and Zodiac were apprehensive about sitting as normally they wouldn't have, until, that is, Mac gave Jim a look that said sit or else. He did so like a faithful dog, sitting next to Willis. Zodiac, on the other hand completely ignored the request, and started slowly wandering round the room, taking in the figurines and the view through the windows, all the time listening to what was being said without getting involved. Mac looked at Willis as if to say what the fuck is she doing, but all the response he got was a small shake of the head, as if to say leave her be, as Zaman started talking.

"How may I be of assistance, gentlemen?" Zaman asked with a grin from behind his beard.

"We believe you were present at the Stones' residence on Saturday evening for Charles's birthday party. We were wondering if there was anything that you could tell us regarding the events that unfolded on Saturday night."

Mac was looking directly at Zaman to see how he reacted to his question as he spoke. "I take it you've heard about the murders?" He followed up with a few seconds later.

"Yes, detective, I have, very unfortunate affair, if you pardon the pun. I sent my car back there yesterday evening to pick up some paperwork from Charles, but the driver was turned away by your officers.

I've known Charles and Caroline for a few years now and at times been very close to them both. I've done business with Charles over the past five or so years and met the lovely Caroline on numerous occasions. We've both made lots of money off the back of some very rich people and prospered very well from that. As you can see around you detective." He had both hands clenched together in front of him as he spoke.

Liz had now returned with the iced water and was placing the drinks directly on the table, Zodiac took hers directly from the tray as she walked past her.

"ساعة غضون في طول على سأكون أنني قائدي أخبري الطائرة وإعداد", Zaman said to Liz after she'd put down the drinks.

"لا حتى بك الخاص جيدا علم كما ساعة ثم أطول ستكون لها الانتهاء نكون عندما تذهب أن يمكن لك يطالب يكون". Zodiac immediately replied. Zaman was somewhat taken aback, along with Mac and Jim. Willis just grined.

"Why I do apologise!" Zaman was now looking straight at her with an annoyed grin on his face, trying to hide his anger that started building up. He'd wondered why this young girl had attended along with the others. He was certainly now aware.

"I simply asked for my pilot to be informed that I'll be along later than I had scheduled," Zaman said.

"Yes, that's true, you did, but it will be more than an hour, won't it?" Zodiac threw him a look that proved she was completely fluent in Arabic and he should not deceive her. She was actually a great linguistic expert, speaking sixteen languages so far and always learning more whenever she had the time. She picked up languages even as people spoke to her, the accent, the use of masculine and feminine words seemed easy to her.

Sabil Zaman gave her an all-knowing smile back before turning to speak directly to Mac.

"Sorry about that, I hope I didn't offend anyone." Zaman actually looked flustered for a few seconds but had soon regained his composure. He then went on to explain how he was first introduced to Charles and Caroline, how he'd attended a dinner meeting with the Stone's at their home when they signed their first contract with his corporation. It was for over £10 million, supplying, and outfitting home tech and security for a major condo tower in Dubai. State-of-the-art tech was required, and AI technology was what Charles Stone was all about.

The dinner had gone really well, with plenty of delicious food which had been served along with lots of alcohol, drunk even by himself despite his religious beliefs. In fact, it had been such a success that Charles had insisted he stayed over because of the lateness of the hour. Charles had explained to Sabil that their marriage was an open relationship and was therefore was very relaxed about him staying.

"Caroline, though, had already worked out during the evening, that I am in fact a man for the boys, Inspector, by that I mean I'm a homosexual. As you can imagine, this in my position and with my religious background is very difficult and problematical at times. Therefore, I asked for the CS to attend today so that you could all assure me of complete confidentiality regarding this matter. I can't in any circumstances have this known outside this room. It must remain that way." Zaman sounded sincere and almost as though he was pleading, something he seemed not to have done too often by the look of panic crossing his face at that moment.

"I will help you in every way that I can, but that I must be guaranteed."

Mac looked across to Willis, who duly gave him the look that said he'd better agree to this. Mac thought for a moment, knowing full well that he didn't really have any choice but still wanting Zaman to be concerned for a few moments more.

"I think we can manage that, Mr Zaman, but I would like to send my officers to inspect and check your plane before it leaves today. We are, after all, still missing the murder weapon, and Charles Stone is also still missing."

"I need to leave by six, detective." Zaman replied with an air of reluctance but also realising that whatever he had planned might have to wait.

Mac looked across to Jim and gave him a nod. They had already set up a team to board the Gulfstream G550, which was sitting on the terminal of the private jet area of City airport. Jim called through and told them to enforce the search warrant, that had been granted an hour before by the courts.

The jet was being prepared ready for take-off at a moment's notice, the crew of three were actively going about the pre-flight checks, making sure everything was in order. The food was being checked and loaded into the kitchen quarters, along with champagne and other liquors.

Danny and Kara led the team with four forensic personnel in close attendance, cars circled the jet, making sure that it had no means of escape. Several armed officers were deployed around the area. Danny and Kara presented the search warrant to the custom officers with while they eagerly awaited the word from Mac or Jim. Once they were given the go ahead to board, they entered via the front set of steps which led straight into the main cabin area. No expense had been spared in kitting out the plane: Its cream leather seats were the height of luxury, a fully equipped bar with gold optics and highly glossed walnut work surface stood out to one side. Plush carpet laid throughout. Danny continued through the plane and Kara went down to the luggage hold, where two of the forensics were already dusting and taking pictures of the cargo. There wasn't much luggage, which helped in their task, but they checked everything no matter what, opening every suitcase and holdall. With only a brief window to operate in, the team had to work fast, and expertly to manage a full and thorough inspection of the plane, and its contents.

Mac continued to ask Sabil questions about his business deals with Charles and Caroline and how they had progressed into larger, more lucrative contracts over the past couple of years. He had learnt a few things, but nothing he couldn't have found out through other sources, but, would check, anyway. His phone buzzed again in his pocket. Kara had messaged that they'd found a laptop and wanted permission to access it.

"Mr Zaman, my detectives have just recovered a laptop in the luggage hold of the plane. I'd like your permission to access it, if you wouldn't mind." Mac said. "After all, we don't want any unnecessary delays, do we?"

Zaman sat a moment, thinking about the request, thinking about the laptop's contents more than anything. Could he risk them looking at it or refuse and have it confiscated?

"I'm sorry, detective, but that laptop is on my plane and its protected by my diplomatic status. It has confidential files and information on your national security and contracts between our two countries. I'm sure you understand." Zaman looked smug as he spoke.

Mac was disappointed, but just sent a text to Kara: "Permission refused. Give it to Hunter and then turn your back, he'll know what that means and what to do." Kara texted back "Okay."

"What about the conversation you had with Charles, the one about the Harley Davidson on the day of the party, Mr Zaman?" Zodiac had seen video footage whereas Mac hadn't. It was now nearly half five and they didn't have much time left. Mac knew he needed the forensic team and Hunter to work fast to finish before Zaman arrived at his plane.

"I only asked if he was enjoying riding the bike. Anyway, how did you know I spoke to him regarding the Harley?" Zaman instinctively turned to Zodiac.

"Mr Zaman, not only am I fluent in Arabic, but I can lip read as well. You had a conversation with Charles Stone at 9.24pm on Saturday, in which you clearly asked him if he was still enjoying the Harley. It seems you obviously hoped Charles might lend or sell you the bike. I've seen all the house security videos as there are several around the house, as you are well aware. How, do you know a character called Mick, Mr Zaman?" She continued.

"He's my close friend and the reason that I wouldn't stay with Caroline that night, detective. His name is Mick Jones. We've been seeing each other for a few months. He comes and goes, usually with loads of my money, but he's a good boy, quiet and reliable."

Zaman felt uncomfortable again. He was now getting very irritated by this young girl, who apparently knew everything about him. Yet she still wouldn't stop asking awkward questions. It pissed him off.

"You then spoke to Mick at approximately 9.52pm, can you tell us what about? Instead of being pleased, he was rather angry and stormed off with the two young ladies you'd brought along for the party. They were a cover for you both, weren't they? Not necessarily for the Stones, because they knew your secret, but for the rest of the guests."

Zaman now was up from his seat, standing looking straight at Zodiac who just stared without blinking straight back at him. She knew how to ruffle his feathers and was doing so with some ease.

"Ok, yes we had a heated exchange of words over Charles' motorbike, I mean Mick and I did. Mick had suggested we take along a couple of girls to look like a normal foursome. They were beautiful and very professional but cost me a lot of money for the evening. Mick also had a birthday coming up, and he wanted a Harley like the one Charles owned. As it happened, I'd already arranged to purchase the bike from Caroline after they returned from their holiday in the States. Caroline had arranged a surprise holiday for Charles, with them picking up a latest model Harley Davidson. Then they were going to spend two weeks doing Route 66 and stay for a week in LA before returning home. Caroline had called me one day, asking for advice. I'd done the best part of the route a few years back, and if I would be interested in Charles's present bike for Mick as a token of her appreciation. I said that I would consider it and let her know. Mick was completely unaware of my dealings with Caroline, of course. Then, after we had argued, he said that he was going to make his own way home and not to wait for him. I didn't. The last I saw of him was when he was speaking to Caroline, and the lovely Emma. I'd only met Emma at the party and was very impressed with her designs and furnishings for the Stones house, and I asked her to contact me regarding work where I'd be interested in her input, so I gave her my contact details. After that, all I saw was Mick going upstairs with the two ladies we had bought along. I knew why, of course. That was the last straw, so I called for my car and left without saying goodbye to my hosts. For that I am truly, truly sorry."

"We'll need to know the contacts details for the girls you hired, just so that we can verify your account and eliminate them from the investigation." Mac said.

"Did you know or talk to Reece at all during the evening?" Jim said, looking up from taking his notes as they talked.

"The contact details would be on Mick's phone, I believe, so please get him to send you those, detective. Yes I had met Reece a couple of times, I must admit, he helped fix a problem on my phone one day at the Stone's office. Seemed an intelligent young man. I met him again at the party and we chatted for some time, but mostly technical stuff. He also got me some food from the buffet at one point, come to think of it. Mick was with me when he returned." Zaman looked as though he was struggling to recall that incident "I also believe Mick wasn't happy about that and I'm sure they had words later on, but that's all."

"Can you verify the exact time you left? We have a tedious task of eliminating people and it would help us," Mac asked, knowing full well that he could get his phone records up if he needed. But this way would save time and besides, he was sure at this stage that Zaman wasn't involved in the murders. After all, he'd invested a lot of money in the Stones and their company and had no obvious reason to murder them, but other things he wasn't sure about. Hunter would enlighten him later.

Mac hadn't finished his sentence before Zaman had his phone in his hand to show Zodiac his call register. She put out her hand to take the phone off Zaman, who was less than eager to let go. He kept a very close eye on her as she whipped through the log and also got her own phone out and blue-toothed the information to her own phone from in her pocket. She handed it back, politely thanking him, she assuring him that nothing had been compromised on his phone. She turned away and grinned to herself.

Mac was now standing and so was Willis. Both had got up almost simultaneously ready to leave, feeling they had what they needed for the time being.

"Mr Zaman, is there any chance that you can give us a DNA sample, please, Sir? We wouldn't want to delay you more than necessary. Oh, and if there's anything belonging to Mick lying around, could we also have that for DNA purposes? After all, I don't want to disrupt your trip unnecessarily, or hold you up at all." Mac made his intentions quite clear giving a sample was compulsory if he wanted to leave the country as planned.

"Liz," Zaman called out. She appeared from another room, as if she'd been waiting for a starting pistol.

"Could you give the officers the bag of clothes Mick left here last week? God knows why he left them, but please hand them over." He waved his hand as if he'd given up on trying to control the situation. Liz did as commanded.

Zodiac produced an evidence bag from her inside pocket and handed it to Zaman, into which he duly put his cut glass champagne flute straight into the bag. Willis was the last to leave, talking to Mr Zaman for a couple of minutes before joining the others outside by the lift. Mac was curious as to their conversation but thought Willis would tell him at some point if it was relevant to the investigation.

Liz accompanied them back to the ground floor where security was still waiting. After leaving the lift, Zodiac smiled at Liz. She commented on her lovely white silk neck scarf and asked if they did it in black. She smiled. Liz looked shocked and embarrassed as the doors slowly closed in front of her.

"What are you on about?" Mac said, looking somewhat confused.

"I think what Zodiac meant, guv, was that Liz is actually a transvestite or transgender man."

Jim and Zodiac were both now laughing at Mac as they walked past security and out into the car park. Willis still looked confused, but Mac suddenly realised what Zodiac meant.

Chapter 6.

Emma Interviewed.

By the time Mac and Jim reached the Thorburn's house in Warren Drive, it was late in the afternoon. Having stopped briefly to pick up a late lunch while talking through the facts they knew at this stage of the case, Mac wasn't ecstatic with the amount of evidence they had so far. It seemed far too easy for it to have been Charles Stone. Especially, as there wasn't much of his DNA to be found anywhere other than on the sheets or carpet. the sheets must have been freshly changed that day. He was just hoping for a better lead right now.

Jim had driven, as usual. Mac had been preoccupied on the phone constantly throughout the journey. Talking to team members bringing him updates. Arriving at the large black metal entrance gates, Jim pulled up alongside the security camera and the caller intercom system, wound down the window and push the call button to talk into the microphone. A few seconds passed before the camera flickered into life. Emma's face appeared on the screen.

"Can I help you?" Emma asked.

"Good afternoon, madam, I'm Detective Jim Bruston and I'm with Chief Inspector Mac Savage, mam. We would like to discuss the party at the Stones residence over the weekend, if we may. Could we please come in?" Jim replied.

"I'd like to see your ID's, please." Emma responded after a few seconds.

With that, Jim showed Emma their ID cards directly at the camera. "Please wait a moment." Thirty seconds had gone by when Emma finally spoke again. "That's fine. Please come in." The gates opened slowly, and they continued up the shingle drive towards the house. An old Tudor House, with large thick oak beams and elaborate brickwork laid between the main timbers. The roof had handmade dark brown clay tiles with interesting gargoyles standing abruptly along the ridge at set intervals, making it quite a creepy looking house. The solid oak door was arched with stained glass embedded within it. It looked as if it was the original one hung a few hundred years before. Either that or it was a very good replica.

As the door opened, squeaking slightly as it did so, Emma stood dressed in a long white flowered print dress, cool in the blaring heat being thrown down during day. She wore opened toed sandals, showing her highly polished toenails in a soft pink. Her hair had been tied up with a hairband and plaited to help her keep cool.

"Afternoon, officers. Please come in." She opened the door fully and gestured for them to step inside.

The hallway was grand, with a staircase occupying a large area leading to a galleried landing, dark oak as the front door, the spindles and ban were large, bulky and full of character. The walls were Raised and Filled oak panels, all capped with solid oak a dado rail. Family and landscape paintings adorned the walls, some of them looking like original masters. The flooring was wide oak planks, with a deep red carpet down the entire length of the hall and up the stairs. Despite the darkness of the wood, the room felt homely and warm.

"Please come through, I was just preparing Dinner." Emma led the way down the hall and into to the kitchen, a large open room with a large walnut and resin dining table along one side. The orangery towards the rear opened out onto the garden and beyond into woods and fields. The kitchen itself looked as if it had been crafted for a country mansion, a big area with a very wide Aga as the centrepiece. The units were all-natural wood with a Corian white worktop to reflexed the natural light from the roof lights above.

"Would you like coffee? What can I help you with?" Emma asked as she entered the kitchen.

"Thank you, that'll be nice. Is your husband home by any chance?" Mac asked. "We believe you were at the party at Mr and Mrs Stone's on Saturday night?" Mac tried to sound as thoughtful as possible.

"Yes we were. Henry has flown to a meeting and I'm expecting him home early in the morning. I'm actually expecting Caroline to call soon. Why?" Emma looked concerned as she spoke to them.

"I'm sorry to tell you this. Unfortunately, Caroline was found dead yesterday morning at home. Along with another man, whom, we haven't identified as yet." Mac didn't want to say any more at this point, but waited to see how she reacted.

Emma just stood there looking directly at Mac and Jim in disbelief and shock. The blood seemed to drain right from her face. Eventually she put down the mugs in slow motion on the worktop.

"I don't understand. How? Why? What about Charles? Is he the man?" Emma took a deep breath.

"Sorry, but at the moment we know very little about the situation and the forensic team are still working on the bodies. Caroline had you down on her phone as an in case of emergency contact, and we got your address from her phone book."

"We were hoping you and your husband could help us with our enquiries." Mac had walked over to Emma now and given her a drink of water, which she accepted and sipped, thanking him. Emma stumbled as she sat down, gently shaking her head in disbelief. Tears appeared on her face. Rolling down her cheeks. She wiped them away.

"Is there anyone who could come and sit with you for a while? If not, we can arrange for an officer." Jim offered.

"My mum lives a couple of mins away. I'll text her to come over."

"Okay, that'll would be useful," Jim replied, sounding very caring.

"I know it's difficult," Mac began, "but is there anything you can recall from the other night that might help us? I mean like, arguments or even cross words between Caroline and any of the guests." Emma as she sat now staring into space. "Ah, sorry, not that comes to me right now." She was almost whispering. She didn't stop looking directly out into the garden where her dogs were now sitting, waiting for their water and to be allowed in.

"Unfortunately, I'm going to have to ask you and your husband to each give a full statement, but that can wait until Henry returns home. Please, there's no need to call him home early unless you feel you need him here with you." Mac tried to sound as sympathetic as possible, something he'd never really mastered, yet something he'd had been trained to do. He'd always struggled with that side of his work.

Jim had in the meantime filled up the dog's bowl with fresh cold water and placed it outside for them. He liked dogs, and this he thought would help Emma as they seemed restless.

"We left Caroline and Charles late Saturday. Charles was drunk and from what I gathered he was feeling randy. He kept touching her and implying things to her, so I took the hint and we left. During the evening I can't remember anything in particular untoward."

"Can you call us when Henry returns, please? I'd appreciate you both coming down to the station to give us a full statement. We'll leave you for now, please call your mother, and we're sorry for the loss of your friend."

Emma called her mother, assuring Mac and Jim that she was fine. So they left her and drove back to the murder scene to see how things were progressing with the forensic analysis. Along the way, they discussed the reaction from Emma. Finding out your friend has been murdered would bring about a reaction of shock. They both agreed her reaction was what they expected, subdued and withdrawn. After all, her best friend had just been murdered and at a party she'd attended as well.

En-route they called in at the station after visiting the house again to get updates from the other Detectives.

While Mac and Jim were at the Thorburn's. Zodiac and Hunter were back at the station, shifting through hours of video footage from the party. The rest of the team had gone to the Stones head office to interview the employees who had attended the party and to search the offices. These offices were in a modern building in Kingston town centre, overlooking the river Thames and occupied the top couple of floors, the office its self was spacious and all open plan. Though there were three separate offices. One had Charles's name on, one with Henry's and another for board meetings and other guests when and if required. The kitchen, shower room and lounge were all located on the second floor, up a flight of stairs at the far end. The team split up into pairs to interview the dozen or so staff. Kara and Eli taking the ladies, while Jude and Danny the men. The forensic team arrived a few minutes behind them and started to set up DNA sampling from the staff. Two computer experts were in the forensic personnel, so having quickly set up a desk to check each laptop they had got everything they needed from each one.

When they arrived back at the station, Mac and Jim discussed some video footage with Hunter, who had found the few seconds of the bike racing off down the drive and then out through the gate. It had turned right towards the country lanes and into the darkness beyond.

From there on, they all knew that any footage would be non-existent. Hunter had managed to locate the tracker device attached to the motorbike through the manufacturer's coding process, and had called, explaining that the bike had been stolen in connection with a serious crime giving them the chassis number and registration code needed to access the data he wanted. So Zodiac was now in the process of tracking its progress and trying to find its present location. Hunter went on to inform the team that Mr Zaman's laptop contained the documents which he had stated, and referred to the contracts between the Government and Stone's PLC, but also a few pictures and images of pornography, backing up his claim to Mac, and The Chief, when they visited him at The Shard.

Mac was frustrated and disappointed in the progress that had been made at finding Charles Stone, there was absolutely nothing. No phone could be found, yet when they tried his number it just rang for six rings before going straight to voicemail. Caroline's phone wasn't difficult to unlock, but again revealed nothing of any importance, or any evidence as to the whereabouts of Charles. There were full details on it of the holiday that Mr Zaman had talked about earlier, which they hadn't been surprised at, along with invoices and the emails between her and the machine manufacturer in the US. Reece's phone, on the other hand, had been more complicated to access. Both Hunter and Zodiac had worked together for some time and eventually got past the complicated encryption signature Reece had installed on it.

Hunter had now managed to get the messenger app open. Putting it onto the incident tv screen, it showed a list of messages Reece had sent, with names to. It seemed as if all the girls in the office were on his call list. Hunter open one to find. "Can't wait till later I'm going to make you scream as I fuck you and cum in your tight pussy." Underneath the reply read, "God, I do hope so big boy." There were several messages in the same vein, six different girls. All had been similarly talking to Reece over the past few weeks. Some content was very graphic, pictures attached along with detailed times, when and where they would meet.

Hunter continued through the phone and went to the album app. There they came across pornographic images of Reece with different girls. Most of the pictures were date marked within the past three months, some went back eighteen months in total. There was one dated Saturday night at 8.24pm and that showed Reece being given oral sex by a black lady and then having sex with her in the bathroom. They all recognised the bathroom, volcanic lava wall instantly in the background. In the video she at first encouraged him, then asking for more as he did she seemingly unaware of him filming, he continued as she wanted until you could hear him call her something. They could quite easily make it out, he was saying that he'd never been with such a sexy black bitch before. She pleaded with him at that point not to cum inside her as she didn't want her dress spoilt and her husband would then know she'd been with someone else. He didn't listen, you could then hear him groaning and slowing his thrusting movements as he held her down firmly and filled her. The filming stopped at that point.

Kara spoke first. "We interviewed Candice Clarke earlier and that coincides with what she told Eli and me earlier, guv. Candice is married with two young children, both not yet teenagers but still a handful. She's had been married to Winston for fifteen years and has been working for Caroline as her PA and in HR since starting there three years ago. She admitted to having sex with Reece in the toilet and that she had to clean herself with her knickers and threw them away. That also explains something else. A couple of the girls in the office told her apparently how good he was and more to the point how big he was. They apparently teased her and encouraged her to try it for herself. Well, it seems she did try it on the night of the party."

"She claims that she needed a pee and went into the bathroom where Reece was taking a leak already, but he hadn't locked the door when she went in and things just went on from there. She pleaded us not to tell her husband, as it was only the once and she wanted to forget the whole thing." Kara continued. "We also have two other girls' statements, saying that they've had sexual relations with Reece over the past six months, both in private and at their own apartments, also in the office on various occasions after the offices were closed. We've searched his apartment in Teddington Lock. He rented a top floor penthouse, a one bedroom place with a large balcony overlooking the river. It's expensive and I would have thought well above his price range. His salary at

Stones, after paying tax etc would have been just enough to pay the rent, let alone his living expenses, which begs the question, how else was he making money? Also, we found packets of Viagra and some weed joints in a cupboard in the bedroom."

"Okay, that explains the black knickers found in the bin. so did he entertain others there as well?" Mac asked. "Did you get DNA from the apartment? We need to find out what he was doing to make extra money. So find out if any of those girls had a grudge against him. Bank accounts: I want to see he's statements for the past few months since taking the job and the apartment. Have you got DNA samples from everyone yet?"

"Yeah, gov, all with Dr Banks now for processing."

"Good. Someone! Please tell me we've made progress in finding Charles Stone. It's been three days now and we have fuck all on his whereabouts. We have technology coming out of our fucking ears, yet nothing on this guy!"

"Guv. We've all watched the footage taken from the house of Mr Stone going up the stairs, which is the last positive sighting we seem to have of him. We think it's him leaving the scene around about 12.30pm on the bike. Zodiac has tracked the bike via video cameras to a certain degree, but that went cold when it went into the country lanes about ten miles from here. His phone has gone dead, I've rung it several times." Hunter didn't sound too pleased with that being the only information he could give Mac at present.

"Okay, keep on it." Mac replied, "I think we need another visit to site, so we'll meet there first thing tomorrow at 8am. There's something that's not right here. What else do we know?"

"We have also established that Reece knew Sabil Zaman, guv, apparently they met when Charles was having computer problems in a meeting and Reece went to fix a virus." Jude had done some cross-referencing from the office receptionist and Charles's emails. There was one from Charles thanking Reece and also asking if he would check out his home laptop at some point when he had time.

"That could be significant as Reece was found with his wife when she was killed. It could well have started an affair which Charles didn't like, which then drove him to murdering both of them. It certainly gives him a motive," Eli added.

"Until we can talk to Charles, we are going to be clutching at straws. Let's put more effort into getting him found." Mac wasn't convinced it was as simple as Charles being the killer. "We need to chat with Henry and Emma Thorburn. But for now let's continue to eliminate suspects and fill in some missing pieces with Reece. I want to know how he got that job at Stones. Are there any connections between Reece and anyone from his past? He's been getting money from somewhere, let's find out where." Let's get to it guys." Jim, get the car, we're going to see the Thorburn's.

Emma sat watching the tv, with a glass of white Kuluma wine. The bottle she was holding was now half-empty, along with the already empty one that sat on the side table. She was starting to become quite drunk and light-headed.

Her mother had gone home. Emma had made her a promise, though, that she'd get some sleep after she left. She didn't. Emma didn't want to go to sleep and so she hadn't, but instead had been catching up with the last episode of GOT, something she'd been told about and heard a lot of good things about from the younger generation at work, stating how good it was and talking about how they couldn't wait for the next episode. Emma had wanted to finish the series before Henry returned from his trip. He wasn't really into fantasy adventure programs as she had been.

It was now late and although she'd thought about calling Henry to tell him about what had happened at Caroline's and Charles's house, she hadn't bothered. He would have left the hotel for a dinner meeting already and then he'd planned to go straight to the airport. Emma knew the flight was due at Heathrow a few hours from now and that he'd be home shortly after that.

She couldn't think much, only what the two detectives had told her. Despite the full on action and carnage going on with the dragons, she was restless. The idea of her friend being murdered was sending shivers down her spine and thoughts spinning round her head. How could someone do such a terrible thing? She raised her glass again for the umpteenth time to Caroline, wishing her all the best in the afterlife. Being a devoted Catholic, Emma believed that there was a life after death of some sort or, other. Just what that was she was unsure.

Henry arrived home when she expected, using the same cab company he usually used. His flight had landed at 6am, and so he'd managed to miss the early morning traffic around the motorway. Emma greeted him with the affection that she once felt for him, despite there being a lull in the sexual side of their marriage over the past few months, despite also knowing what Henry was like and what he'd really been doing the last couple of years behind her back. She felt sick every time her thoughts brought that back into her mind, but now Emma was now only thinking of her predicament with Caroline as she greeted him, not who or what he was. Her thoughts returned to the day of their wedding, the times before her unearthing of the gruesome, disturbing truth. Putting her arms round him she gave him a deep, passionate kiss. He responded with a surprised and confused reaction. Henry had now become accustomed to her chilled affections over the past few months, knowing that something was deeply worrying her. Yet he couldn't help her with her thoughts. This was good, Henry said to himself as they went through to the lounge.

"Henry, there's something I need to tell you before you hear from another source." Emma gave him a subdued look.

"Okay," Henry looked puzzled and confused.

"I had two officers round late yesterday afternoon. They told me that Caroline has been murdered in her bedroom along with a man. I assumed that would be Charles, but as yet they haven't confirmed."

Henry stood motionless with the shock of what Emma explained to him. "What?" he eventually stammered.

"They say that she's been killed and there was a man with her. I think that must be Charles. But I don't know yet and I don't know how to find out. I've called Charles's number, but it just rings and goes to voicemail." Emma said, fighting back the tears.

"What did the police actually say about the incident?" Henry was now holding Emma firmly as she'd started crying. "Have you got the detective's number? I'll call him." Henry held Emma tighter and with a firm grip.

"They've said they want us both to make statements at our earliest convenience." Emma was now whimpering into Henry's shoulder.

"Okay, I'll have a quick shower and then we can go."

Henry called the number Emma had been given by Mac the previous day. Jim answered after a couple of rings explained they would appreciate them coming down to the station to see them for an informal chat. Jim carried on explaining that it was important to do this today, as they might be able to help them with vital information. Jim put the phone down. Henry had asked if they minded going to their house, as it would be easier for Emma at the moment, Jim told Mac that they were both at home and after the meeting, they could go over to interview them.

Henry then contacted the office to let them know he wouldn't be coming in and to cancel the conference call he had planned later that day. Candice had answered the phone and told him of the police presence at the office yesterday and two detectives today. She said they were still interviewing all the staff but didn't fully know why. Henry couldn't think at this stage. Did everyone need to know the truth before speaking to the detectives? He pondered for a brief moment. He needed to do that in person. So he told Candice he'd be along later, and that everyone needed to stay until five.

Mac and Jim arrived at the Thorburns' house a little over an hour later, Jim driving as usual while Mac answered calls and went through the case with him as he drove. River had been one of those who spoke to Mac. She had some important and significant information, which he was keeping to himself for the time being. They pulled straight up the drive as the gates were already open, assuming that was done on purpose for ease. After giving a rather loud bang on the impressive brass lion head knocker, they waited just a few moments before Henry opened the door. He greeted them both and took them through to the lounge, where Emma was sitting reading a magazine and drinking a fresh cup of steaming coffee.

"Please take a seat," Henry asked, making a hand gesture towards the sofa.

"Thanks for seeing us this quickly. We appreciate you have things you need to arrange with work and other personal matters." Mac and Jim sat on the sofa opposite

Emma, taking in the furnishings and massive open fire place, it felt homely and peaceful.

Mac opened the conversation. "First of all, I need to tell you we've identified the body of Caroline Stone and the man they we believe to be Reece Jones, an employee at the Stones' offices. We are trying to put together a timeline of events for Saturday night. So we would like you, please, to tell us in your own time everything that you remember. You know the sort of thing. Time you arrived and left. Also, anyone you talked to etc. As I said we're still finding out who was there and trying to contact some of them. Anything at all at this stage would be of great help, no matter how insignificant it might seem to you." Mac turned on the recorder app on his works phone. Jim had been very impressed with the way Mac had learnt and adapted to new modern technology, especially over the past couple of years, despite his age and older traditional methods he'd been brought up with and used in the past.

Emma and Henry explained as much as they could remember about their movements, from arriving at Caroline's, right up to when Emma decided Henry had had, too much to drink, and that it was time perhaps they left. Henry, after all, had a flight the next day to Berlin to meet potential new clients from Dubai, who were important government officials. She also explained how Caroline had insisted they get a lift home, and how she collected the car early the following morning. Getting an Uber there before Henry got up as he was still sleeping.

Henry spoke first, explaining how the evening had gone for them. Both had mingled round most of the guests, chatting to some for longer than others. But no matter how much they tried the conversations were shorter than they'd really like to have been. Emma at some point had managed to tear herself away from Henry, who started talking golf with a couple of older guys. She had assumed that they were members of the club both Henry and Charles were also members of. After a few minutes, the dogs started barking in the back garden. Emma apologised and said she'd better go and sort them out, offering coffee or tea to Mac and Jim as she walked into the kitchen.

"Actually, do you mind if I have a glass of water?" Jim asked as she got up.

"Why, of course you can, come with me I'll get you one while I sort out Jack and Jill. There the dogs by the way." Emma encouraged Jim to follow her.

When they reached the kitchen, Emma explained that she'd had some very interesting conversations with some of the office girls that had turned up at the party. To be honest, they were all there. But Emma wasn't familiar with too many of them. She didn't go into the offices that often and they seemed to come and go regularly.

The conversation had been mostly about guys and who they were seeing at the present. Talk had inevitably turned to Reece. Most of the girls had fancied him, and Emma got the impression that the two of them knew more than they were saying about him. She then explained that she'd gone to use one of the upstairs toilets as the one downstairs was in use. When she was in the bedroom, she found the bathroom door locked. So, she decided to wait until it was free and have a sit down. While quietly sitting on the bed, she could hear a couple in the bathroom, laughing and joking about, then moaning and noise coming out of the room told Emma only one thing, that they were having sex in the bathroom. So she decided she'd better wait somewhere else until they had finished. She heard the woman giving some very encouraging instructions to her lover and had to have a smile and have a giggle to herself. Someone's getting a good seeing to, she thought, and thoroughly enjoying it.

Emma had been sitting on the chair in the dressing room, off the main bedroom, with a long walk-in wardrobe, with a dressing table and cupboards down both sides, all full of clothes, shoes, and other distinctive designer wear. She pushed the door, almost closing it, but left a crack for her to see who came out of the bathroom. Several minutes passed before they stopped, and sure enough, a minute or two later a man came out, it was none other than Reece, still adjusting his hair while heading for the bedroom door, a big smile beaming across his face. Emma was becoming interested as to who he had been giving a good seeing too.

And Candice, one of the PA's from work, appeared a couple of minutes later. She had obviously been reapplying her makeup and was still adjusting her dress on her way out. She looked hot and flustered, but well satisfied after her session with Reece. Emma's first reaction was envy of her, but that passed when she remembered that Candice was married, her husband was in fact downstairs chatting with Charles and Henry when Emma had needed to pee. Emma explained to Jim that she hadn't liked Reece from the first time she'd met him; he seemed so full of himself and cocky around the girls in the office. Whenever she'd met him at meetings or get-togethers she'd thought him creepy to a certain degree.

Emma thanked Jim for talking to her separately without Henry; she hadn't wanted to disclose that information in front of him but had thought it could be important or relevant to the investigation.

Henry, meanwhile, had been detailing to Mac how he'd talked to most of the guests throughout the evening, some far more than others. He really didn't have much in common with the younger generation and office employees, a bit of an age thing, really. He'd spoken to the more distinguished guests, though. Both Henry and Emma described how some of the girls had brought bikinis in their handbags, knowing full well that there was a pool to use and being determined to take a swim as it was still very humid and hot. The men had mostly enjoyed the spectacle as well. A couple of girls had forgotten costumes but being a bit tipsy they just went topless anyway. Emma had also seen that a few men smoking weed and thinking how disgusting it had smelt to her. She had to escape at one point and went told Henry she needed fresh air and a walk. The drink had flowed throughout, the music had most people up dancing and enjoying the night, Henry commented even he had a dance at one point.

"Did either of you know that Mrs Stone was pregnant?" Mac got Emma out of her own thoughts in a split second. Henry looked bewildered and looked at Emma to see her response.

"Yes, I did actually, Caroline had told me a week ago that she was expecting and was about ten weeks gone as far as she knew, which I must admit was a surprise to me, knowing Charles's condition."

"What condition was that, then?" Mac responded, looking a bit bewildered.

"Not a hundred percent, surely. All I know is that they had discussed other forms of conceiving. and having a child. Caroline had been getting broody over the past year and really wanted to be a mother. If you take a look at his medical records, I think you'll find out. I'm not sure personally, as I say, it's a condition he's had for a while, I'm not a doctor, sorry."

"We were at a coffee, come, breakfast meeting when she told me. She just couldn't wait, apparently, to tell Charles, but it was his birthday coming up and she was going to tell him then. But she wanted to tell someone and share her excitement, so she told me. Caroline said they'd found the right sperm donor a while back and she had been to a private clinic and had artificial insemination, which had taken first time."

Emma had known that this was a white lie, and that Caroline was testing her loyalty in a roundabout way, trying to see if she questioned her story and hoping Emma wouldn't say anything to Charles until she'd had the opportunity. She asked her not to let on to anyone she was pregnant until they announced it. Emma, had of course, agreed.

Emma also knew deep down that no matter how Caroline had conceived this child, Charles would be so pleased and overjoyed about becoming a father. He'd wanted children as much as Caroline had., just as Emma knew Henry would too, but Emma hadn't plucked up the courage to tell him yet, she had been in two minds as to keep her baby or not, but in that instant decided she would keep it and tell Henry when the police had gone.

"Why would she tell you before her husband?" Mac was confused.

"She wanted to surprise Charles for his birthday since it was his 50th and a special one, simple as that." Emma's mind started to wander at this point, beginning to wonder about the bodies and Caroline fucking Reece, then realised instantly who the father was. Until now she'd had her suspicions, but now it totally clear to her.

"Wasn't Caroline with Charles on the bed, you know, when they were murdered?" Emma quired.

"As I said, we believe that the young man was Reece Jones, not her husband." Mac allowed her to take it in once more.

"Yes, you said earlier, sorry,"

"Do either of you know where Charles might be? He's not been seen since you last saw him at the party and his phone is now dead. Anything at this stage might well help us find him."

"Sorry, we've told you everything we know." Both Henry and Emma were sure that they had given a truthful account of the afternoon and evening's events. They then decided they had as much information that they would get for the time being and decided to leave Henry and Emma to themselves.

Henry walked them to their car and watched as they drove away.

While Henry was gone for those few moments, Emma cleaned up her face and re-did her makeup. She wanted to look her best when she told Henry about the baby. When she came into the Kitchen after doing her makeup Henry was making fresh coffee.

"You remember the other day at the party I told you I wanted to go for a walk and felt funny, and you put it down to the drink, well, it really wasn't the drink. Henry, I'm actually two months pregnant with our child," Emma said and waited for his reaction but didn't need to wait for long.

"You're kidding me! Oh my God that's amazing. I wondered what was going on. Now it makes sense! When's it due?" Henry couldn't believe what Emma was now telling him. It took a while. But he was so happy.

"It's due in seven months." Emma said feeling relieved by Henry's reaction. They then spent the next few hours discussing the baby and toasting Caroline at the same time.

At the station, Kara had been busy contacting the two escorts Mick hired for the evening, managing to get in contact with them through his phone records. The girls confirmed exactly what Zaman, told the others that morning, adding that they knew Mick had had an argument with Reece at the party, when he'd interrupted them in the bedroom. Reece had apparently laughed and had taken the mickey out of Mick as he fucked one. Asking if he wanted a real man to show him how to satisfy her. Apparently the two men nearly had a fight over it. Reece seemed to enjoy ridiculing Mick about it for quite a while. The girls said that Mick had been worried that Reece would tell Sabil Zaman.

"This might have pushed Mick a bit too far and could have given him a motive for murdering of Reece in particular." Kara concluded.

Mac now had more reasons than ever to want to interview Mick as soon as possible.

Chapter 7.

Mick Jones.

Michael Jones had been an unruly teenager. His mum Maggie always worried about how he was going to get on in life, how this boy was going to make a living, find someone to love and be happy with. Mick, however, seemed happy and content with his odd lifestyle. He'd grown up quickly learning to drive fast cars and more importantly riding a motorbike. Much to his mum's frustration, Mick's dad was a massive motorbike enthusiast and had owned several fast machines when Mick was young, eventually showing him how to ride properly and safely. It was then an ironic tragedy that his father got killed when Mick was in his early teens. A lorry didn't see him coming one dusky morning and pulled out, giving him no chance to avoid the inevitable collision, breaking practically every bone in his body. Mick had mourned his dad's death ever since, as they were very close. But still he wanted to ride bikes because it reminded him of his father.

Mick had been the youngest of the family, his sisters continually making him feel the least important of the three of them, constantly teasing him and winding him up about his sexuality along the way. Mick was always the one who, when it was raining, was made to walk the dog and go shopping if there was no milk. The things they made him do were endless. Years later, Maggie still had her oldest daughter living and caring for her at home in the cottage, despite Lucy having a child of her own to look after. The cottage the Joneses now lived in was a smaller house, but comfortable and affordable, being mortgage free, since the life insurance paid out and the sale of the large family home in the exclusive Berkshire countryside.

Mick became resentful over the years of the attention that his sisters received from their parents, the love and affection their mother showed them, all the time, and keeping her distance from him. Maybe she could tell Mick was different in so many ways. But what was different these days? The wider acceptance of those who came under a different and so-called unacceptable sexuality had now completely changed. Mick, although born a male, considered himself to be a binary person. He'd slept with both women and male friends and at one point had lived with a couple in a polyamory relationship, which he felt had ended unfortunately and far too soon.

Maggie very rarely saw Mick nowadays; he seemed to be always busy, even though she knew his employment wasn't always continuous, as a freelance consultant for a construction company. He was always seemingly away on business, here, there and everywhere. But she did get regular calls from him, along with surprise presents arriving through the post and by delivery vans. He'd sent her the most up-to-date gadgets on the market, including phones, laptops, and jewellery. At one time Maggie had been concerned about the continuing arrival of parcels and asked him to stop, but with no response. The parcels kept appearing. Mick was trying to please her, doing what he thought would impress her. Showing that he was a responsible and loving son.

Since meeting and starting a relationship with Sabil Zaman, he'd considered he'd won the lottery big time in so many ways. Not only was he in a sexual relationship, but he was never short of money, Sabil had always seen to that. Mick carried on seeing women as and when Sabil was away on business. Sabil knew full well that their relationship would not be in the public domain, all the time it allowed Mick that freedom and Mick also knew that when he asked for money or almost anything, he would be allowed it. Mick had the power and means to destroy Sabil Zaman's reputation simply by saying the wrong thing to the right people, and Sabil knew that too well.

Maggie was now wondering why she'd not heard from him in over a month, especially as it was the bank holiday weekend when, he would normally at least text her at some point. Maggie waited.

Mick had first met Sabil Zaman in a Soho night club. It had been wet and cold, and he'd only really gone to the club to get out the cold weather but thought he might see if he could pick up a girl for some fun. Inside there wasn't much happening, just the usual people having a good evening out, seemingly being mostly couples. A young girl caught his eye and he'd been watching her and thought about approaching, vanished along with a rather tall, mean looking black man, so that frustrated him somewhat. Deciding then to get himself another drink from the bar, he accidently knocked into Sabil sitting on his own, a pint of lager in one hand, and a vodka sitting alongside it. Mick quickly apologised, to Sabil offering to replace the spilt pint of lager. That was the first and last drink Mick ever bought for Sabil. After sitting and chatting for an hour, Sabil decided to invite Mick back to his room for a night cap, in his hotel across the way. Mick agreed enthusiastically.

Sabil after that night had seen Mick regularly while in London on business. Every time he returned he'd called Mick to meet him; and they had amazing sex together and had become good friends and companions over the past couple of years. Things started to go sour as far as Sabil was concerned, when Mick started getting greedy, always asking for more money to live on, and hinting to Sabil that they're were benefits for his silence about their affair. After all, Sabil had become a wealthy man over the time they were together, making millions from being in the right place at the right time, getting construction contracts for luxury apartments and buying land to develop condos and large shopping malls. The list seemed endless.

Mick arranged for Sindy and Tammy, the two ladies they hired for the evening party, to be picked up by a limo and brought to the car park in the Shard. They all became acquainted with each other as they were driven to Surrey in the blacked-out Mulsanne Grand Limousine, a luxury car with its seats facing each other so that the passengers could talk and drink together, which they duly did. The girls were everything Sabil had asked for even if they were getting paid quite handsomely for it too. chic, elegant and both stunning to look at, Sindy was a tall redhead in her mid-twenties and Tammy a natural blonde just a couple of years older than Sindy. They both showed their figures to the utmost with plenty of leg and cleavage, just as Mick had stipulated when contacting the agency and transferring their fees in advance via his phone.

As they made their way to the party, the conversation was mainly about what the girls could expect during the evening. The drinks were flowing, throughout the journey so the girls were relaxed and very much looking forward to what lay ahead. Throughout the evening they duly chatted and laughed with other guests as well as each other, getting along really well and seeming genuine partners for the two men. Neither girl, however, had met before, so to hear them talking like old friends helped relax the atmosphere. Sabil realised that during the evening Mick disappeared with each of the ladies for half an hour or so, but he was under no illusion about what Mick was up to. Sabil actually felt jealous, along with annoyance. While Mick was off with Tammy, Sabil was in conversation with Charles and Caroline about the Harley motorbike Charles currently owned. He had thought as a favour to Sabil about allowing him to borrow the machine for Mick for a couple of weeks while they were away, with all the right insurance in place, of course. However, Sabil refused very quickly, saying that Mick probably wouldn't want to risk damaging such an expensive and personal item, knowing full well that that wasn't the case and Mick would undoubtedly want the bike. When Mick returned, he heard Charles say to Sabil that if he wanted to change his mind about the bike to let him know, and he asked Sabil what they were talking about just as Charles had been called away by Caroline to greet the local MP arriving late from a Parliamentary debate.

Sabil ignored Mick's question as just then Henry brought over some guests, introducing him as David, an electrical supplier Stones used, along with his wife Sarah. The conversation then completely changed, and Mick had left in a huff before he could be involved into their conversation. He headed off down to the garage, and sure enough there was the Harley all shiny and gleaming. Its big chrome chassis highly polished. He decided that he wanted to sit on it, to feel what it was like to sit astride the plush leather seat. As he did, Caroline emerged behind him and caught him getting on it. She stood watching for a minute as Mick indulged himself on the bike.

"Nice machine, isn't it? So much power, and such a great ride too. Your Sabil's boyfriend, aren't you?" Caroline startled Mick for a brief moment.

"So, what if I am?" He was still feeling the anger from his conversation with Sabil, but then realising that there was an attractive lady standing behind him, he quickly smiled.

"Well, if you like, I could arrange a ride for you. can you handle a bike like that?"

"I can ride anything." He'd now turned and was looking at this beautiful woman now in front of him. "Especially someone as sexy as you, babe."

"Before you say anything else, let me introduce myself. I'm Caroline Stone, your host."

Mick completely changed his attitude towards Caroline. Apologising for his last comment, then trying to hide his embarrassment, but not managing too well, so, looked foolish for a moment.

"It's fine, I get that a lot, don't worry." Caroline replied.

"I'd like to ride this sexy machine though. Harley Davidsons are such masterpieces and great faultless engineering as well." Mick was now running his hand over the machine as though it was his latest female conquest.

"I'll arrange something for you. You're, not sober enough today, but drop by Monday and I'll arrange for someone to be here to give you the keys." Caroline sounded sincere and very genuine as she spoke, and knowing what she'd discussed with Sabil earlier, had reason to be.

"Thank you. I'd appreciate that. Wow, I can't wait that'll be fun."

They chatted more while they returned upstairs to the other guests, Mick was feeling his usual cocky self again and thanked Caroline for her tolerance about their meeting. He then went to find Sindy.

Charles had brought the Harley Davidson when the company had turned over nearly half a billion pounds in contracts, leaving him the luxury of being able to order this special bike, and purchasing it without it affecting the company bank balance too much. He'd ordered a design to be sprayed on the Harley that matched Stones' company logo colours, it was stunning in the red, white, and blue. now looked like a British bike and not an American product.

Charles had always owned a bike when he was younger. Caroline often teased him about it being a mid-life crisis purchase, how it reeled back the years for him. He had special leathers made to fit both himself and Caroline and matching the leather seat on the bike to. The suits were also embossed with the Stone logo, the colours of the patriot he was. Charles had been a patriot all his life and tried to make and keep all his businesses and work force in Britain, despite having pressure put on him to move abroad with the manufacturing side of the business. He refused frequently and instead increased the workforce after the pandemic. He'd kept his word. The company was even stronger now. He'd also had been several times to a private race track at Loughborough with the bike, managing to get the bike round for few laps, getting it up to incredible speeds along the straights and having a great day out with his mates, he even persuade Caroline on board for a few laps and knew she really enjoyed the experience, too.

Mac was now trying to locate this expensive piece of machinery, hoping that its driver could explain a lot about the events that night. It had been in the garage without question during the afternoon of the party, a couple of the chefs had also been to have a look on their break and admitted sneaking down to photograph themselves sitting on it. Mac now had the bikes original documentation, along with the serial number for the engine and subframe. Hunter had come across the documents in the main vault where Zodiac had been shifting through the piles of papers and found it. Built in the US and custom made for Charles, the paint was a one off, and the leather soft as a feather, and a tracker had been enabled and fitted into a specially formed compartment under the fuel tank. It was unmistakably a fine piece of engineering and a status symbol like no other.

Tracking it had been difficult to begin with, but the further it went away from the house it became easier as the tracker could be activated. Hunter had already tracked it down to Dover and beyond to Calais via the Channel tunnel. From there they tracked it to Marseille, where it seemed to vanish into thin air. The tracker showed it was static for about three hours late on the Monday evening, then it was disabled and disappeared from the computer screen.

Hunter had already contacted Mac to ask that they got help from the French Police Nationale. When they arrived at the Harley's last known location there was no sign it, only an articulated lorry full of tools, and the tracker. There were no finger prints on anything left in the lorry, no sign that the bike had even been present other than the tracker. Someone had done a thorough job of cleaning the inside of the vehicle and if it hadn't been for the tracker no one would have suspected anything. The device to all intents and purposes appeared to be left to torment the police and anyone who came looking for it. The bike was now thought to have been stolen to order and would have been taken to pieces before going to its new owner for to be reassembling.

Mac considered at one point sending someone to France to investigate, but felt that it was a waste of resources. The French authorities had provided video footage along with photos and a full written report on what they found. They had even given a list of port and ferry departures, along with cargo manifests for ferries, leaving the ports on the dates Hunter had asked for. They were still checking CCTV footage for passengers boarding to verify whether Charles Stone had tried to abscond further along with his bike, the face recognition software being used was a reliable and accurate programme, but hadn't bought up any results.

Mac, however, was satisfied that the Harley was no longer in France, but in a container being shipped to a client elsewhere and felt pretty certain that this was either payment for help to escape or stolen to order for someone. Mac and the team were going to have to dig much deeper and find out more.

Hunter contacted all the companies and relative authorities where ships were scheduled to dock. He'd persuaded the freight border controllers in all the docks to report back what was in their cargo. This hadn't been a straightforward task, but Hunter informed them that they were looking for possible drugs and Diamond smuggling along with the bike. Hunter knowingly they would take more notice and react to it quicker, helping as much as possible.

The only aspect Hunter didn't have control over were the private yachts, those that had already left port, three had left port during those few hours, all without indication of their next destination, let alone their country of origin. The harbour master at Marseille had been as helpful as he could, but was refused to disclose the owners identities, because of confidentially clauses in the documentation, he implied it was more than his job was worth.

He did, however forward information, a contact who might be willing to help. The hotel situated on the cliff, just outside of the docks that looked out on to the warm sunny waters of the Mediterranean and had security cameras overlooking the beach and exit from the port. The harbour master called his contact, explaining the situation, after which Mac had rung the Hotel. He was put through to a Monsieur Batiste, the chief security officer in charge at the hotel. Yes, Mr Batiste would help and was already preparing the video footage that Mac required. He also had a file already being loaded with some other information, just waiting for an email address to forward it to Mac. He had written the names of all yachts that departed the port over the past seventy-two hours, along with clear and precise descriptions, a total of three expensive yachts that he could only dream of owning on his meagre salary. One was Russian, one was Saudi registered, and one was a South American vessel. He'd already taken still pictures from the footage and made sure that they showed the names and registration numbers attached to each vessel in turn. Mac asked these he'd emailed immediately over, along with any info he could manage to find out about the craft.

True to his word, Batiste emailed Mac, and included the destination ports according, to the logs he had sourced from his brother. Batiste's brother worked at the port loading cargo. He'd worked there for years and knew everything that went on and everything that came and went.

The boat heading across the Atlantic wasn't due to dock until the weekend, four days away in Tampico. Unfortunately, the other two yachts were already at their next ports of call, one in Algiers and the other in Valencia. Both were now docked, and the occupants seemingly long gone from the vessels when the local police came calling.

"We need to inspect those vessels and try to find out if they were carrying any cargo, and if so whether it off-loaded. Can you get on it straight away?" Mac said across the room to Danny, copying all the information he'd received from Batiste to the entire team to have as a reference if required.

Mac called Superintendent Willis to bring him up to date, but mainly to ask him to contact and arrange the necessary permissions with the Mexican authorities to search the yacht. They would need special diplomatic permissions to board and search it when it docked at Tampico, a lot of red tape that needed to be sorted quietly and quickly.

Willis agreed to try and contacted the embassy in London, to start the arrangements for the necessary paperwork. Then, he had to explain the situation and reasons behind their request to his own boss. This was going to eat into money, and he was well aware of that.

The sun hadn't risen when Katie was out running with her two greyhound's, they always enjoyed a good run in the morning before the park and towpath got too busy, and far too hot for them. The Thames meanders slowly along this stretch at Runnymede with canal boats often moored overnight. The dogs this morning seemed very excitable and Katie was having to run faster than usual just to stay with them as they race along the towpath. Suddenly up in front they stopped, and disappeared down towards the water's edge, Katie stopped, too, to see what had distracted them from their constant running, usually nothing did.

She immediately took a step back as she realised why the dogs had stopped. They were sniffing round a black object washed up in the clay and weedy thick mud at low tide. A large black sack which had been torn practically right open. Poking out were an arm and a leg, both badly blotted and turning rather grey. The body looked as though it dressed, but as the body was covered in mud and difficult to be sure. Somehow she managed to drag it onto the bank, all the time trying to stop the greyhounds from biting it and causing more injury to the already decaying corpse. Without hesitation, Katie took her phone from her running belt, calmly rang for the police, and told them the What3words that would bring them straight to her GPS location, all the while still struggling to control the dogs from doing any damage to the body.

Katie didn't have long to wait before the police arrived. The flashing lights were visible long before they pulled into the car park and made their way along the path to her. Several other passers-by had stopped to take a look as more and more emergency services began to arrive.

Katie was now sitting down on the grass verge, in shock and being comforted by a female officer as she took her initial statement. Eventually her husband arrived to take her and the dogs home.

Mac's phone rang as he sat at his desk going through the guest list with Kara. They'd substantially managed to reduce from when they had first compiled it, always good news. From the original number they were now down to the last twenty and the staff employed that night, those who couldn't give exact times and reasons for their whereabouts.

Mac picked up his mobile; a withheld number was on the screen.

"Chief Inspector Mac Savage," he said as he pushed back in his chair.

"Good morning, sir. It's Detective Blake Harris from the homicide team in West London. Thought I'd better tell you that I think we have one of your suspects for your murder investigation. He came up on our register when we ran a basic remote data search. We believe it's Mr Mick Jones. There was a note on file saying you wanted to know his whereabouts and to question him."

"Great, that's good news, where have you taken him? I'll be along to chat with him soon," Mac replied.

"That might be difficult he's in a black body bag as we speak. He has been washed up on the river bank at Runnymede, I'm afraid. He was pulled out of the water by a passer-by on her run with her dogs earlier this morning. Looks as if his been in the water three or four days, according to the forensic team."

"Fuck," Mac said. "Who's your forensic doctor down there?"

"Dr Jenkins, I believe you might know him. When I mentioned that the victim could be related to your case, he also called in Dr Banks. I believe she's on her way here as we speak."

"Okay, I'll send a team down to get a full report, if that's okay with you?"

"Of course,"

Eli and Kara arrived at Runnymede an hour later. Through the heavy traffic of commuters trying to get to Heathrow Airport to catch flights and make it to the office on time. The M25 was slow moving as usual. All lanes chock-a-block, Kara still drove through the traffic with siren and lights flashing as she eased her way between the lorries and cars, not wanting to use the sirens as most of the traffic then gave way without hesitation.

The Thames at Runnymede meanders gently working its way down stream, before reaching The Bell weir lock, its width substantial and with signs placed along that section warning of how deep and how fast flowing the water could be at certain times of day. It was also very murky along that stretch of river and during the recent spell had left thick clay and silt clinging to its drying banks.

Pulling into the car park Eli and Kara were greeted by two uniformed officers, who asked to see their identification, before allowing them entry and directing them to the cordoned off area to park in. They were directed along the towpath by another officer, walking for a couple of minutes along the narrow stone path before they reached the spot where the body had been washed up, now covered by a white tent. Two small police search boats were patrolling the water, protecting the scene from inquisitive boats as they chugged past. There were divers waiting at the side of the river, being briefed about the search area. Over on the far side were the ruins of the old Benedictine nunnery which had stood for some considerable years, along with the Ankerwycke yew, a beautiful, centuries old tree that for walkers and tourists is a wonderful sight and experience to visit. The body had been more exposed by the forensic team over the past hour as they carefully pulled him in further onto the safety of the dry grass and reeds. Over on the other side there seemed to be lots of activity and looking across Kara and Eli could plainly see why. There was clothing caught up among the trees and bushes protruding into the river. Only time would tell whether they were part of this or just coincidence, but the divers were on their way, so they left them to do their job.

Approaching the white tent, they were greeted briefly by Dr Banks and Dr Jenkins, both with the usual Hazmat overalls on, both looking as if they could do with a few hours' sleep.

"Morning, guys, Mac sent you on this one did he? Mac isn't brilliant with washed up bodies, never has been; he doesn't mind the bloody one, though," River grinned.

"The body's been in the water a good three or four days as far as we can tell and has been decomposing quickly in this hot sweltering weather. I'm surprised no-one spotted it before this morning, but there was an extra high tide yesterday. The clothes he was wearing have all but disappeared. Whether that was because of the time in the water or because he was without any when dumped further up river, we don't yet know. Cause of death at the moment we believe to be to be a blow to the back of the head with a blunt instrument, fracturing his skull. Most probably a hammer or instrument with a small impact area. The body is, as you would expect after that amount of time in water, swollen and beyond recognition. Also, the blow to the head caused a large gash six to eight inches in length. There is something else that we found somewhat strange and could also be a factor in his death, he was actually castrated. We won't completely be sure until the post-mortem whether that was before or after death, both penis and scrotum were removed. I'll be back at the lab in a couple of hours, so I'll text you when we start the post-mortem. Okay?"

"Four days ago, would put it within the time of the party and the other homicides we're investigating. Any idea about where the body might have dumped into the river?" Kara reminded her.

"Yes, it would be around that time. As for where he was put in the river, I'm not sure as yet. The tide speed and regularity would affect the time factor." Dr Banks needed time to answer fully, which Kara really knew, but thought she'd better ask.

"When can we expect a full post mortem report?" Eli spoke abruptly. The truth was that he was a bit freaked out by the condition of the corpse, it felt as if he had entered a walking dead scenario. He felt queasy seeing the body lying in the mud half-expecting it to jump up and attack him.

"Dr Jenkins and I will conduct the post mortem this afternoon. Want to be present?" River asked Eli, with a bit of sarcasm in her voice. Before he had time to answer. Kara replied with a positive "Yes, of course, we'll see you there." Eli gave her the filthiest of looks as she turned smiling back at him, but knew she was right: they needed to know as soon as possible when and how he exactly had died. Before returning to the station.

When they arrived at the medical examiner's office they were shown through to the autopsy viewing area. Dr Banks was already doing her pre-check routine of measuring body parts and telling her assistant, Dr Sam Rogers. She didn't even look up as she welcomed the two officers. Dr Rogers was a young man who had recently joined the forensic team, River had taken him under her wing after recommending him to her bosses.

There was an extensive amount of swelling of the body. Indicating that the time of death would have been between twenty-four to thirty-six hours before it was pulled out of the river. Still, the water hadn't swollen the body as much as River had expected. She decided that other tests on the skull, lungs and blood vessels would be necessary to give her what she needed to know, before she could conclude the cause of death was a combination of a blow knocking him unconscious and the ensuing blood clot.

I think then he was castrated and dumped in the river which gave him no hope of recovering from the attack. The head wound was caused by a blunt object approximately three inches. She'd concluded because of the amount of bruising around the impact area, the skull was fractured, and a clot had formed on the brain, before being dumped in the river. As the post-mortem continued, Eli looked and felt uncomfortable watching, so turned his attention to taking notes instead, trying not to look what at the doctor was doing, seemingly unaffected by the incisions being made into the skull and torso. It was all in a day's work for her, and natural.

"Why would anyone want to castrate him after they killed him?" Kara asked.

"Could be for any reasons really," Came the reply from Sam.

"It could be a trophy. Most murderers, as you are well aware, will take a souvenir from the victim or crime scene to keep as a memento. I expect that's what happened. But, also it might have been considered necessary. I mean to remove any trace of DNA or other evidence that could link them to the body."

"Okay, thanks for that." Kara replied. "Think we've seen enough for now. I'll let Mac know and we'll await the written report. "With that, they left the doctors to do their work and went to report back to the team at the office.

It was now possible for them to piece together the last few hours of Mick Jones's life, from how he left the party to being washed up on the river bank at Runnymede. The fact his corpse had been castrated made things more difficult for them. Detective Harris had been assigned the investigation into Mick's murder as it was part of his case, but assured Mac that he could have access to any files and documents he needed. With two other corpses having turned up along the same two-mile stretch of the river over the past four months. Harris had his hands full now. All of them were in their mid-twenties, good looking and both single free men. Harris and his team assumed that all three had been dumped upstream when the river's tides were at their highest, so the bodies could travel as far as possible downstream when the tide went out. All the men had been struck across the back of the head with a sharp instrument and then castrated, left to die if they weren't long dead already.

Because of the warm sunny days, all three bodies would have been put into the river late at night. The cover of darkness giving the necessary cover, making it easier and far less obvious what was going on. All three were thought naked, without jewellery or watches, items which would be of some value when sold, something Harris suspected had already been done. Mick, on the other, hand had a couple of tattoos to his upper arms, in the form of an, Angel, and one of a skull. Both the others had designer hair stubble, and bright blue eyes.

Harris's team thought that the castration would have been done post death; the blood loss from the victims hadn't been sufficient for them to have been removed while they were still alive, in his opinion. Dr Jenkins had performed the autopsies on the bodies when they were washed up, with the help of Dr Banks, in Mick's case. All three showed signs of alcohol use, not in any significant quantities, but still enough to put them over the limit for driving. Mick Jones they knew had almost certainly been riding the bike stolen from Charles Stone's garage, despite the bike no longer being anywhere to be found. Yet here he was, dead.

There were scratch marks on all three men's backs, leaving marks of between two and six inches and all contained the same DNA profile, leading to the conclusion that all three had been having sex or had sex with the same person at some point shortly prior to death. Despite this, there were no known matching DNA profile on any of the databases they could access. The scratches showed minor signs of nail polish in the cuts, Eli suggested that perhaps Hunter, might follow this up.

Mac sat at his desk. His paperwork was now beginning to pile up, but it was getting to where the press and media were pestering, wanting to know what was happening up at the Stone's house. Someone had apparently tipped them off about the police presence. Mac wasn't surprised. To be honest, he was half-hoping to keep things quiet until the morning, but that now seemed a futile task.

He got a call from Willis. He confirming a press conference in a couple of hours, time. Mac now had to work out what was the least and best information he could give them, with Charles Stone still missing. He needed their help in many respects but also didn't want to get government officials involved and to asking problematic questions.

Eli and Kara had now returned in from the autopsy and were waiting to share the information that Dr Banks gave them. There was now an arrest warrant being issued for Charles Stone, and Mac was sure that that alone had been the cause for the media attention. Charles Stone had been missing now for possibly four days and could in theory be anywhere in the world. It would be a mega task just to find him, let alone interview him. So, he decided that with today's social network it might actually help them and boost their task. Mac knew full well the release of the news that it wasn't Charles Stone murdered with Caroline, but of an unknown male, was going to raise a lot of awkward and unanswered questions. They had little on Reece, even after three days, they needed a break in finding out more about his background. They were beginning to wonder where that was coming from.

The press conference went better than he expected, and he was now he waited for some help from the social media in response to their appeal. This could go either way, help or a burden. Although he was well aware of the false and cranky calls, now they would probably receive. He remained optimistic.

Chapter 8.

Scandal. Eight months before the party.

One sunny evening in the previous Autumn, Henry and Emma had just returned from their local church. The service had felt even longer because of the recent hot sticky weather, the church had been full, with the sixty or so people, but they were, back at home. Sitting and enjoying a glass or their favourite chardonnay in the orangery. The Sunday tabloids were spread out across the table, with Henry deep into an article on the progress of solar power. Unexpectedly, the front gate security system activated on the monitor across the other side of the room, showing a man standing waiting for a response.

Henry got up, putting his wine and paper down on the table as he left to answer the front door, it was at the far side of the house and it meant going through the lounge then into the long hallway. By the time Henry reached the door and the intercom monitor, it had been pushed yet again, making Henry a bit annoyed and frustrated. When he finally opened the door, he had a better view of the visitor; an adolescent man dressed in black shorts and a white tee shirt with plain black sandals; he looked like he'd just walked off a beach not for an autumn day.

"Can I help you?" Henry asked, as he pushed the intercom system.

"Hi, my name is Reece, is that Henry?"

"Yes. Do I know you?"

"Hope so, from a few years ago at school, but you probably don't remember me. Can I talk with you please, sir?"

"What about? I'm busy and I'm with my wife."

The young man turned to look straight into the video camera. He smiled.

"Oh, it won't take long and I'd rather we chatted in private, Henry, I'm sure your wife won't want to hear what I've got to say." Reece was determined, and Henry could sense it in his voice. He began to remember the face, but certainly not the name. Where had he seen this young man before, what did he want? His heart started to race. Oh, shit, he thought to himself without saying it out loud.

"What do you want? What's this about? You come here on a Sunday knocking at my private house demanding to see me. What do you really want, boy?"

Henry was getting flustered and very anxious now. He certainly didn't want Emma to become suspicious and start asking questions, so he agreed to let him in, only if he would come into the study and wait for him there. Reece nodded his agreement and Henry begrudgingly pushed the button and the gates opened. He showed Reece straight into the study, then offered him a drink from the small fridge that had been fitted in the study a few weeks earlier. Reece thanked Henry and took out one of the bottled waters, drinking it almost in one gulp. Placing the empty bottle in the waste basket.

Henry left Reece while he returned to Emma, who seemed to be in a world of her own. She was still reading the latest issue of H and H with a glass of wine in one hand. She looked up as Henry re-entered the room.

"Who was at the door?"

"I'm sorry, I forgot I told a new employee of the accounts department he could drop bye. We need to go over a couple of figures regarding the Government contract we are bidding for. Do you mind taking the dogs out for a walk while I see to him?"

"Of course. They need a walk anyway. That'll give us some time later for a swim and some proper quality time together later, before dinner." Emma smiled, and gave Henry a peck on the cheek.

Henry and Emma had two old English sheepdogs, Jack and Jill. They'd rescued the dogs last year when Emma had seen them at the local centre, looking very neglected and mistreated. They'd been abandoned by their previous owner in a very sorry state when they became too large and needed a lot of attention and grooming. Emma couldn't resist their cuteness and decided she must take them home. Since then, she walked them a couple of times at the weekends and a dog walker came to take them out on weekdays. Both dogs now were very healthy and thriving in their new surroundings and loved walking in the woods out behind the house. Emma had recently had them both trimmed, so their coats were short and looked very tidy and cute.

"I'll take them out to the woods. That'll give them a bit of exercise." Emma was now putting the magazine down and getting up from her chair.

"Thanks, love, we shouldn't be that long, I'll call you soon." Henry felt relieved as he watched Emma calling for the dogs. He now returned to his unwelcome guest. Reece was still where he'd left him, sitting in a large leather armchair, He had inherited from his father a few years before and loved it ever since, dark green leather and button fastenings on an old frame-work of oak. It had seen better days, but Henry liked it anyway, so hadn't bothered getting it refurbished.

Emma had the dogs' leads and whistle, something that the trainer advised. Jack and Jill were already in the garden, she blew the whistle once, and the dogs responded, getting up from their beds and running over to where she was standing. Then she remembered that she needed to post some party invites to her parents. Caroline's surprise party was a few weeks off now, but she knew her parents always liked a lot of time to respond. They were so old-fashioned that way and would only send a written RSVP.

She went back into the hallway to pick up the envelopes from the hallway table. Passing the partially open study door where Henry was talking to Reece, and so she stopped for a brief moment, listening to the heated conversation going on within the room. Something Emma wouldn't have normally done, but for some reason today was different.

"What do you want from me? Why have you changed your name to Reece?"

"Why, Henry, I would have thought that was fucking obvious. I needed to move on. So how could I without changing my life completely? The abuse I got from you and some of your so-called mates at those parties at Rose Manor have never gone from my head. Day and night I see those things over and over. You abused me. Hurt me. And just destroyed everything I went to private school to learn. Now it's payback time. I need money. But better still a proper paid job, something that will set me up and let me move on with my life, you know, compensate for those traumatic times. You know I've got the qualifications and knowledge to work for your company, so let's get something sorted or I can destroy your life far more than you could imagine." Reece was standing now right in Henry's face sounding vicious.

"It's not my company, but you probably know that don't you. Haven't you got a job?" Henry asked.

"Yes, I have, but, Henry, remember what you did to me back then. You raped me, caned me and made me do things that a twelve-year-old boy shouldn't been put through. You abused your position as my headmaster, tormenting me and the other boy Giles. Bet you didn't know that he's in a home after having a serious fucking breakdown after you fucked with his head?"

Henry was now getting worried. He'd been to special counselling sessions after leaving the boy's school, trying to put that period of his life behind him. Even Henry was ashamed of his behaviour, He had been Head of Maths and Economics at the boys' boarding school and lectured regularly at the University. Putting those memories behind him had been a long journey for him over the years. He however got to the stage where he was beginning to feel better about that period in his life. He'd joined the church and become a devoted Catholic. Although feelings were beginning to flood back and he hated himself as much as Reece, standing in front of him obviously did.

Emma was still standing outside listening, now in complete shock at what she'd heard. It was so harrowing and as much as she could do to comprehend what she was hearing. With her head spinning and mind whirling, she managed to pull herself together, managed quietly to return to where Jack and Jill remained patiently sitting waiting for her.

Henry now had a dilemma. What should he do? He managed to persuade Reece that he'd need time to sort out an opportunity and a suitable position for him. He would need to make it appear Reece was necessary within the company. Until that time he'd have to make do with some cash and be patient. Henry went to his personal safe and produced a large envelope of cash and handed it to Reece.

"This will have to do for now. It's all I have in the house." Henry was now very annoyed to be put in this situation it had come completely out of the blue.

"Okay, Henry, I'll give you a couple of weeks to sort me something out. But I'll be in touch, don't worry. Oh, don't let me have to tell your very sexy wife about this. She's a looker, Henry, it'd be a shame for her to find out what you did, won't it?" Reece left the house with a pocket of cash and a big grin on his face.

Walking the dogs down the garden path through the gate and out into the woods beyond, Emma was in turmoil. It was cool under the trees for the dogs to run and play, but it wasn't cool inside her head; so many questions she could think of, yet none she could imagine had a decent or plausible answer. What should she do? Or more to the point, what could she do? How could she manage this revelation in her life? She continued to walk. It was supposed to be a quick walk around the woods but turned into a long ramble, a nightmare of questions and confusion spinning in her mind.

Her phone rang, it was Henry. She took a deep breath and trying to sound calm and collected managed to answer the call. Henry said he was worried, she'd been gone for some time and he thought it was time for them to get ready to go out. Emma succeeded in sounding convincing when she answered him, explaining that she'd dropped the whistle and had to re-track her footsteps to find it, and that she'll be back shortly. All a complete lie, of course. Still trying to compose herself as she walked back down the garden. The dogs were well ahead of her now and making their way to the bowls of water left out on the patio. Lapping up the water fast, they were tired and thirsty after their long walk. Henry came out as Emma walked up the steps, greeting her with a glass of wine in one hand and a smile, that Emma was sure was one of guilt and embarrassment. She managed to force a smile with a thank you as she took the wine and sat down at the patio table opposite where Henry was now sitting.

"You okay?" Henry asked. The perspiration on his face.

"To be honest, no, I've got a migraine coming on, the long walk didn't help so if it's okay, I think I'll have some tablets and go have a lie down."

"I'll cancel dinner. I'd booked a table at the local Indian."

"Why not go on your own? I don't want you to go hungry. Besides, didn't you see Philip and Gillian this morning at church? Didn't you arrange dinner with them as well? I'll be okay here." Emma wanted to get him out of her sight as well as out of the house and have time to herself.

Henry had forgotten that he'd mentioned meeting with their friends for a meal and finally agreed to go, but he said he wouldn't be long.

Once she was alone, Emma thought back to her marriage to Henry. The two of them had been introduced at one of Charles and Caroline's parties a couple of years before. Emma had been assigned the lead architect role in the design and overseeing of the house at St George's Hill, with Caroline's insistence. Emma consequently had been invited along to a party by Caroline, but without a plus one she nearly didn't go. She couldn't think of anyone to go with either, not even from her own office.

At Bath university she'd gained a diploma in Architecture and Designing, which she was extremely proud of coming from a poorer background than practically the academics at the University. If only her natural mum had lived long enough to see her graduate, she would have been so proud. Her foster mother and father had been present at her graduation and been ecstatic at her achievements, telling everyone they knew how clever they thought she was.

Henry had also attended the party on his own that night. He'd just joined Charles's company from working as a tutor at the Oxford University, teaching advanced maths and accountancy to under-graduates. He became a member of the Stone's board when he joined, having invested five million pounds into Stones' PLC, money he'd received after his father's death in a car accident. The party was, in fact, part of the celebrations around his appointment, that had allowed Charles to acquire major supply contracts with Sabil Zaman, consequently expanding the company, taking on new members of staff and new, more efficient offices.

They introduced Henry to Emma when she arrived, and eventually at Caroline's insistence he asked Emma for a dance. They danced and chatted a lot throughout that evening, and Emma became quite smitten with Henry. They arranged to meet for dinner two days later. They slept together for the first time that very evening, a time Emma always remembered, as it was her first time. Emma was very inexperienced in the boyfriend stakes, she'd only ever been out with one other man in her life. But was Henry her Mr Right, she thought to herself.

Now Henry was out of the house, she picked up her mobile and texted Caroline, a simple text asking if Caroline could meet her for breakfast at their local café as she needed desperately to talk a few things over with her.

Caroline answered almost instantly, wondering what was up and hoping that Emma was okay. Her text had been out of the blue, yes, they knew each other professionally and met at the gym a couple of times a week, but Emma had never asked to meet like this before. Caroline thought to herself that it might be better if Emma came to her home instead, she obviously wanted to chat privately. Suggesting she came to hers, as the new pool man was due and she wanted to be there when he arrived. And anyway, souffle would be on the menu. Something sweet and fattening was always an excellent remedy for troubled times. Making going to the gym far more important and meaningful on other occasions.

They arranged to meet at nine am at Caroline's.

Chapter 9.

Breakfast at Caroline's.

Emma woke early as the sun came into the through the bedroom windows. Not that she'd slept much with the revelations of the day before. The beginning of yet another day ahead with bright clear blue winter skies. It was a far cry from her bed sit days in Bath when she rented a small pokey room while studying at University.

She felt relieved that Henry was still in a deep sleep when she woke and managing to slip out of bed and get dressed quietly before going downstairs, without doing her makeup or having done her teeth or hair. It was still only 6am, but light enough to take the dogs out for a good long run.

Jack and Jill were up, tails wagging as they heard Emma enter the kitchen and put the kettle on. She made herself a cup of tea, as she did every morning. Sitting at the kitchen table, her thoughts were still going round and round in her head, but suddenly she became aware Henry was surfacing from his sleep. She heard him toss around in bed, as he usually did before he got up, like he was trying to escape a bad dream. Emma had meant to get that squeaking floor board fixed some time ago, but right now she was relieved that they had forgotten it. Henry was now in the bathroom. Putting on her shoes and grabbing the dogs leads she left silently through the back door leaving her cup on the table half drunk and still warm.

When she returned Henry was clearing his breakfast dishes into the dishwasher and wiping down the granite worktops, something that he did most mornings, to be fair to him.

"Hi, love, I thought you'd taken the dogs out. Did you have a pleasant walk? What you got on today?" Henry seemed to be full of small talk this morning or sheer guilt. She replied with the best smile she could muster.

"I'm having breakfast with Caroline at nine, then I've got a meeting with a Mr Zoltan this afternoon. I've no idea how long that will take. We have a lot to get through, wallpaper and décor pieces, the usual stuff. I think it might go into early evening."

"Okay, that's sounds a busy day love," he replied. "I'm off now myself unfortunately, there's a meeting at 8.30 with one of our suppliers I've got to be at. So I'll see you later." With that he picked up his brief case, gave Emma a kiss on her cheek, gave her bum a tap and left. Emma felt like slapping him across the face, but that wasn't an option yet. She stood at the window and watched as Henry got into his black Jaguar F-Pace and drove off without a care in the world, or so it seemed to her.

Emma showered and got dressed in a smart skirt and blouse ready for her meeting that afternoon with Mr Zoltan. Driving to Caroline's took only a short while, taking the back roads to avoid the morning rush hour and the school run mummies in their 4x4's. As she drove up to the gated estate entrance, Benny came out of his little security hut to greet her.

"Morning, Ms Emma, how are you today?"

"I'm good, thank you, Benny. How's things with you?"

"I'm great, thanks, missing seeing your lovely face each morning, though."

Benny was a big black man. He always worked out regularly and had fancied Emma from the first time he'd seen her. He was always looking out for her during the build at the Stone's house, they chatted regularly and had some great laughs, too, mainly about the time the contractors were taking. Benny seemed to be their time keeper.

Looking at Caroline's house, it still made Emma feel proud that she'd designed, and project-built it for them, and she would always be grateful to them for that. She knew every little nook and cranny. Stone's PLC had naturally supplied the technology in the house, but the rest was all her imagination and creative knowledge.

Walking up to the front door, she heard a quiet buzz as the mechanism engaged and the door slowly opened. It was big and heavy, needing a mechanical motor in the steel core. This helped to heighten the security level necessary to comply with the building's insurance, along with putting Charles's mind at ease after an attempted break-in.

As soon as she'd passed the internal sensors, the door began to close slowly behind her. She continued to walk past the impressive staircase and aquarium into the kitchen, where Caroline pouring coffee into two large mugs. Dressed in just a skimpy bikini and loose-fitting dressing gown, she handed one of them to Emma.

"I'm just going to put something on more suitable, won't be a moment, I've just done a few lengths this morning to work up an appetite." She smiled cheekily at Emma. With that, she sprang up the stairs behind the lift and straight to the main bedroom.

Emma wandered around the house, eventually going over to the pool and looking out across the beautiful garden. The sun was warming up a bit now. All of a sudden, she was startled by a male voice behind her.

"Morning," came from the other side of the pool.

She turned around to be greeted by a young man testing the pool for chemicals. It was only then that she remembered Caroline had mentioned she was expecting someone this morning, and the reason they were having breakfast at Caroline's.

"Hi there," Emma replied.

"I've almost finished so I'll be out of your way in a couple of mins," he replied, in a soft-spoken but polite voice.

Emma watched him as she sipped her coffee, then sat down on one sunbed as swept and clear the patio outside. The guy obviously worked out, as he had a nice six pack and what she could see of his stomach showed his bronzed skin. He was dressed only in white shorts with a white tee shirt. He wore no shoes as he went about his work, knowing full well he was being watched by Emma.

Caroline returned, coming down the stairs she'd gone up, seemingly a long time ago, but in fact only fifteen minutes. She was now dressed in a casual yellow dress down to her knees. She apologised for being a while as she needed to have a proper shower, her morning swim and exercise activities having left her sweaty and uncomfortable. Emma had a good idea what she also meant by that.

"Eggs benedict okay for breakfast?" Caroline asked, knowing full well that it was one of Emma's favourites. Caroline had introduced her to them a couple of years before over a development meeting, not long after they first met.

"Anyway, what was pressing you so much that you wanted to come over for breakfast? We normally do lunch or dinner."

"How much do you know about Henry?" Emma just blurted out.

"Sounds ominous, why you ask that. Why, what's he been up too?"

"Don't know, that's the real problem. I thought we were soul mates and meant to be together, but we had a visitor yesterday that made him very anxious and angry, someone he knew from his past, and I believe from his lecturing days at Oxford, I believe."

"Sounds really interesting. What did he look like?"

"Couldn't see him, just heard the conversation though the door. I'd forgotten to pick up my post and keys from the hallway table and just caught some of the conversation through the door it wasn't quite shut. This guy must have something on Henry. He sounded as if he was blackmailing him into something, saying that if he didn't give him what he wanted, then Henry would suffer, and he'd ruin him. When did you first meet Henry?" Emma sounded very on edge.

Caroline placed plates of food down onto the oak dining table. The table had been made from an old oak tree that had been part of the grounds when they brought the land. It had been cleaned and dried before being made into this magnificent oak and resin master-piece. It had so much character in the grain and the blue coloured resign used between the planks made it look as if a wild river ran straight through it.

Caroline already had arranged the table for breakfast before Emma arrived. She was always good at organisation with everything, and everything was done just so. Along with the eggs was orange juice freshly squeezed that morning and chilled, toast and freshly prepared ground coffee. The aroma of the coffee filled the room and made Emma feel hungry suddenly. Caroline continued.

"I first met Henry at the party we went to on Halloween, quite a laugh actually. He was there because he knew a client of Charles. Mr Steven's, I believe." Caroline thought for a split second before continuing.

"Anyway, I was later told that he wanted to invest in Stones PLC. He wanted to buy 30% of the shares, as he had just inherited a fortune from his late father, although from what I gathered, he didn't actually like his dad and hadn't seen him in years."

" He told me his dad died twenty-seven years ago, a car accident, apparently." Emma sounded surprised that Caroline didn't know that.

They continued to eat their breakfast as they chatted. The pool man finished, cleared away his equipment and finally popped his head into the house by the patio doors to confirm that he was leaving. Caroline quickly got up from the table and went over to talk to him.

"Sorry about today, I must make it up to you another time," she whispered to him so that Emma couldn't hear. She handed him some money and off he went, smiling.

Caroline gave him a smile too and puppy dog eyes that she often used when she wanted to get her own way or for being naughty and forgetful. She'd perfected this throughout her life, but no one had been foolish enough to resist her mysterious charm.

"I take it you've researched into his past?" She almost instantly turned back to Emma with an even broader smile as she spoke.

"Done some," Emma replied, "but mainly on the internet and social media. He seems to be highly praised by people who know him and have worked for or with him. He was a brilliant lecturer, with most of his pupils receiving top grades. He still does special seminars for them at Eton."

"Okay." Caroline looked as though she was thinking very hard and deeply.

"Fancy doing a bit of research and having some serious girly time? What I mean is, let's go shopping soon and explore his claims."

"We could go to one of his lectures and see what happens, I think you can as a member of the public provided you pay. While we're there see if we can find out any more from his peers at the University. Also, it'll give us an excuse to do some shopping!"

With that in mind, Emma reluctantly agreed to find out when Henry was next going to Eton and whether they could listen in on a lecture. They finished breakfast and sat chatting for a while. Eventually, Emma's phone rang. It was a client from Paris, asking to meet her that day for dinner. Nazark Kasparkov had got into town earlier than expected and wanted to go through the plans for his company office in Mayfair. Emma knew full well it wasn't an office per-say, but a very expensive penthouse for his blond English mistress. The finery that was being proposed wasn't that of an office, but, a unique place for relaxation and continuous one, on, one private meetings. It was going to contain some very exotic art work and furnishings, large vases especially made on Murano island in Venice, and fine Italian silk bedding to hand-woven rugs from India.

Emma had been speaking a lot to young Scarlet, the so-called lady involved, not particularly liking her attitude either, she was obnoxious and mostly rude towards Emma and to her ideas, but she was the person Emma dealt with despite her obvious pain in the arse attitude. She'd been putting up with it now for a few weeks and Emma had always thought her name quite fitting for her, along with the way she dressed, nothing short of tarty and slutty. This young so-called lady was really getting on her nerves, calling her almost daily to find out what she'd achieved and where she was up to, and starting to pester for a completion date to move in. As far as Emma was concerned, it would be even longer the more she moaned. She explained that she had a meeting at two but would gladly meet after that and dinner would be a good idea to chat and explore their requirements.

Emma turned to Caroline, saying she needed to go, but that she did want to go and find out whatever they could. She would be in touch when she found out when Henry was next due away on a lecture visit.

Chapter 10.

Searching for the truth.

Emma returned home and before she changing her mind, looked through Henry's diary, searching for his next scheduled lecture. It turned out to be sooner than she thought, this coming Friday at the Oxford lecture theatre. Henry was scheduled to be there for an early afternoon lecture on business management strategy and financial stability for new businesses after COVID-19. There would be an early evening dinner as well, according to the information written in the diary which she knew meant with the other lecture's.

Emma knew at once that Henry wouldn't be coming home until the following morning, she'd got used to his routine, over the past couple of years. He'd phone her early in the evening, explaining that he'd been drinking with some old friend or colleague from the Uni, then asking her did she mind him staying over and coming back in the morning? Emma had never really objected and was often relieved he was staying away, leaving her to have the house to herself and do the stuff she wanted. She'd watch her usual soaps on the tv or read a good funny book on her Kindle or sometimes just take a long evening stroll with the dogs.

Emma phoned Caroline, who was true to her word. Between them they planned to meet for coffee at the house before going shopping in Oxford. Caroline wanted to buy some new underwear and shoes, apparently, so it was great for combining the two, and have some girly fun.

Friday came around. Henry started packing his holdall, Emma surreptitiously taking far more interest than usual in what he put into his case other than papers and files. It became far more obvious to her this time. Watching what he'd been putting into the case, seemed far more than he needed. She asked him what time the lecture and dinner would finish and if he planned to stay over, to which he smiled and laughed, saying that she knew him far too well, and hoped she didn't mind if he stayed.

He went on giving her full details for the day's planned events, something he hadn't ever done before, and it only deepened her anxiety even further. Emma became very suspicious. He almost did a full artillery of the events for the day. She felt almost freaked out by it now, and if she should ask why he needed to drink and stay away. Henry kissed her on the cheek, thanking her for being such an understanding wife, Emma turning her head slightly to show her annoyance as he did so.

"I'm meeting Caroline to do some shopping later, we might even take in a show or pictures later if we feel like it," she announced.

"Brilliant, sounds like a good plan to me." Henry replied, with a look of relief on his face. Henry did seem delighted and gave her a big cuddle, which Emma had to put up with and endure. She hadn't forgotten the drama of the Sunday before with their unannounced visitor had played on her mind all week and still did, even as he packed.

Henry contacted his usual Uber driver, Billie, to take him to the station. He always tipped her well, despite it only being a short drive, so it made it worth her time. Emma just thought he was lazy, as it was a fifteen-minute walk. She would have taken him but made the excuse that the dogs needed to be walked, so she left him to his own devices. When she returned, Henry was just getting into the car and gave her a wave and a grin as they passed each other along the road. It was all she could do to give a far less enthusiastic wave back.

Caroline arrived a couple of hours later, dressed quite conservatively for her, Emma thought, a black jump suit very plain in design, but still a low cleavage and also with a zipper that she could easily pull up enough. This was a good sign as far as Emma was concerned. Caroline rarely wore a bra, but today she did, and Emma was pleased about that. The last thing they needed would be to attract too much attention walking around a large University.

Stopping to have lunch and a drink by the Thames, they chatted about a lot of different subjects. They even discussed the way the company had prepared for the leaving of the EU: Stones had invested over two million pounds in stock, just in case the scaremongering in the news did actually happen. Not that Charles and the rest of the board were worried, they traded mainly with a very affluent clientele. Charles even describing it as a load of bollocks on more than one occasion, implying that the politicians, just wanted to stop Brexit for their own agenda. Trying to make themselves look good and important, it seemed more about what they wanted, how they could make a name for themselves, not what was good for the people or the country.

Shopping in Westgate centre was a completely different experience from their normal range of designer boutiques and stores. Although pleasant, neither bought anything of any importance. Caroline had taken Emma into Ann Summers and got a couple of pieces of lingerie that made Emma blush somewhat. And of course there were the coffee shops.

The time soon came around for them to make their way to the Uni and the lecture theatre where Henry was giving his business talk to the graduates. It wasn't far, so they decided the walk would do them both good. Walking up the entrance steps and into the reception hall they made their way to the information desk and the female attendant busily tapping away on her computer. They explained to her that Henry Thorburn was Emma's husband, and he'd invited them as they were shopping nearby. She gave them a big smile, as if she knew him personally, and duly pointed them in the right direction for the Nelson Mandela Lecture Theatre. The ladies' rest room, which they both now needed, was also along the same corridor. The lecture room has the capacity for up to 317 students and the Uni's modern feel and design made it quite different from what you would have expected from Oxford University facilities. The modern glass entrance hall was enormous and light. Round pillars supported the high ceiling, and wooden oak flooring made it quite noisy, especially with the echoing of busy people chatting and walking round, going to and from lectures.

Emma and Caroline made their way along the corridor and up a flight of small steps to the lecture theatre, trying carefully not to be too conspicuous. They just wanted to find out if Henry was giving the lecture he'd said he was there to deliver. His phone was turned off, as Emma had been tracking it with the GPS app on her own phone. She'd managed to activate Henry's phone a couple of days before when he was showering. She hoped he hadn't noticed it, which it seemed he hadn't.

When they arrived, Caroline and Emma could hear Henry's distinctive voice beyond the doors in front of them. It was deep and slow, making sure that everyone present couldn't do anything except take notice of what he was saying. Henry was giving an introduction, to the key points and was now taking questions from the delegates before carrying on.

Time to leave, they said almost simultaneously, looking at each other. Walking back outside across to the grass area opposite the main entrance, they sat watching and waiting for Henry to emerge from the building. He did so a good two hours and twenty minutes later, walking along with three other men all about his own age and all wearing the traditional gowns. Crossing the paved courtyard they got straight into a black SUV parked up in the slip road, waiting for them. The driver got out and opened the doors politely as they walked towards to him.

Both women looked at each other and said. "Car," standing up and brushing the grass off their clothes, grabbing their shopping, and making their way quickly back to the car park, fortunately, they'd not far to go. Caroline drove, following Emma's directions, as the black SUV had a good head start on them now. Emma was just praying that Henry didn't turn his phone off before they had a chance to catchup with them.

Heading out of town into the countryside, the houses became more infrequent but larger, as they made their way down the narrowing and darkening lanes. The light was fading quickly, which would help them be more discreet and undetectable when they caught up, which they seemed to do fairly well. Emma's eyes were transfixed to her screen as they sped along. Fumbling in her clutch bag, she found a charger and quickly plugged it into the cigarette connection, as her phone gave her a warning of a low battery.

They'd been following the GPS for twenty minutes or so when, the signal from Henry's S20 stopped moving, so Caroline slowed down a bit, but kept driving. A house came into view and they thought was where Henry's phone had gone off or out of signal: the drive time and disconnection period were approximately the same. Continuing, they drove past a large gated drive with rose bushes covering the house and hedges on either side. A few hundred yards down the road they came to a turning point, stopping to check on the signal from the phone to see if it was still active. As Emma held her phone, waiting for a signal to emerge, it did for a few split second then disappeared. The phone had just been switched off.

Driving slowly back along the lane, Caroline pulled into a small lay-by, Caroline turned the headlights off. The lay-by was an old entrance to a corn field, so the car would be difficult to see unless you were right on it, fortunately the field gate was blocked and made impossible to open by a large rusting farm vehicle, that had been there for some considerable time. This was ideal for them, if Caroline parked neatly it would conceal the Range Rover well enough for the time being. She lent across and opened the glove compartment, taking out a small yet powerful pair of binoculars.

"Where'd you get those from?" Emma asked.

"I bought them a last year when we went to The Derby. Charles was quite adamant that I have them, he didn't want me to miss anything, especially the horse he'd backed losing a couple grand of our money!"

Caroline got out of the car, so Emma felt as though she should follow and did so. The ground wasn't now as hard, but still firm enough for them to walk on the grass verge. Looking directly across the small field in front of them was a rose-covered manor house, the whole front of the house covered with multi-coloured roses growing up over the dark oak timber framework. The first-floor timbers protruded beyond the lower floor, giving the appearance that the rooms were larger on that floor. In fact, they were designed like that to allow for the sanitary facilities of the 1500s. White rendered bricks in-filled between the timbers and had obviously been repainted recently, as the lights shone over them giving a bright white shine. The roof was all higgledy-piggledy, with handmade clay tiles, but would have probably been thatched when originally built, the tiles didn't look out of place though.

The house was very wide and looked grand, having three floors, the upper windows were dormas set in the roof, another addition at some point later, of this magnificent looking house. A wooden structure set to one side had open doors and a large enough entrance to allow for coach and horses to enter many years ago. A covered walkway went from there to a side entrance of the main building. Several cars were parked on the shingle covered drive, while a man stood at the front door checking the identities and credentials as they went into the main home.

The subtlety placed lights lit the drive well as Caroline panned across the area with her binoculars. She noticed that the old coach-house next to the house were open. A newish Mercedes mini bus was parked as far as it could go inside the old wooden structure. Working her way back across the area slowly, she pointed to the front entrance, where they both could see a group of older gentlemen gathered, talking, and laughing. Finally, they all entered the front door. The door man acknowledged each of them as though he knew them well and saw them regularly.

Caroline lowered the binoculars and turned to Emma, beckoning her to follow quietly, and she started walking round the outside of the field beside a freshly cut hedge, just tall enough to cover them without having to duck down out of view. Both of them cautiously moved ever closer to the house, both in complete silence, even the footsteps unheard between them. Getting closer, they worked their way round the back of the gardens. A small yet adequate gap appeared before them in the hedge. Both on their hands and knees, they crawled up a small mound of long damp grass to get a proper view into the back garden.

The garden area was well lit, with LED lights strategically placed along the pathways and patio area. An open log fire pit was blazing away on the patio. The Ratan chairs around it were occupied with three very elderly gentlemen, smoking, and drinking without a care in the world, or so it looked to the girls.

A waitress came over to them with more drinks. Her outfit was very controversial for this day and age, that of a 1960s bunny girl. The velvet black uniform was cut very low at the front, and the ears stood long and tall. As she turned to move away, the costume might well have been a simple thong for all it covered: her camel toe showed clearly and her bum cheeks were in full view, but the traditional bunny tail was still fitted at the bottom of her spine, all fluffy and pure white. She waggled her way back indoors, all the while being leered at by the men she'd just brought drinks to.

Caroline let Emma have the binoculars for a while, although she didn't really need them to see further into the house. The large retractable doors were fully open and standing just inside were a couple of groups of men and women chatting away. Emma then noticed Henry. He was taking a drink from a bunny girl and in doing so caressed her. She just smiled at him and went about her duties as though that was the standard thing that went on and she had to accept.

Emma became agitated at this point, and sensing it Caroline put her arm round her. Now was not the time to get emotional. It was a time to remain calm and not be discovered, so Caroline kept her wits about her, which was more than Emma looked like doing right now. They continued to watch for some time, Caroline taking pictures on her camera whenever she could get a suitable shot. They could see clearly in the background a flight of stairs, and men were being accompanied up the stairs by a more mature hostess bunny, with an electronic tablet in her hand. There were distinct groups of men and also some women, some disappearing down to the left of the staircase, rather than going up.

Emma could hardly watch as Henry was led away and climbed the plush carpeted stairs. Her heart fell as she realised that Henry must have been lying to her for some time, unless there was another explanation. She doubted it. So many thoughts were whirling round in her head yet again, about tonight and about the visit they received a few days ago. They'd both seen enough now. Caroline had the feeling that Emma was about to explode and do something foolish, so she took her by the hand and led her back to the car as fast as she could without attracting attention. As they walked, Caroline had a really creepy feeling that they were being watched, but shrugged it off as they continued to walk as fast as they could.

"What the fuck did I just see?!" Emma raged as she got into the car. "I'll cut his fucking balls off when I see him. That fucking arsehole, I'm ten years younger than her! Why would he want her? I do everything he asks for, too, no matter what!"

Caroline looked in shock as Emma went on. She'd never heard her swear, let alone carry on in a frenzy like this. She was seeing a different side to Emma, which she was now getting concerned about.

"Calm down, it might not be what you think it is." Caroline didn't sound very reassuring nor did she feel it.

"You wait, I'm going to kill that bastard when I see him."

"Wait a minute." Caroline said calmly to her. Think before you get too carried away. "I'm sure we can work out where we go from here and what's best to do. You don't want Henry to know we were here tonight. We need to get more information and evidence before getting too carried away. After all, he might be innocent and there might be a logical explanation as to what happened."

"You are fucking kidding me, he went upstairs to do God knows what!"

"Precisely, God knows what, but we need to find out more." Caroline had her arm round a sobbing Emma now, tears started to roll down her cheeks.

"I know a couple who will help us to do some investigating for you. I've used them on various projects, and I think they could help on this one, if you want them to, that is?"

"Why don't I just fuck him where it hurts and take his money, he deserves that at least."

"Think about it for a moment. You signed a pre-nup, didn't you? Or so I was led to believe. Which means you'll get nothing if you kick him out. Let's get some more information first, build a case. Then you'll have a much stronger position and he might even offer you money later."

Emma started to become calmer now. She sat quietly for a few minutes, thinking and crying at the same time. She felt helpless and confused. She'd thought her and Henry were soulmates, she was looking forward to having his children and living a full and happy life until they married and gave them grandchildren. How could she stay with him now? Her life had been turned upside down, inside out and fucking thrown down the toilet, then flushed away.

Eventually she spoke to Caroline.

"You're right, I'd get nothing. I want him to suffer as I am now."

"Okay." Caroline looked at her sitting there, her face starring out the window, out into the darkness as the traffic slipped by. They'd made their way back to the motorway and round the M25, back into Surrey and home.

Caroline connected her phone to the car's Bluetooth and dialled a private number under the name of Marcus.

"Hi, Marcus," Caroline said as the phone connected.

"Hi, Caroline," came a deep voice from the speakers.

"How are you both? I need your help with something, a job for a friend in need. It might be difficult, but I know you will do what is required, it needs discretion and diplomacy. Are you able to do that for me?"

"Hi Caroline." A new voice. Abby had returned from the bathroom and was now standing next to Marcus.

"Oh, sorry, forgot the time, did I wake you?"

"No, we were just going to bed," Marcus replied.

"Can you come to mine first thing? Breakfast, if you'd like of course."

"Yes, of course we will. See you tomorrow," Abby replied.

"Sorry, Marcus, have fun and thanks." Caroline put the phone down. She drove almost in complete silence back to her house. It was very late as they pulled into the driveway.

Caroline made them both drinks. Emma hadn't felt like going to bed now, so they stayed up for a couple of hours, drinking and discussing the way forward, forging an action plan to find the truth. Night seemed to run through to morning, as they talked, with only having a few hours sleep before the sun appeared over the trees, and the mist cleared from the damp grass.

Caroline had the coffee percolating as she slowly walked round the kitchen isle. Her pure white silk gown flowed in the breeze from the open bi-folding doors. She hadn't yet put on her makeup or put a brush through her long dark hair, but she looked as beautiful and attractive in this unprepared state as she'd look dressed ready for a night out on the town.

Emma emerged from the guest bedroom, looking as if she'd not slept at all; her hair was a mess and the nightie she wore just covered her. Emma had established her own wardrobe at Caroline's. having stayed over several times in the past. Henry even teased her about having an affair with Caroline on one occasion, but he knew that this wound her up, so hadn't done so since. Emma mainly stayed over when Henry was away on business for days at a time. She'd get lonely. But she knew the dogs would be looked after by the neighbour and the dog walker, so didn't get worry about them.

Chapter 11.

Awakening.

Emma sat at her laptop, looking through the workload, but suddenly the screen froze, and a blue warning message appeared flashing on the screen.

Great, she thought to herself, I've so much to get through and now this! She sat there, pushing all the buttons, making things worse and then the screen died completely. She hoped that by some miracle any combination of hitting the keys would work, but to no avail.

She needed the computer urgently, so decided that her only option was to call Henry for some advice, She knew he'd be in the office at that time of day as he had a business dinner at seven with a couple of clients and Emma knew that would go on till very late.

He answered the phone quite quickly. "Hi, Love." He sounded quite out of breath.

"You OK?"

"Yes, just finished using the treadmill. I did a few minutes on that, I've got to be sitting down and eating later." Henry knew very well that he needed to exercise more these days, that he's blood pressure would go very high if he didn't keep to a very strict routine.

"I've got laptop problems here. I hope you've got someone who can help me." Emma explained the computer crash and the warnings signs that had come up on the screen before it completely died.

Henry was reluctant to mention that Reece was still in the building working on a network project in one of the other offices. He knew that he'd mentioned at breakfast that Reece was now working for Stones PLC and didn't want her getting suspicious by saying that he wasn't there, when she knew differently.

"I could ask Reece if he could pop over after he's finished here, if you like?" Henry was concerned about saying that, but decided to anyway.

"That would be great. I've a couple of quotes I really need to send to suppliers tonight to meet deadlines and I've an early start in town, so can't make time in the morning. What you say his name was? Have I met Reece?"

"You could well have; he went to sort out Caroline's laptop and a security camera that was playing up at their house."

"Okay, I think I know who he is and what he looks like then, didn't want a complete stranger to appear at our door. What time you home tonight, sweetheart?" Those words made her cringe after hearing what she'd heard a few days before.

"I might stay over in town after my meeting tonight. These guys know how to drink, so, if that's ok with you?"

She was thankful and pleased to hear those words and could hardly contain her relief.

"Okay, I guess I'll see you tomorrow then for lunch?" trying to sound genuine.

"Yes, brilliant. About one, Bye, love." Henry put the phone down and went through into the main office area where Reece was working away on a computer over in the far corner.

Reece was pleased, but certainly not surprised to see Henry approaching him. This meant only one thing. The email virus he'd sent had been released onto his wife's computer and she needed help. He grinned to himself. Reece, had managed to get onto Henry's laptop earlier while he was uploading a new software programme to his system. He'd purposely attached a virus to Henry's email listings, which meant Emma Thorburn had received an email from Henry, and that meant it had attacked her email settings, exactly how he'd planned it. His plan was working out well.

Emma decided that she'd like a Chinese takeaway that evening and had already decided to make sure that Reece would have to stay too. She needed an evening of complete freedom, she wanted to find out more about him and his past.

Her phone chimed; a text message flashed up.

"Hi there, Mrs Thorburn, it's Reece. I'll be over to yours in an hour, just finishing up here." Emma smiled to herself with the anticipation of meeting him.

"That's great. You eaten?" she replied, leaving it long enough to seem as though she'd not planned anything.

"No," pinged back.

"Okay, I'll sort out something, see you in a while."

Emma sat back and started to get tense about meeting Reece while she picked out her favourite dishes from the menu. She decided she needed to shower and slip into some more casual and relaxing. She also wanted her makeup re-done in subtle, pale colours and her hair tied into a topknot with a white hairband to keep it off her shoulders.

She looked at herself in the mirror; looking good, she thought, grinning. Back in the kitchen, she poured a large glass of white wine and set the dining table for two in the orangery. The doorbell rang, startling Emma. It was the Chinese delivery man. He'd been as efficient as always, forty-five mins and there it was, piping hot and smelling as if the orient had just arrived in her house. She put it into the hostess trolly to keep hot. As the delivery man pulled off the driveway, Emma caught a glimpse of a small white car pulling up at the gate. The intercom buzzed.

"Hi, it's Reece about the laptop."

Outside the front door, Emma greeted him.

"Wow, you're Henry's wife. I'm so sorry I didn't realise that the other day. I should have guessed, as you were around Caroline's. How are you?" His charm flowed as though it was genuine and sincere.

"I'm great." replied Emma, feeling flirtatious as this young man stood there in front of her.

"Well. I'm just here to help you out, Emma, may I call you that, Mrs Thorburn. Where is the laptop?" He didn't want to sound too unprofessional, and there was plenty of time to chat later.

"Of course you can," Emma replied as she led him through the hallway to the kitchen. She could feel his eyes watching her as they walked, her bum as her cheeks swayed a little as she walked. She'd always liked her bum, it was perfect in her opinion. It was as good as anyone she'd ever see on the catwalks or any of the bum of the year winners who seem to be praised for theirs. Henry never complimented her about it, but then he was more a boob man, anyway. She started to get aroused by the thought of Reece watching and eyeing her up.

"The laptop is actually in the kitchen. I usually use it in there, it's easier to make tea when I'm working." Emma tried to sound as calm as she could.

"Okay, that figures. It won't take long to fix, I hope." Reece told her, knowing full well that it wouldn't as he was the one who'd sent the Trojan in the first place. He'd just needed to get an invitation over, and it had worked.

"I've had a Chinese takeaway delivered, so I hope you like Chinese?" Emma asked as she poured another glass of wine and handed it across to Reece. He reluctantly accepted the drink and asked for some water to go with it.

Reece quickly sorted out the computer problem. He also started running lots of additional tests for other viruses and updates. It seemed to take a long time to load a software update, so he left it to its own devices for the time being and joined Emma.

While Reece was doing what he needed to do, Emma had served up the Chinese and taken it through to the orangery, opening another bottle of Sauvignon Blanc and placed it on the table.

They drank the wine and talked throughout the meal. Emma explained about her work and how Caroline loved and commissioned her designs. She described to him how the design and installation of the water feature had been a complete nightmare, with the structural glass having to be made really thick and bespoke to specific requirements. The coral and tropical fish came from an aquarium supplier in Australia. Getting the right water temperature and salt content had been a stressful challenge, even for the expert they had contracted to oversee the installation.

Reece listened politely to her, laughing, and agreeing with her when needed and asking some very pertinent questions about the design process. They finished most of the Chinese along with the second bottle of wine without really noticing, but both were now beginning to feel the effects of the alcohol, and the conversation started to get far more intimate and lewder.

As soon as she started to worry about the amount of alcohol they'd drunk. Emma thought she'd better offer Reece a coffee She started to clear the plates, making her way to the kitchen and to the coffee machine, turning it on and offering to make them a latte. Reece replied with a, yes please, along with a broad smile as she left. While Emma stood waiting for the coffee to finish, he'd joined her in the kitchen with the glasses. He walked up behind her, gently moved some of her hair which had dropped to one side, leant forward and placed a gentle kiss on to the back of her neck. Emma gave a gentle moan of pleasure, closing her eyes as his lips began gently kissing round her neck, slipping his arms round her waist as he did so. Emma reached out her hand, to the back of his head encouraging his advances. She felt his hands moving up to caress her breasts, her nipples beginning to harden to his touch. He continued to stroke her, slowly caressing her. Emma did not stop him, nor did she want to. Her breathing was getting deeper and her heartbeat was racing.

Turning around slowly to face Reece, they met in a deep kiss, both full of passion and lust all in the same moment. Emma felt herself falling more under his spell as his hands slid down her back onto her bottom. caressing her and squeezing her gently. Emma still did nothing to stop him, she wanted him now. Moving her hands down and could feel his increasing arousal. Managing to unbuckle his belt, she got her fingers on his shorts and boxers, managing to pull them down slowly. Emma now had him firmly in her hand, stroking slowly back and forth with her soft hands, as he seemed to grow with every movement from her. Emma broke off the kiss, then looked down at him in her hands.

"Well that's big," She looked straight into Reece's eyes as she spoke to him.

"I want you. Let's go upstairs. Would you like that?"

"Yes, I'd love that." Reece was pleased that his plan was starting to come together, far better, and quicker than he'd expected. Emma was turning out to be a shameless lady, so who was he to disappoint her, and eagerly followed her.

In the bedroom they continued to kiss for a while. Reece had removed Emma's dress and started caressing her through her knickers, feeling her move her legs further apart as he did so, to allow him to continue. She felt him gently working his hand under her gusset, where he found her damp and warm. Moving his hand up slowly, he caressed her and gently eased a finger into her warmth. Emma took a deep breath and moaned as he did. Reece felt Emma's hand on his and she started to remove her own knickers. He told her to lie down on the side of the bed, took hold of her legs, gently easing them apart while kissing her inner thighs. Emma was now on complete show to him. He could see then she was ready for some attention, encouraging Reece to move from kissing her thighs to using his tongue on her. He could taste her sweet juices and aroma as they started to flow.

Moving gradually, he got her rose bud into his mouth, gently running it round in his mouth and kissing it slowly. Emma let out a long deep moan and arched her back. He sucked her gently at first, but then getting firmer and deeper as he continued. Emma tasted sweet. The hot musty scent engulfed his nostrils as he gave her an orgasm that made her tremble, and her hot creamy fluid began flowing. Reece swallowed as much as he could as she quivered under her orgasm and continued to kiss her while she recovered. He started to enter her and gently pushed deeper into her. As he slowly pushed, she gasped for breath. He began to stretch her open as she'd never felt before. The sensation was incredible. Inch by inch. Thrust by thrust. He was now deep inside her and touching her sweet spot and cervix as he began fucking her faster now, knowing just how much he could thrust into her without hurting her, but still pleasing her. Over the years he'd had to master this, knowing full well that only a few could accommodate the length and thickness of his manhood.

Emma seemed to be in constant orgasm and was screaming for more. She wanted him to release inside her. She was starting to lose total control until she felt him harden even more. Then he started to ejaculate, filling Emma fully. She loved the feeling of it filling her up, every squirt prolonged her own orgasm and it was amazingly hot inside her. Reece eventually stopped. He pulled out of her and the combination of their lust followed. Without any encouragement, he gave Emma a cuddle and watched as she regained her composure, her body feeling satisfied. For the first time in many months, if not for the first time ever.

"Think you'd better stay tonight," she finally said to him.

"You sure? When is Henry home then?" Reece knew the answer to that already. He'd heard him on the phone to his client, telling them he was okay for meeting that night.

"Not till lunchtime, and I want more of that before he gets back."

They both slept until early the next day. Sunlight gleaming through the window, waking Emma from a deep sleep. The dogs were in the garden already, they always stayed at night in the kennel, made for them. It was behind the garage. They had freedom of the garden with enough food and water to keep them happy. It was still early, so she went downstairs and made tea, bringing it back up to find Reece still fast asleep. He'd kicked the covers off and lay there completely naked. Emma put down the tea and stood looking at this young man in her bed. Smiling to herself, she got on the bed and started kissing him, bringing him out of his slumber to enjoy her attention. She'd so rarely given oral pleasure to Henry. Maybe only a couple of times throughout their time together. But here she was giving oral to a man she'd only met properly the night before. What's more, enjoying the experience and not wanting it to end too quickly. But it did.

"Wow, I hoped you'd do that" Reece said, smiling as he'd been watching her play with him.

"My pleasure," Emma replied, "I think you need to get going. I've got a lot of clearing up to do. I don't want to leave these sheets on the bed."

Reece showered and drank the tea even though it was now cold and although he didn't normally drink tea but wanted to be polite. Emma felt quite embarrassed as she said goodbye to him, even though she hoped they'd meet again. As Reece drove away, it left her wondering what she was going to do. After all, she was a devote Catholic girl, contraception wasn't allowed, and she'd not taken any, not even with Henry. This guy hadn't just made love to her, he'd fucked her hard several times throughout the night and not used protection. So she could well be pregnant. She hoped deep down that she was, but this wasn't the optimum time for her anyway. She now knew the difference between love and sex, and that was sex.

She continued thinking about the consequences and what was best to do, but the only thing she could do, became a nightmare for her. She must have sex with Henry. At least if she became pregnant, then she could try to convince him it was his. But looking on the bright side, there was this unstoppable urge to meet Reece again as soon as she could. She was dreading Henry's return, and the thought she had to have sex with him sent shivers down her spine. Could she ever again?

As she stood in the utility room putting the bed sheets into the washer, her phone buzzed. A text message from Reece, thanking her for the evening and wondering when he could see her again. Emma just smiled to herself.

Chapter 12

Funeral.

Edward and Isabella Baker-Smyth had been very tolerant and patient with the police and the forensic team up to this point, but they were now insisting that they were given back the body of their daughter, Caroline, for a respectful and decent funeral. They commissioned a solicitor to act for them, and things became far more formal. The Baker-Smyths, had offices based in the Cannery Warf part of west London, occupying space on the tenth floor of the Canada One area. Mac explained to them the science team procedure of the as best he could without going into gruesome and unnecessary details. Knowing, that no one ever really wanted to know the graphic details of a loved one's death, especially when murdered with these types of face injuries. He explained that case complexity meant that releasing the body for burial was a long and tedious process, having to be done methodically so that nothing would be left to chance or left un-investigated, or even forgotten.

With time passing, Mac became more and more aware that the situation was becoming agonising and frustrating for them as well as for the police. Mac had been doing his best to keep them informed about any developments in the case, but he had to admit that there were very few at this stage. This had been complicated by the fact most of the information they accrued was from confidential sources and needed to be kept that way for all concerned. Without Charles Stone being found, along with no further evidence coming to light, and lack of any breakthrough in the investigation over the previous couple of weeks had brought its own problems. The bosses above Mac had been reluctant to allow the bodies of both Caroline and Reece to be given back to their families. Mac had asked Mr and Mrs Baker-Smyth for their permission to hire a specialist for the reconstruction of Caroline's face, since most of it had been disfigured with the exit wound for the bullet. They agreed to this for the sake of Caroline's dignity and the rest of the family's, glad that they wouldn't have to go through the ordeal of seeing her disfigured. The work was done with great accuracy from photographs and video clips from Caroline's phone pictures by the plastic surgeon. Both Edward and Isabella were reduced to tears seeing Caroline for the last time. They still hadn't come to terms with the fact that Caroline had not only been murdered, but that another man and not Charles was with her, thinking this must have been a mistake, their daughter wasn't like that, or so they had thought. The truth was only just beginning to start to take effect on them after the past few weeks.

No family had come forward at all for Reece. Even in death he was a complete mystery. No family to be found, and the only people he seemed to know were the workers at Stones PLC. Mac had to make a sad but necessary decision that his body. A pauper's funeral looked the most likely option, but until that could be arranged, he was to be put into a more suitable deep-freeze facility at the infirmary. Mac still had a glimmer of hope in his heart.

The only information they had managed to gather about Reece so far was that it wasn't his actual name, and that they would need to dig much deeper to find out more. The information that he had been submitted to Stone's PLC when he started work had been forged, and obviously for a reason. There was no trace of a national insurance number or any tax references, even his Facebook page had very little on it, nothing older than three years. It showed only six friends, all of whom had worked with him over the past few weeks. Any pictures on his page showed him with the office girls, a couple of other guys, a cat, and a labradoodle, neither of which belonged to him.

Reece had lived in an apartment along a stretch of the Thames at Richmond. It was kept immaculate and clean. The bed looked like a military man had made it but hadn't been slept in for days. Tracy the cleaner had been there to confirm this when Mac sent Eli and Kara to check out Reece's home. A small book shelf stood in one corner, with only a dozen books piled up on top of each other all of them about computers and internet technology. Eli carefully rifled through each one, finding an old school photo that had been slipped in between a couple of pages. It showed a group of students, twenty in all, no date or other indication of any names, not even which school. There were no other pictures or anything else that would help identify Reece or help with the ongoing investigation. His WhatsApp profile picture was a selfie taken off his phone less than two years before, but again the only messages registered in the history were of him chatting to ladies, mostly through chat forums, but certainly no family.

Mac had Hunter and Zodiac scouring the internet to find out more plus, Kara, Eli and Jim also doing some background checking to help out. They had only managed to contact the companies he'd apparently worked for and had been given as references to Stone's. But they all turned out to be illegitimate and umbrella corporations, none of which had any traceable addresses. Most seemed to have been made up and the only one that existed had closed down and the owner had died two years earlier. His picture came up through a dating site under the name of Reece; he had several responses and likes, according to the personal history. Zodiac had been onto the administrators for more information regarding the profile and account details, but the only thing they would confirm was that the account was accessed regularly over the past six months. The email address linked to the account was reece104U, that was until Zodiac implied that she could acquire a search warrant if necessary to get into their servers, though with her skills, she really didn't even need that. Zodiac had been examining the emails from the ladies, mostly chatting with Reece about meeting with him and why he had the number 10 in his email address. Reece just replied with a smiley face. He'd even had a couple contact him, and they'd arranged a meet, but that was for next week. Zodiac took down all their names and email addresses so, Jude and Danny could try to chat to each of them individually.

The only other thing that they were certain of was that his finger prints and DNA weren't on file. Not even face recognition technology had returned anything to give him a proper name. Who was Reece and how had he stayed off the digital radar in this day and age. That must have taken some considerable knowledge and expertise. Mac believed that if they could find anything out about Reece, then they might get to the bottom of all the mystery and solve the murders.

Caroline's parents had arrived back in London almost demanding the release of their daughter's body, to lay her to rest. They had just travelled from their retirement villa in Fuerteventura, where they had gone to retire some years ago. Both were now in their sixties and had travelled throughout the world over recent years, going on world cruises and expeditions to some extreme and beautiful places. Edward had made a fortune through the internet company he'd started back in the seventies, programming software for banks and investment companies mainly. Selling his media company to a consortium for the odd few million a few years back. An offer he couldn't resist back in the late nineties when computer technology was worth far more than it is nowadays.

Caroline, along with her brother James, had come along late in their marriage, only a year separating them, but Isabella had been in the prime of her life when she conceived the children, and devoted very little of her time and energy on their development and upbringing, the company business seemed to always come first. Teaching the children had been the responsibility of the nannies and tutors they employed until, as young adults, they were both packed off to different boarding schools. Caroline, at the tender age of thirteen, was sent to a strict Catholic convert school, while James went to a specialist school in London to advance his academic knowledge. His IQ fell into one of the top thousand for his age even when he was only a teenager. He had two doctorates by the time he was twenty-one and been head-hunted before even finishing his University degree. However he took over from his father in running the family company, expanding, and enhancing their portfolio.

Childhood had been one of strict parenting and increasing frustration as far as sister and brother had been concerned. This eventually led to Caroline moving out of the family home as soon as she became eighteen, finding a bedsit of her own at university. Her parents couldn't comprehend her reasons for this. In their minds they thought they had bought up the children correctly and with a really excellent education, with love and affection. But with the constant arguments and bad feeling between them, Caroline and James were unhappy at home. The arguing and bickering died down once they had transferred the company to James and things had returned to what seemed the normal marriage, Isabella and Edward rekindling their love for each other even to this day.

Now they had the unenviable task of burying their daughter, with no real opportunity to reconcile with her, let alone tell her how much they really loved her, and how proud they had become of her amazing achievements.

The wicker coffin had been a request by Emma, with Isabella's blessing, Emma remembering a conversation between her and Caroline one lunch time. It all started through a news report they had both seen watching over breakfast one day. It seemed so weird that it was so soon after that conversation that Emma was now arranging one for her best friend.

Bright, colourful rainbow roses and white lilies covered the coffin as it arrived at the natural burial grounds, the hearse drove slowly down the hard shingle roadway, slowly following the female funeral director as she walked to the chapel of glass, built in the centre of the grounds. Behind, the cortege followed slowly, no one talking, just the sound of silence. Edward, had purchased the small spot here in the woodlands after speaking to Emma at length when they had first learned of the tragedy. Emma seemed to know more of what Caroline wanted than her estranged parents, so they took heed of her comments.

Mac stood watching along, with his team. They had made themselves inconspicuous around the glass building, watching and waiting to see if Charles would attempt to attend his wife's burial. The day was dull, overcast, with mist in the air. It had been this sort of dreary weather for a couple of days now. The blazing heat from the summer had gone, nights were drawing in and the leaves showing signs of falling off the trees. Autumn had arrived.

The guests turned up dressed for the rain that had been forecast, but as yet not yet materialised, just the dark grey clouds were lingering overhead, more people attended than Mac had been expecting. It felt as if everyone that Caroline had ever known had turned up, old school and University friends had heard through social media and felt the need to pay their respects. A young Catholic priest Emma had become close to at church over the past few months conducted the service, a favour to Emma more than to Caroline's parents. He'd felt honoured and blessed to be helping in these sad and tragic times, somehow out of what Emma had told him about Caroline he had created a eulogy for her that was both, fitting and joyful, with some light laughter among the mourners.

The music was non-religious, something Emma had recommended to Isabella from a playlist left on Caroline's iPod. Mac could only stand and admire the way the ceremony was being conducted. Everyone had been asked to wear colourful and inspirational outfits, which helped lighten the mood. Emma had sent out the announcements, telling those she knew that it was to be a joyful occasion. An obituary had been posted in, The Times, for those who still read the broad sheets. Mac wasn't surprised at the number of people; he'd been investigating Caroline for a few weeks now and had been impressed by how many of people loved her manner and presence. When she walked into a room, everyone knew she was there without looking or comment, her charisma and personality shone through without question.

The congregation slowly followed the casket. It was carried by four bearers down the few steps and onto the pathway, where it was carefully and respectfully slid into place onto a small cart with a white shire horse tethered to the front waiting as still as a statue. Then the horse led the way down the narrow pathway leading towards the lake, and the chosen plot for the body to be laid to rest. On arrival the casket was placed across two bearers before finally being lowered slowly into the neatly dug grave.

Mac and his team followed, keeping their distance, showing full respect for the family and friends while still watching and listening to various conversations going on around them among the mourners. He could only think how tranquil and picturesque the surroundings were, no grave stones, no goulash statues of gargoyles. Nothing watching over unkept and unattended graves, only the flowers of autumn were left in full blossom, filling the area in colour and tranquillity. He thought to himself how nice and refreshing the whole experience had been, having never attended a funeral quite like this one, only the usual church and funeral parlours. It got him thinking about his own funeral and how he should really organise something that would suit him, but then again he hoped he had many years in front of him yet.

People began to leave the burial ground, gradually starting to head back to the wake at the country lodge down the road, only a couple of miles away. Mac had told the team that it would leave that part of the ceremony. Allow the family and close love ones to mourn their loss.

He's thoughts returned to Reece and wondering again why no one had come forward to claim his body. He still lay in the morgue back at the hospital, DNA tests still being performed on him to find out who he really was.

Mac hoped someone would eventually do the right thing. Only time would tell, he concluded.

Chapter 13.

Bunny Play.

Out in the Hampshire countryside the evening sun had just set, the weather making the days now warm, but as the sun went down so did the temperatures. The days were longer and the ever increasing lighter nights helped with their task tonight.

Both Marcus and Abby were both in their mid-twenties, both fit and well kept at all times. Abby could have been mistaken Caroline's younger sister. Both had the same face structure and almost the same sassy figure, the only difference being their hair colour; Abby was more a mouse blonde. Marcus was built like a rugby player and worked out daily in their home gym. He was six foot, clean-shaven, and the ladies seemed to love the way him.

They'd been watching the rose covered manor, for some time. Waiting, seeing who came and went from this tranquil, looking place hidden away from everyone and everything. They'd been returning and watching for several days now. Deliveries had come from food suppliers and laundry from a dry cleaners, a specialist cleaning company came in one afternoon, four men entering the house and two hours later leaving. Their equipment included a large industrial hoover and wet machines for deep cleaning of beds and carpets.

There always seemed to be some activity going on at Rose Manor, people coming and going continually. Two people were always there, though, an elderly couple, who both looked in their late sixties, in quite the country dressed posh style. The man walked with a stick as he limped frequently to his car; she seemed far sturdier and capable of walking briskly and unaided. Early one evening a mini bus arrived with four ladies all in their twenties got out and entered the house via the side door just behind the garage. Abby waited until they returned to the mini bus a few hours later and told Marcus to follow the bus. They did for twenty minutes until it turned into the service station car park at Chobham on the M25. Two of the girls got out and had words with the driver before waving him away. Abby followed one of the girls to the ladies' toilet, hoping to chat with her and perhaps find out more about them.

The girl was in her early twenties, tall, blonde and with a superb figure. Even in this late hour, adjusting her hair and makeup in the mirror as Abby walked in. She went into a cubicle and had a quick pee, all the time listening to the girl on the phone as she spoke heatedly to someone at the other end. She abruptly ended the call, calling the person a fucking bitch. Abby walked to the basins to wash her hands.

"Hi," she said. "Had a good evening? I'm loving the costume."

The girl was still partly dressed in a bunny outfit, her coat slightly open. She had removed the ears, but Abby could see the soft black velvet of the bodice underneath.

"Oh, what's it to you?" came a snappy and angry reply.

"Sorry, just thought it looked like an old-fashioned bunny outfit. I had a client who wanted me to wear one a while back, but I couldn't find a nice one. They all seemed to be PVC and leather nowadays." Abby had coated the situation and had the girl's attention.

"Yes, apparently this was one of the original ones," She turned and opened her coat, showing her the costume. Abby did think she looked very sexy.

"Our clients insist we wear them. Apparently, they remind them of when being a bunny girl was prestigious. Still it's also better than having to lie on your back while the old gits have their fun. It also beats trying to make out they're the best fuck you ever had." The girl was opening up now, which Abby had hoped for.

"Tell me about it." Abby thought that she'd try her luck, as the girl was almost finished reapplying her makeup. "Things we do for money." Abby added with a slight hint of laughter.

"Well, we get paid by a Mason 'come fraternity' thing, apparently. They insist we stay loyal to them and don't go with other clients, and because of that we get paid good rates. Besides, one of the rules is that we're not supposed to discuss what goes on behind the doors. But we all know. They must think we're thick idiots."

"How you get into that? it sounds fun," Abby was hoping for more detail, but, the girl headed for the door instead. She didn't answer Abby as the door closed behind her joining her friend sitting in a cubical outside with her burger and chips waiting. Abby left it a short while before following her out and when she did, she casually walked over to where they were tucking into their food as they chatted away.

"Sorry, ladies to disturb you, but can I leave you my card? I'm getting old to compete with the younger girls now, and if you ever want an extra bunny girl, please call me any time." Abby put a business card onto the table. It depicted her as a high-class escort and male companion, she made sure she had a business card for whatever occasion demanded.

"There's a website you can check out on the card, too." Abby took a small step back, and turned away from them, hoping that one of them would pick up the card. She sat down on the other side of the coffee shop and kept an eye on them as they looked at the card. The other dark-haired girl looked as though she was on the internet searching for the website. She was. As Abby's phone flashed to alert her to a hit from the website. She grinned to herself, bingo.

She discreetly watched as the redhead girl got her phone out and took the card from her friend, dialling the number on it. Abby was pleased she'd set up a page some time ago; Marcus had created several websites for all different reasons from e-commerce to escort pages. Being well prepared for clients was one of their strong points and, being a very professional team, they were always ready for anything. Abby felt happy with her progress, she couldn't do any more without looking suspicious or too obvious. She finished her coffee and left, calling Marcus as she walked out.

A couple of days went by before Abby received an email through the website regarding some special work for a client. A phone number and a contact name had been attached to the email, asking her to call if she was interested. Abby left it a couple of hours before calling the number, she didn't want to sound too eager before she did. When she rang, a deep male voice answered.

He explained that were Abby to accept the position, it would be on a weekly contract and would pay £1500 for each shift she worked and twice a week. They would be ten-hour shifts and she'd be expected to work exclusively for his agency, without question. Stating she must close her own account on the adult websites to comply with this, and that he would check that she'd done so. He explained what would be required of her, telling her to keep herself looking her best at all times and, if touched by the men or women to treat it as a compliment and just shrug it off. She was to be at the service station at 2pm the following day, where the mini-bus would pick her up and drive her to the venue along with the other girls. Abby agreed and thanked him so much for the opportunity to work for him. She sounded sincere and as genuine as she could and pleased that her plan had worked out so far.

She turned up at the services and sat waiting in the coffee shop. Marcus had dropped her off early, sure enough, the mini bus arrived with its blacked-out windows, the sliding door opened, and a blonde girl leant out of the cab and told her to jump in. The other girls introduced themselves as they drove off.

"What's your name going to be for these meetings?" one of them asked Abby.

"Well, I suppose the name I usually use for working, Ally," Abby replied.

"Ok Ally. There're rules we have to abide by at these parties. First, your there to serve drinks and snacks, nothing else. The grumpy old gits once they've had a few drinks will of course grope your arse, tits and everything else they feel they can get away with," Viv said, looking straight at Abby.

"Okay, anything else I need to know?"

"If they spill drink on you, which quite often happens, drunk bastards do it on purpose, there are spare outfits in the changing room. We also take a break every two or three hours and change uniforms and unwind a bit. They become sweaty and uncomfortable when they're damp."

"We'll handle the special requests for the first few times," Dee said, looking at Abby.

"What's a special?" Abby asked.

"You get, these certain types of gentleman, who come along and ask for a personal tipple. In which case we can make extra cash. So, if a guy asks you for a special, just get one of us for now and we'll explain fully later on. You'll soon get used to what they want."

They drove slowly up the gravel driveway to Rose Manor. They were greeted by a large and well-dressed security guard who looked as if he'd give any super hero a good run for their money in a fight.

"Afternoon ladies." He spoke in a deep and cheerful voice.

"Oh, we have a different face with us tonight?" he asked, looking through the driver's window.

"This is Ally, Jenny couldn't make it, we think she's off ill," the driver explained. Viv knew full well that last week Jenny had upset one client and been told not to return. Viv and Dee had felt bad for her and had tried to get her job back for her, but to no avail. One mistake and your out was the policy.

"Okay, make sure she's up to speed on everything ladies." The guard smiled at them.

Making their way through the large oak door into the manor house, Abby was surprised at the plush interior. The entrance was old and traditionally oak-beamed. An old fireplace was framed by two large leather chairs on either side, the carpet was a lush deep red, something that looked as if it had been left over after a refurbishment of the Houses of Parliament. A small oak table sat against the wall on the right as they walked in. On it were two large black leather-bound books and one smaller red leather one. The girls went over to the red one and opened it up. It was a diary, and each girl signed her name, with the date and time of their arrival. Abby followed, almost forgetting to put her pseudonym down, but managing to change the b's just in time.

Looking across as she was signing, she saw one of the black books was open and showed a blank page. Along the top were three columns marked as name, signature and number, and the date. Dee gave Abby a quick look as to hurry her up and follow them. She did, but, made a note to get a proper look later.

Following the girls through the wide hallway, a door was left open ahead for them, continuing through and down an old rickety staircase, which was obviously the original pitch pine one. Led into a small but quaint dark corridor. Following it along to the end, they came to a smaller room. Inside the room were dressing tables. One wall made from complete mirrors, but on the far side was a hanging rail holding twenty or so bunny costumes all neatly ironed and arranged ready to use. The entire room must have been no more than eight metres by six metres, no windows, with a slight musky feel, but at least it had a radiator fixed to the wall opposite the mirror. There was just another small door at the far end.

Both Viv and Dee didn't hesitate. Quickly stripped down naked and worked their way through the rail of hanging costumes.

"Don't leave your undies on, it'll be hot enough without them and far more comfortable if you don't put them on." Dee advised Abby, who looked as though she was wondering what to do.

Viv had already picked up a chic velvet bunny costume in her size. It was more one size fits all scenario. Abby followed suit and soon all three were now putting on makeup chatting as if they had known each other for a while. Abby was making up stories as they talked and had them all laughing several times. She thought to herself that she was pleased she'd had a proper Brazilian treatment the day before. Both the other girls looked clean shaven and needed to be with these very tight costumes. The ears and tails hung neatly at the end, fluffy and cleaned well. In front of her at her dressing table was a flowered name tag. Abby carefully picked it up, looking to see how she'd be able to use it. Sliding her hand into her makeup bag, she took out a bright red lipstick. Gently she opened the lid and watched anxiously in her mirror as she extracted a small micro 4K camera. She placed it into the flower arrangement around the name tag, making sure it was securely fastened. She jotted her working name onto the card and attached it to her costume, fixing it with two safety pins above her left breast. She could only guess what it would pick up, as she couldn't test the camera's alignment. Standing up and making her final adjustments she felt quite exposed, but sexy and confident in the uniform. Her fluffy ears were now fixed into her hair, which she had arranged into a top knot. The tail had a series of poppers that attached it to the top of her bottom, so Dee helped her.

All three girls went out of the door at the far end of the dressing room, out into a long and dimly lit corridor. They passed two rooms on each side, all with the doors firmly shut. Each had a name which Abby found quite intriguing, Matron's room, Training room, Wet play room and Detention room. These rooms at one point many years ago had been the stores or cellars to the manor house, but now had a more sinister use according to the door sign.

Winding their way round to the left and back up another flight of wider stairs onto a landing, they pushed open a pair of old doors, to emerge into a large lounge area. There was a bar along the wall on the left, with bottles of fine wine chilling or being kept at room temperature, depending on what it was. The two other girls walked across to the barman and greeted him with kisses to each cheek.

"Oh, I see we have a new friend tonight," he said in a rather camp and girly tone. Abby immediately thought he wasn't really interested, just that she was different, but to be polite, she smiled.

"This is Ally, she'll be with us for tonight, probably longer if all goes well. Especially since we haven't seen Jenny for a few days," Dee remarked, while looking at Abby. "Think she might have taken a long holiday somewhere hot and sunny. She said she was going to." She didn't sound very convincing.

"Hi," Abby said with a bright smile showing her gloss red lipstick and her pure white teeth.

"Right then, Ms Ally, take a tray of drinks over to the reception table, please, our employers and humble important guests are going to be arriving soon." He said with sarcasm, pointing to a table by a pair of doors in the far corner.

She did as she was asked. Walking as though she was a top fashion model, she deliberately made sure the other girls saw her walk with elegance and style. As she approached the doors, they gently slid open and disappeared back into the walls. On the other side, there was the small reception lounge she'd see on the way in. A complete and utter contrast of styles from where she'd just been talking to the others. Sitting in one of the leather arm chairs was a sliver haired old man in his late seventies. His head buried in one of today's broad sheets, which was open across his legs.

Through the window across the room, she could see a couple of cars pulling up the driveway. It was now gone four, and the occupants of the cars were being led down to the side entrance. They all looked happy and excited.

Abby went over and offered the gentleman a drink from her tray. On the table in front of him was a bowl of assorted nuts and crisps and with a bowl of fruit. He smiled at Abby and accepted a glass of champagne from her. He had a small yet unmissable badge on his lapel, bright golden with the number 1 clearly visible.

"Why, thank you young lady, you're new here, aren't you? Tell me. What's your name, sweetie?" he muttered to her as he looked over his glasses.

Abby thought she recognised his face but couldn't put a name to him right now. She would later though.

"I'm Ally, sir, I started here today."

"Mm, I see, well, I'll expect to see more of you later then." He gave her a smile.

Abby turned away, thinking that if he wanted to see more, she'd have to remove her costume completely. Her arse cheeks and most of her tits were already on show.

Purposely walking past the open black leather book, she could see that he'd signed in with a long number and been allotted the number 1 beside his name. Next to that was a column for activity order of preference, which read the numbers 3 and then 4. She wondered what the numbers referred to but didn't want to linger too much. The front door opened, and three other men now stood in front of her in the hallway, as she stood looking at the books. Quickly, she returned to the table and placed her remaining glasses down before returning to the bar and refilling her tray.

The guests all signed the black book as they entered, discussing with each other what numbers they were going to nominate for their entertainment that evening. They all seemed to have a small leaflet with them, to be able to choose their allotted numbers. As they finished, each one took a number badge and entered the main bar and entertainment lounge, taking a drink from her on their way past.

Classical music was playing quietly in the back ground, Abby wasn't sure what was playing but really didn't care. The guests started talking and greeting each other as if they knew each other well. Within an hour, twenty men aged from early sixties to their nineties had assembled in the lounge. The large glass windows across the back of the building were today closed, as the weather had turned cooler, but one door was still ajar. Viv, Dee and Abby had been weaving through the groups with drinks and canapes all the time.

Abby was well aware who several of the men were. In her line of business, she'd come to know the businessmen and women who run our country, who they were and how important they thought themselves. Senior judges, barristers and politicians were among the motley crew gathered in the room that night. These people were supposed to be pillars of society, yet here they all were in this den of iniquity, polite and friendly to each other. Abby wondered whether their wives and partners knew about this place. Not likely, she thought, and then wondered if they did, would they care?

An older woman probably in her sixties and dressed in an expensive black dress appeared from a side room. The black leather book from the hallway firmly in her hands, and head buried, looking at the open page.

"Gentlemen, please may I have your attention." She struggled to make herself heard above the chatter and noise, so she repeated herself but with much louder voice. Eventually there was silence.

"Numbers one, two, six and twelve, your rooms are ready. Please go down into the cellar area, where you'll be met by your respective door keepers. Three, four, seven and nine; upstairs, please, for your rooms. Thank you, the rest of you all please be patient, as your turn will come soon enough." She turned and walked away, closing the book, and disappearing back to the room she'd come from. The room thinned out as the men disappeared to where they had been instructed.

As Abby walked round, she'd made sure that she had filmed everyone on her camera. She'd also managed to record some of the conversations going on, several boasting about how they thought the public were idiots not wanting to stay in the EU and what did they know, anyway. This made her quite frustrated, but she couldn't in her present capacity put them right on a few points, although she wanted to. She knew that by this time the camera battery would be getting low, so she went to find Viv, telling her she needed to powder her nose and change her outfit to one that fitted better. Viv agreed and told her to take a half hour break as it would be a while before the changeover of clients.

Walking down the old oak stairs back to the changing room, she was aware that no one else was in the corridor. It was still dimly lit and there wasn't a sound from any of the rooms. Slowly and quietly, going to each door, she tried to see if there was anything she could find out, but to no avail; all the doors were locked from the inside. Eventually, she went into the changing room and striped off the bunny outfit. Grabbing another off the rail, she felt as though she was being watched. A weird feeling came over her as she stood in front of the mirror. It felt creepy, so she turned her back on the mirror, and carefully changed the camera and the SD card. She now felt even more determined to find out what was behind those locked doors. First, she thought, I need to get upstairs and see if I can find anything going on in the rooms on the first floor. She turned back and looked into the mirror, adjusted her ample breasts, and smiled at her reflection. She was even more positive that she was being watched and played up to it, turned her bum and wiggled it. Abby knew a two-way mirror when she saw one, there's something different and disturbing about the reflection, a feeling you can't escape.

Abby didn't find out much more from scouting upstairs. It was the same result as in the basement, all locked, although she could hear people and activities from inside. There were eight rooms in all on the first floor, all numbered and all completely locked and no doubt sound proofed too. Only one thing to do, she thought, she and Marcus needed to get in when everyone had gone.

The evening continued with three changeovers, some men going into different rooms but others staying in the same one all evening. Abby continued filming and tried to talk to everyone she could. Some were a lot more talkative than others, as the drink took effect and with her ever increased flirting.

Abby left with Viv and Dee after the men had all gone home to their wives and partners, seemingly without a care in the world. Another, night full of perverted and sinister activities. Even the coach had disappeared from the garage, along with the people who had arrived while the girls had been getting ready.

Abby texted Marcus, who had been camped outside in the bushes all the time, waiting recording times and car number plates as they drove off into the night.

Driving back to the service station, the girls talked about the events, they'd all been paid in cash, Dee remarking that she'd made nearly four hundred pounds on extras, which was a record for her.

"How you managed that?" Abby looking surprised as she spoke.

"My dear Abby, so much to learn. So, when a punter says to you: - can you put a wee special into my glass then that's what you do. There are a lot of guys who don't actually do anything but watch and ogle us, if you know what I mean. Normally it's the really older ones who sit in the corners or little alcoves and like to be left alone to a certain extent. But they do like to be paid a lot of attention. So we look after them. Then there's the old guy you spoke to when you first arrived. He likes to sit behind the mirror and just watches all evening. He always leaves a good tip under the door when he's gone. Perhaps next time you can look after a couple of them," she laughed. Abby suddenly caught on. They'd now reached Chobham service station at, where Abby had said she'd left her Mazda CX5. She bide them good evening, making sure she clutched her bag tightly. The next party at Rose Manor was due the following week, a special lodge party for the most senior member, who was celebrating his ninetieth birthday. Abby was expected to attend, as the manager had told her so after meeting her during the evening and being impressed by her.

The other girls drove off and as they did, so Marcus pulled up alongside Abby to checking that she was okay. Let's go home he said to her through the open window.

Marcus let Abby have a lie-in the following morning. She'd obviously felt uneasy the night before, and he'd decided to let her chill for a while. He made her a late breakfast, including all their usual healthy and energising food., and laid it out nicely on the table, along with fresh fruit drinks and coffee.

Marcus had been busy loading the two micro storage cards from Abby's recordings. Both of the cards were full, and with over six hours of recordings to go through, so they would be busy all day, he'd connected his second laptop to make life easier for them. Abby became upset and anxious as they looked through what had happened the previous night, despite Marcus reassuring her she was only doing her job. She needed to get a perspective on the nightmare, she'd already donated her payment to child charity. Marcus on the other hand had started creating folders for each of the people. Whether or not he recognised them from the videos, Pictures of the men, in clearer detail, on every one of them, to save time and enable a better and far more informative report back to Caroline and Emma. It was plain that many among this gathering of people were considered the high flyers of the British society, now seen drinking together, discussing the ins and outs of political processes, and how they could make money out of the less fortunate public.

Marcus continued to gather a dossier of the clients. Finding out who they were, how had they earned the right to be where they were in society today. Going through the video slowly, almost frame by frame as Abby wandered around serving drinks. He froze the screen suddenly as the familiar figure of Henry came into shot for the first time.

"That's our man," he said, looking closer into screen. Abby had now joined in watching couple of hours before Henry finally came into the footage. He was well dressed and polite as he took a drink from Abby's tray. He gave her a smile and commented on how nice she looked in her bunny outfit; he asked about her perfume and what make it was. Abby had thought it creepy at the time. But, now thinking about it, she felt as he had been flirting with her, trying to pick her up in a bar or club, despite the proximity of other members. Marcus felt Abby's unease and looked at her.

"He's not only trying to chat you up, but look at his body language, his eyes are all over you. It's almost as if he's gone back in time and seen a girl he fancied in school or uni, a teenage boy again trying to talk to his first girlfriend." They watched the footage a few times, and agreed it was as just as Marcus had said.

"Look at his reaction to the other girls. Both Viv and Dee he almost ignores except to put down an empty glass for them to collect. Every time Henry wants a drink, or you walk near him, he looks straight at you and then tries to make himself seem more friendly and approachable. That is typical Jurassic male mating behaviour." Abby cringed at the thought.

Leaving Marcus to continue to examine the footage, she decided to do her own bit of research to check. She had a theory of her own. She called Caroline, asking if she could send over some pictures of herself as a younger girl, preferably a teenager, and also asked if they could meet for coffee later. Caroline said she had a couple of school photos, her mum had sent her them a few years back and agreed to come over when she had finished her workout and had a shower.

She turned up ninety minutes later with a bunch of roses for Abby, to thank her and told her how much she appreciated what she'd put herself through the day before. Marcus was still working on his computer and insisted that he take a shower before coming to chat with Caroline. With Marcus out of the room, Abby asked Caroline if Henry had in the past ever shown any interest in her sexually. Something beyond that of a business partner. Her theory was that Henry had an infatuation with her, or just the way she looked.

Caroline said she had always, since she'd met Henry, found him to be strange and eccentric in several respects. The first time they were introduced, he'd been rather enthusiastic when talking to her, speaking fast and quite loudly. Even when he found she was married to Charles, it didn't stop him either, in fact it seemed to encourage him even more.

"Since then, whenever he knew I was going into the office fresh flowers appeared from nowhere in my room, along with fresh coffee. I always assumed that this was the office girl being efficient. Jesus," she said, as she remembered other instances of various other things that occurred, now seeming fucking obvious, she thought.

Abby took notes as Caroline spoke and felt convinced that this was all part of why Henry was attracted to her last night. Marcus returned freshly shaven in fresh clothing, he'd bought a bottle of wine and a couple of takeaway menus with him.

"Ah, great, you're still here. I've taken the liberty of ordering dinner and it will arrive soon. I've ordered curry for us all with some little extras I think you both like."

"Great, I am hungry now, but I need a pee first." Abby got up and left, leaving Caroline to help Marcus lay the table. He told Caroline how unset Abby had been by the evening, despite her trying desperately to make light of it.

During the meal they, discussed the previous day's events and showed Caroline some footage of Henry. Caroline had bought along the pictures that Abby had asked for, old school ones of when she was sixteen; the resemblance between her and Abby was remarkable. Marcus decided to do more digging into Henry's back ground, to find out if he knew anyone resembling the picture. After they talked for a while, before deciding to contact Emma and let her know Abby wanted to meet with her the following morning after her karate and yoga sessions.

Emma was apprehensive while she waited for Abby. Coffee was on the simmer and a good healthy selection of fruit and nuts were on the table. Henry had gone off to work early fortunately, because there was an audit going on, much to everyone's frustration, and he was needed there. Abby arrived on time, and although they had only spoken on the phone, she and Emma hit it off. Abby took her time going through the report with Emma. She didn't want her to misunderstand the findings. She was pleased and relieved with Emma's reaction to seeing her husband flirting with her, even touching her where he wouldn't have in normal circumstances, patting her bum and caressing her arm for what seemed far too long.

"I can't understand why he did that to you. He's hardly ever touched or spoken to me like that. This is another side I've not seen. I'm sorry on his behalf, he shouldn't have propositioned you like that." Emma was taken aback by what her husband was doing and saying in the footage. No woman should be placed in that position unless she wanted it. Abby reassured her and just said that unfortunately there were many people who thought they had the right to treat women like that.

"It's been a long while since he made that sort of suggestion to me." Emma looked withdrawn, trying to work out what she was seeing. When Abby showed her the photo of Caroline as a young girl, she looked shocked, suddenly she realising that Abby was almost the spit and image of Caroline, with just slightly different hair colouring. She really wasn't expecting the resemblance.

"I've a theory I'd like to put forward," Abby spoke as though she was looking for a particular reaction from Emma before carrying on. "I think Henry has an infatuation with Caroline Stone. He seems to want to please her and do things for her, mainly at work, but also in other small ways. When I mentioned it to her, she was genuinely surprised but then started to realise what I meant."

"What?" Emma interrupted, confused.

"I know Caroline didn't suspect it either, by the way she reacted. But nevertheless, I think it's a fact that Henry does have this thing for Caroline. I also think that you need time to digest this, so I'm going to leave you to go through it by yourself. But I'm on the end of a phone if you need to ask anything." Abby left Emma with the memory stick and pictures taken from the micro cam she'd worn.

Emma tried to make sense of things and work out her what her next move was to be. Caroline had been helping her fill in all the missing areas up to now, but could she go on doing so? Questions span round her head. Did Caroline really not know that Henry had this schoolboy infatuation? Then she decided that she was being unkind to Caroline and knew in her heart that she wouldn't have encouraged any of this. Emma finished the coffee and calmly cleared the table, locking her laptop into her own safe, along with the pictures. Henry never used the safe she had here and didn't even know the combination number. He had always insisted on using the larger, more complex one that had been specially installed in the office.

Marcus called Emma a couple of days later to see how she was coping, and asked if there was anything else that they could do to help her. Emma came across as being in full control when she replied.

"I'll transfer payments for the invoice to you later," She said.

"There's no need to, it's been settled. Caroline transferred the full money last week, she's always paid up front. But thanks anyway." Marcus hung up the phone and had the feeling that Emma did need more help than they could give her at the moment. He'd mention it to Caroline later on.

Chapter 14

Burning.

The dark figure walked along the same unmade path Caroline and Emma had taken a few nights back, along the side of Rose Manor. Rucksack over their back, efficiently moving round to the back of the Manor. It was a still night, with the moon was lighting the way. Slipping into the garden through the small hole in the hedge, the figure made their way to the side entrance, unconcerned about any cctv. Breaking one panel of the glass and wrenching the door open, the alarm burst into life. The countdown had started. Within a couple of seconds it had been immobilised, bolt cutters saw to that, snapping the cable supplying the alarm with its power. A hammer smashed the alarm casing open, allowing the batteries to be ripped out, and preventing a full scale trigger scenario. The assailant continued into the main kitchen area off the corridor; he'd been here many times before. He Placed the rucksack onto the table, now knowing full well they had ample time to complete the task they wanted to do. Inside the rucksack were four candles, a box of matches, along with a small metal crow bar. Carefully placing the candles on a couple of old plates on the old wooden dresser and lit them. Leaving the room, he moved silently along the corridor to the wooden staircase that led up to the main living rooms or down into the darkness and the small wine cellars. Pausing for a brief moment, to stand and stare down the stairs as though it brought back darker, more disturbing memories.

Now out into the main living area, which was in complete darkness, except for moonlight showing through the large bi folding doors. They continued across to the office door hidden within the bookshelf. Without hesitation he used the crowbar, sliding it into the door jamb to ease door to open, then giving it a firm push, forcing the door to break its hold, it had no resistance from the strong dark figure. The room inside was completely enclosed, without windows. Putting the light on, he could see its purpose. The office had cabinets of books and files, filling the shelves all round three of the walls, some of them looking as though they had been in the same spot for years. Finding the section that seemed to have little, or no dust settled on them, without hesitation he emptied of books onto the floor, revealing a small hidey-hole. Just a quick jab with the crowbar broke the front, it revealed a Phoenix Millennium Duplex DS4656 safe, set into the wall behind. Opening the safe was easy enough, as the code was only six digits long and the combination had already been bought from one of the regular cleaners, a price worth every penny. At the back of the safe lay a pile of black, leather-bound books, all piled up in a numerical order, along with a smaller red leather one.

Quickly stashing the books into the rucksack and then placed a small metal box which they put into the safe before shutting the thick steel door. Zipping the full bag up and turned the lights out, then left. The figure ran quickly and silently up the stairs, going two at a time, quickly reaching the top floor in the attic, the landing small and dark. This far into the roof there wasn't much room to move, but they knew the door in front led straight into a surprisingly large bedroom. Turning the handle slowly and quietly, easing the door open. The snoring became louder in the room, the two distinct tones almost in sync. Taking the key from the inside rim lock and closing the door as gently as possible, then relocking it from the outside, leaving the key in the lock, the figure returned via the stairs to the kitchen, touching nothing, leaving no trace. Double checking the exit route and checking they would have enough time to escape the building before turning on the gas. The Aga sat in the centre of the far wall of the kitchen, old and worn but still clean and working. Without looking back, running along the corridor, out of the door and into the field next to the house, putting enough space behind them as quickly as possible.

 The explosion took a mere twenty seconds, igniting the gas-filled room, the blast taking out the windows throughout the lower floor with a deafening bang, splinters firing across the surrounding grounds. The explosion would have been heard miles away, that was for sure. Fifteen minutes and counting. The figure emerged from the shelter of a large oak tree, avoiding the glass and flames as they flew out into the night sky. Glancing again at the watch, it would be at least another fifteen minutes before the fire crews could get here and that was only if someone had reported the explosion within two minutes. Plenty of time to return to the bike in the bushes on the other side of the field. Standing and watching briefly, the flames were now engulfing the lower floor, spreading quicker throughout the fifteenth century building. The second-floor windows now started spontaneously bursting, one after another, flames pouring out of the old oak frames, lighting up the night sky one by one. Twelve minutes and counting. The dark figure now started to jog across the ploughed field, with the heavy rucksack on their back. The farmer would probably be the first to respond to the fire. He lived the nearest, but still nearly half a mile away, in a separate small cottage on the edge of the old estate. With the flames now well into the roof and smoke billowing out across the night sky, time seemed to pass rapidly. Reaching the motorbike in just over six minutes brought its own slight problem. Six minutes and counting. Passing the fire crews arriving from the opposite direction would cause unnecessary problems. Revving up the machine and giving it full throttle, they must get to the junction before crossing over with them. The sheer noise from the machine might be heard, so playing devil's advocate, they roared into the distance. Blue lights came into vision three-quarters of a mile away. Slowing the bike to the speed limit as they drew closer. Three engines went blazing past and behind them came two squad cars, one slowing as they passed each other. The bike had been seen, so although the number plate would be difficult to recognise, it now needed to be disposed of. Pissed off by that thought, the throttle once again opened up and raced into the distance.

The fire crews continued to fight the increasing heat from the flames and intense smoke throughout the night right the way through into the early morning sunshine. Drenching the old wooden manor house with all those gallons of water was going to save what they could of the Grade 1 listed building, it felt like killing history as it crumbled into ashes. The oak beams still stood solid, remaining and standing strong, charred, burnt and smouldering, but still binding what was left of the house together. The roof was nothing but a collapsed pile of rubble and ash. The intense heat had destroyed most of the flammable materials throughout the building. Fire investigators were now shifting their way through the ashes. Two German shepherd dogs and one springer spaniel were let loose into the building, making their way through the still warm rubble, checking there was no one trapped in the debris. On the ground floor a team of four were ahead of them, securing every room, ensuring the timbers were supported and safe. The main staircase was mostly intact, fortunately it had been recently refurbished and treated with fire resistant lacquer. Carefully, acrows were erected under what was left standing of the building, giving extra stability to the weakened structure. The dogs suddenly started barking loudly as they headed up the staircase in front of their handlers, and the Investigators finally reached the top floor a couple of minutes after them and came across the burnt out bedroom.

Inspector Andy Cardell and his Sergeant Beth Jenkins had been onsite from first light, having waiting for an update on the Manor's condition of the from the Chief Fire Officer. Eventually they were approached by a couple of fire fighters as they left the smouldering house. One was carrying what looked like a small burnt black box.

"Think this will be of importance to you guys," he said, handing over the blackened metal container. "We found it in a vault which had been left open we assume, as it's an expensive piece of kit."

Taking the still warm metal box, Cardell tried opening it, but to no avail. Looking around, he called to the firemen as they walked away to a well-deserved tea break.

"Can I borrow your axe for a second, please?" Cardell asked, putting on a fresh pair of latex gloves handed to him by Beth. Taking the axe from the fireman, he beckoned over one of the forensic inspectors. Gently at first, he tapped the latch on the lock mechanism, getting firmer with each strike. Eventually, after half a dozen whacks, it gave way. Gradually lifting the lid off with a pen from his pocket, and without touching it, he managed to ease it open. Inside was a folded piece of paper, perfectly untouched and wound, with a silver cross attached to a chain.

Picking up the chain he placed it in the evidence bag Beth was holding open, ready for him. Turning his attention to the piece of paper that was neatly folded into a small square. He started slowly to open it, a camera flashing away as pictures were recording every step as he eased it open. When completely unfolded it read: -

Thou shall be judged at the Gates of Heaven.

My maker will receive me with open arms.

For what I do is for humanity itself.

For those who attend this place for evil gratification without morality, retribution will be thrown upon them at the

Gates of Hell by the DEVIL HIMSELF.

Cardell read the note several times, as did sergeant Jenkins after he'd finished with it.

"Okay, what the fuck does that mean? Maybe we have an arson case on our hands." Both looked stunned, wondering who would want to burn this place down.

The chief Forensic Scientist was now standing next to them.

"Not just an arson case, but potential murder as well, detective; We've just discovered two bodies in one bedroom in the attic. That's what all the noise was about with the dogs. They're burnt to a cinder and on the bed together, so it looks as if they didn't even know what was going on, or couldn't do anything about it. The smoke probably killed them first. I've got a forensic team up there now, so bear with us for a while."

"Okay, I must get in there, Beth, we need a full team in here and get me as much info about this place as possible. Seems this wasn't a run-of-the-mill country home after all."

"Right on it, guv," Beth started calling the team together.

Emma sat alone in her local pub, deciding that while Henry was away for the next week, she would enjoy her freedom. The torment in her head over the past few weeks was getting to her now, and she was still trying to decide on what course of action to take about him and about her current situation. She'd had her lawyers draw up divorce papers and a settlement that suited her and her unborn child. She'd just eaten a carbonara but without her usual glass of the white wine, just water instead. Then the waiter returned with the coffee she'd ordered and gave her a note from the man seated at the other side of the pub lounge bar. Emma cautiously took the note and started reading it to herself, only looking up when she'd read it through twice. Over in the far corner of the room was a man dressed in black trousers and black shirt. He looked a very smart well-groomed around her own age, or so she thought at first glance. His hair was short, raven black, and he was clean shaven. He was staring in her direction continually as Emma had read the note, waiting for a response from her.

Emma put the note down on the table and sat motionless for a few minutes, considering her response, and weighing up her options, finally looking across and nodding her approval for him to approach her. This brought a bright smile across his face and without being asked twice he got off his stool and walked to where Emma was sat drinking her coffee.

"Thank you for allowing me to talk to you, Emma." His husky voice sounded pleasant and welcoming. "I'm Father Jason Moore, a Catholic priest and a genuine friend. I hoped that you would accept my invitation. I would like to share your burden and help ease your worries, my sister."

"How do you know my name? Have you been following me?" Emma was getting annoyed, she was just about to tell him to go fuck himself, but just as she was going to, he spoke again.

"In a certain way. I've been searching for you for some time. Please, before I continue I would like you to phone your mother and say that you've been contacted by me. I hope she will confirm who I am and that I mean you no harm."

With his words still ringing in her ears, she picked up her phone and dialled her mother. Four rings later, she answered.

"Mum, how are you? I've called because I have just met a priest called Jason Moore, he told me to contact you. What's going on mum? Are you ill?" Emma felt concerned and confused as she spoke to her mother.

"My love, please listen to him, what he has to say is the truth and you need to know the complete truth now. Just remember that I love you," her mother sounded very sincere and sad.

"Okay, really, if you think so, I'll call you later, love you too." Emma put down the phone looking at Jason "Okay, what's going on?"

"What has your mother told you regarding your upbringing and childhood?"

"Very little, just that I was adopted when I was a baby and that my mother had died giving birth to me, Why?"

"Please believe that what I'm going to tell you. It was a shock to me as well. I'm your twin brother. I was adopted at birth by a different couple."

"Whoa there!" Emma interrupted Jason as he was just going to continue. "You can't be my twin brother! I don't have a twin and besides, we're not identical or even look anything like the same."

"I know this must be a shock to you at the moment. But I need to continue. I will of course answer all your questions at the end, but please let me continue.

Our birth mother was a beautiful girl called Mary Anne Thomas, she was only fifteen when she gave birth to us. She died a couple of years later. She'd been in a deep depression for eighteen months after the birth. Mary was told by the authorities that she couldn't keep the babies, us, as she was too young and was too mixed up. I've only got one picture of her, as the rest were destroyed as far as I'm aware, but this is, what she looked like then." Jason removed the picture from the pages of the Bible he was holding and handed it to Emma. She looked in bewilderment across the table as she gingerly took the picture from him, and saw a beautiful girl dressed in her school uniform, a massive smile on her face. Her long brunette hair shone in the sunlight; she looked as though she didn't have a worry or a care in the world. The photo made her look older than she was, but she looked a wonderful young teenager. She stood alongside two other girls as though they were her best friends.

"She had us shortly after this picture was taken." Jason interrupted Emma's thoughts.

"Our dad?" Emma whispered under her breath.

"Can't say, sorry. She claimed the father was unknown to her and anyone else. You have to remember that in those days, DNA wasn't a common thing. But there were also other aspects regarding that." Jason didn't really want to hear the next words, but he felt Emma was going to say them anyway.

"Why didn't she know who got her pregnant? Was she a slut, then?"

"Okay, do you really want to know? I'm reluctant to say more. But I can't allow you to misunderstand what I mean." Jason paused for a few seconds before Emma threw him a look as if to say, carry on or else.

"You have become aware of Rose Manor, and what it represented, also for what purpose people use it for. Well, Mary was apparently one of the girls and boys that was forced to attend."

"Stop!" Emma shouted at him, "I get it don't say anymore!" trying to hold back the tears now as he spoke.

Emma was now breathing deeply, and tears had appeared running down her cheeks. "I want to know the good things, not those horrendous images. Not the ones I've already got in my head."

Jason stopped and sat in silence for a few moments.

"I heard on the news that Rose Manor was burnt almost to the ground last night. I'm pretty sure that it wasn't a coincidence either. Someone has given divine justice and intervened in the activities that occurred within that place. I am certain that Mary, our mum, would have approved of its downfall, and gain peace in her grave for that."

Emma was now looking straight at Jason, as the priest within him appeared from his heart and soul. Being a Catholic when she was younger had taught her the rights and wrongs of humanity.

"How do you know about Rose Manor?" She asked him. He was drinking his third cup of coffee, but looked directly into her eyes when he replied. "I heard about the manor when my step mum passed away a couple of years back. On her deathbed she made a confession to me regarding my twin sister, of your existence. She told me we were both put up for adoption during our mother's pregnancy, and she explained the adoption wasn't at all legal and kept quiet. Before she died, she gave me two letters, one addressed to boy, the other addressed to a girl. Our actual mother didn't even know what names had been given to us. Mum not only met Mary several times, but those meetings persuaded her to have me, Mary apparently was mentally unwell. Mum also explained how complicated the situation had been for Mary, how her own parents had disowned her when she got pregnant and that they weren't sure of the father's right even to be informed of the pregnancy. By that, I assumed they didn't really know who the actual father was.

"After my Mum's funeral I quit my parish and decided that I wanted to find you and get to know you, connect with you, and the natural starting place was of course was our birth place, Rose Manor. Then imagine my total surprise when I found you there. I saw you and your friend sneaking along the field and hiding in the bushes and guessed that you were doing the same as me. Naturally, I wanted to know more about what had happened to you and our mother. It felt like fate when I saw you there that night. God's way of getting us together again, I thought. Was it that or was it about your husband, Henry? I recognised him while I was there from pictures I'd seen on the internet and on your Facebook page. Henry hasn't been faithful to you so far since your marriage is concerned, has he? How often do you think he's been visiting the manor?" Jason waited for a response from Emma at this point.

"I don't really know. But even once was one too many and I know he's been there a couple of times within the last month. I have a rough idea of why he goes, but not the full story." Emma was laying her trust directly in this man now, someone she'd known only for an hour. He seemed to know her entire life story, filling in the things she'd always felt missing.

"Would you like to visit Mum's grave with me tomorrow?" Jason thought that was enough for Emma to digest, she needed thinking time to process the information. Visiting her mum's grave might well bring home the reality of what he was telling her, and also bring her some peace.

"Yes, of course I would. That would be wonderful." Emma managed a smile at Jason "Thank you."

They sat chatting for a while longer, discovering that they weren't dissimilar in many respects, their food tastes, music, and clothing, along with lots of other small yet significant areas. The time passed quickly, but then Emma's phone vibrated on the table. It was Marcus. She spoke to him for a moment or two, then looking at Jason directly as she spoke, "You're sure they're from Rose Manor? Okay. Can I come over this evening? Fine, I'll see you then." Emma put the phone down.

"Did you send a parcel to my private investigator, Marcus, by any chance? I take it you know about Marcus and Abby?" Emma was now wondering how much Jason knew. "What do you know about these diaries that have turned up at their house this afternoon?" Jason grinned before he spoke.

"Before I joined the church and became a priest, I was in the SAS and did two tours in Afghanistan. That is, until I caught a bullet in my shoulder from a sniper in Iran after just a few days there. That meant that even though I fully recovered, I could no longer meet their fitness levels due to the injury. So I quit and decided that I'd like to become a priest. I could then give back something to people who really needed my help, trying to educate the mindless people who caused these unnecessary wars." Emma was now in no doubt that Jason had been the one to start the fire at Rose Manor. Emma really wanted to hug him, or at least thank him out loud for what he'd done, but thought better of it for now.

Jason decided that Emma had heard enough for today. He promised her that he'd pick her up at her house the following morning at nine and they could chat more then on the way to their mother's grave. He left her deep in thought and still somewhat perplexed, but something told him she'd be okay.

Next morning, as promised, Jason turned up, ringing on the intercom a couple of times before the gates started to open, he drove slowly up to the main house. Emma stood waiting, dressed in a black dress that fitted and covered her pregnant belly. Emma had slept little and had only a coffee that morning, not really fancying anything to eat for breakfast.

"Morning, sister." Jason had waited a long time to say that, while the smile on his face echoing the words.

"Morning." Emma replied, though with little conviction, just a small expression of recognition. "I had a long chat with my step mum last night. She confirmed what you were saying, or at least the bits she knew of it. She couldn't tell me much about you though, other than that she knew of your existence. But Mary she knew everything that I asked her about. When I asked her why she'd not mentioned anything about you to me before, she managed to say was that they had all decided it wasn't in our best interests, so they made a pact, deciding it would be in everybody's best interest if there was nothing said."

"Okay, let's go say Hi to mum." Jason held out his hand to Emma, hoping she'd accept the gesture. She did, and picked up an enormous bouquet of lilies before shutting the door and following him to his car.

As Jason drove, they talked about their childhoods and experiences in life, several being very similar but in different circumstances. Emma talked about events over the years where she'd always felt that someone else was present, watching and guiding her. Jason had been brought up in the suburbs of New York; With a loving, caring family and a step sister, he'd had a great childhood and everything that he'd wanted from his adopted parents. The family having to move back to the UK in his early teens, as his step father had been relocated by his employer.

As they approached the cemetery, Emma went quiet again. They stood side by side, tears in their eyes. The grave was simply marked with a small round plaque with Mary's name and dates on it, nothing else. Jason had brought along a new and better one, with his and Emma's name engraved on it. They stood together as Jason gave a loving prayer for their mother. The rain started drizzling as they stood there under the umbrella reminiscing. But even that didn't matter now.

Chapter 15.

Building renovations.

It had now been eight months since the discovery of Caroline's and Reece's horrifying bodies lying across the white silk sheets. Mac and his team had worked methodically and relentlessly to find the killer, following every avenue that came up to the bitter end. Every person involved, their movements and times were accounted for, and still nothing. Stories were verified and found watertight. All except one. The man they couldn't find or account for; Charles Stone.

Charles Stone. The most obvious man, having the motive and an obvious reason for the murders. Yet no one knew his whereabouts at all, and he remained missing, and still in hiding somewhere. All the law enforcement agencies round the world had been contacted and spoken to, but yet still they were without a lead of any description.

Mac didn't believe or didn't want to believe that he couldn't resolve the case, but his team had so little to go on. Days and weeks had gone by, with nothing to show for the hard work the team had put in, no footage of Charles being on any CCTV in the house other than when he was last seen going up the stairs. He'd looked drunk, but not too unsteady to climb up the plush carpeted stairs, even with a large whisky in one hand and the bottle in the other. Still sober enough to be able to pull the trigger.

Hunter and Zodiac had scrutinised all the footage of that night's events, many times over, yet they still found nothing suspicious. The disappearance of the motorbike had been a major part of the investigation, but so again had the bodies found in the river that linking Mick Jones into a separate crime investigation from their own. Mac had taken a lot of interest into that case as well, the discovery of Mick Jones's dismembered corpse made it four young men who had been murdered in the same way. Then at five, with yet another being found less than a week before. Mac had been called upon to take over both investigations by Superintendent Willis, with the aim of co-0rdinating the search for a sadistic serial killer that needed to be stopped.

It was now middle of winter. Although the weather was now mild, having rained consistently over the past month. This was good in many respects as water levels had got desperately low after the long hot summer months. Reservoirs were now finally beginning to fill and return to normal levels.

Mac was continually looking through the case files to see if he'd missed anything along the way, trying to reassure himself that only Charles Stone could have been responsible for the murders, albeit strange murders. It was mid-morning. Jim had just been out to get them both a fresh mug of coffee from the canteen. Mac's mobile rang, it was the Superintendent Willis.

"Morning, Mac, I've got some extremely interesting news for you, I've just received a call from Detective Baker, at the Stone's house. I suggest you get down there.

There's been building works going on there over the past couple of weeks, and something surprising has turned up. The house was bought by a building company a couple of months back after Caroline's parents decided that they couldn't keep it for sentimental reasons. Just get your team down there, Mac, you'll see what I mean when you arrive."

"What's going on, Guv?"

"Think they got another body for you," came the quiet reply.

"On our way," Mac sensed this was some sort of reprieve, his second chance on the case. Grabbed his jacket from the back of his chair and flung out his door into the main office area.

"Listen up, people. Get this, we've had another body turn up at the Stones' house. Where's Hunter and Zodiac?"

"On location, guv. They went back to Runnymede for another look round where Mick Jones turned up guv. I'll call them," Jude piped up, phone already in his hand.

"Well, let's go, people!" Mac shouted as he clapped his hands, encouraging them to move quicker.

Three cars sped through the post school run traffic with sirens blazing and the lights flashing. Only a set of roadworks slowed them down as they made their way through town and down onto the A3 to the St George's Estate.

Mac remembered the first time he'd approached the Stone's impressive house. Its long tree-lined drive and the sparkling windows had impressed him on that occasion, but not so much today. Today beneath the rain, and dark sky it looked like a house lacking the love and attention it required but had now been left to diminish. The garden hadn't had the attention and care it so much needed. Mac remembered he'd been told the gardener attended most days. He'd been so proud and meticulous in the way he looked after the gardens back then. The trees were now hanging over far more than they should, the grass was long, and in bad repair. The once highly polished glass windows hadn't been cleaned for months, yet the front door was still glossy, although looked un-friendly now.

Getting out of the car Mac and Jim were approached by PC Blackwood.

"Morning sir. I've made sure the house has been cordoned off. We have six officers round the perimeter, mainly to stop the builders from re-entering."

"Anyone inside?" Mac asked, looking around as he spoke.

"There's a couple of forensic guys upstairs and more on their way."

There were several builders' vans parked along the drive that led round to the garage, so Mac had presumed that they were still around somewhere. Building materials had been stacked under tarpaulins beyond them, a port-a-cabin sat in front of the large garage entrance. The lights were on and Mac could see people inside. Outside, he could also see two officers standing at the main entrance doorway like guards of honour.

"Apparently, one young carpenter was working in the main bedroom and accidentally smashed the mirror. It mostly shattered into a pile on the bedroom floor, but behind the mirror was a scene he described as horrifying, and sickening, the smell horrendous. I believe he was sick on the stairs, too, as he ran down them."

"Has anyone else seen the bedroom?" Mac asked. Still surprised at the thought of how they could have missed a body before. How could there possibly be another body? Was it even Charles Stone?

Mac had so many questions, but some answers should come soon; a white Transit van pulled up on site behind him, along with two other SUV's.

Dr Banks was one of the first out, her equipment case was over her shoulder as usual, and phone in one hand, already dressed in her white hazmat suit, fitted with a chest cam and ready for work. Technology had moved on, and a suit camcorder was now a standard piece of forensic kit. Everything was recorded from start to finish, every piece of evidence, every word recorded. Nothing could be overlooked, and it wouldn't be.

"Hi, Mac. Came as soon as we could." She smiled at him. "Shall we go up?"

Mac had been handed a white suit the same as River's and was struggling as usual to get into it. He had always struggled when putting these suits on, and today was going to be no different. Eventually turning on his camera, he followed her to the front door.

Jim had asked to Kara to be in charge of getting statements from the builders. Jude now followed her round the outside of the house to the tea room. They knew that the builders would want to get away, but they needed to get statements. Plus names and addresses for follow-up interviews.

The work hut was a typical builders, mess, a large table in the centre, a dozen chairs round it, a messy counter at the far end with a largish tea urn, a bag of sugar next to the urn, with a stack of biscuits and boxes of tea bags and coffee. The windows looked as if they hadn't been cleaned for some while, but someone had made an effort today. With nothing else to do, why not? A bowl of water and a dirty cloth lay on the table.

Jude took down details, asking where they were living and if they could give statements tomorrow morning, informing them that until further notice the site would be closed. That cheered them up no end. It was approaching Easter and they had been relying on a nice bonus from the refurbishment for the holiday period. Jude could only sympathise with them, he assured them that they could return as soon as the forensic teams had finished, and the crime scene cleared.

Kara in the meantime had taken the young carpenter who had found the body to one side. He was still in shock, but Kara needed to get as much detail out of him as soon as possible, while he had it clear in his mind. She got him a hot cup of sweet tea and sat him down. At first it seemed he had been more upset about puking up on the stairs than the actual body. All the other men had been winding him up about it for the past hour, making fun of him, telling him that now he'd have seven years of bad luck for smashing the mirror. He wasn't amused; Scott only started working for the company a couple of days before after qualifying from college. He was just twenty and new to site work and all the banter that went with it.

He said again and again, it was an accident, he didn't mean to break the mirror, his screwdriver had just slipped from a screw when he was removing the architrave around it. His boss had asked him to take it off as it had a mark along the bottom, as though the mirror was tarnished. When it smashed, Scott had turned his head away quickly, so that the glass didn't go in his face, but unfortunately he still had some blood on his hair where he'd been hit by the shattering glass. Before turning back to look at the damage, the stench had hit him hard. He said he only looked for a fraction of a second at the corpse before rushing for the door yelling.

Mac and Dr Banks entered the house. The building redecoration was quite an undertaking. The floor was covered with a carbonate sheet protector and the walls were partially painted, two step ladders stood in the hallway; paint tubs were piled up at the doors to the cloak room cupboard along with sets of brushes and rollers. Piles of newly polished oak had been stacked on either side of the now empty tropical fish tank, the fish had been taken away by collectors and found new temporary homes, but the tank now looked unattractive without fish or water, waiting for a complete clean. Mac remembered how impressed he'd been with the concept and ingenuity of the tank when he first seen it and walked over the landing. The fish had been colourful and mesmerising, he could have sat there watching them all day. It was indeed a mind-relaxing piece of modern art in its own right, an architectural master-piece. But no longer. Making their way through the hall, Mac also remembered the art works he'd that also been on these walls, the abstract paintings from local artists that were so impressive and colourful.

They continued on straight upstairs, and they approached to the top landing, the smell came into its own, that unmistakable stench of death. They passed Scott's vomit on the stairs, covering several treads, and staining the dust sheets over the lush cream carpet. Mac gagged a bit as he got to the top of the stairs. River just smiled at him.

"I'll never get used to that." He commented. They both then put on full breathing masks and continued through into the bedroom. They stopped dead, staring across the room. The mirror had gone, fallen into a thousand pieces of shattered glass, the shards covering a large area of carpet and into the exposed room.

"What the fuck is that?" Mac eventually managed to ask. "How the fuck did we miss that?" He looked at River in dismay.

"Shit," She eventually replied, in a soft whisper, something Mac hadn't heard from her before. He'd always thought of her as lady. Perhaps working with him over the last few years was catching up with her.

It was a couple of minutes before either of them managed to move again. Both staring. The aroma of decaying human remains filled the room. The vacuum that kept that confined and hidden for so long, now finally broken. Before them was a sight neither hadn't witnessed before. The bed had gone, the furniture stacked in the centre of the room, covered with dust sheets. But across the room and to one side was a dark black cave, as they were now seeing it.

It was approximately eight foot wide from floor to ceiling and had been completely hidden behind the mirror. In the centre was a chair perched on a platform and approximately level with the bed height. It was made from solid oak, padded with red leather that covered the arms and with a padded back support in the same leather. It was like a large throne.

Sitting strapped in the chair was a decaying corpse. Its arms were clamped with metal rings to the armrests, and the feet had been strapped to the chair legs. Thick leather restraints with silver belt buckles and chains were fastened around his ankles. The head of the corpse was strapped and held in place round the forehead, the strap going through the back of the chair and buckled up behind the head. The head had a red ball gag, where the mouth was, and yet still attached to the victim's lower jaw. The body was naked, decomposing slowly due of the lack of oxygen in the room it had delayed the onslaught of the organic decay. They could see a stainless steel cage on the floor, that could have been strapped round the man's penis and with several rings that had engulfed the length of his manhood, restraining any arousal he might get.

Mac and River edged slowly towards the chair, her camera clicking almost non-stop, as they did so. The victim's skin had started to turn grey and was at the point of starting to flake off onto the floor. Dust to dust as it decomposed. The corpse was well-preserved, without the oxygen, the bugs and bacteria couldn't multiply and consume the flesh and organs, Dr Banks now had to work out the time of death, the vacuum would have helped in that aspect, she could calculate the time of death by the volume of air present within the chamber and comparing it to how long he would have lasted against the time of when the murders occurred.

River had put her equipment case down before entering the bedroom just in case it interfered with crucial evidence, but now she needed to get on with her work. Time really mattered. With the vacuum broken and the body exposed to the natural elements, she needed to work fast. Mac had now walked round the back of the cave and into the bathroom, trying to work out how this room could have been accessed.

Despite her growing experience. River always been enthusiastic and excited whenever she came across a different type of murder situations, especially one so abnormal as this one. So often she did autopsies on bodies that were still practically warm, with rigor mortis just setting in. This was a very different and a much more complicated situation. Had he died from lack of oxygen?

Or had he suffered a heart attack? Her camera was in full flow, shot after shot going onto her SD card.

Mac returned to the room and now stood closer to the corpse, his hands in his pockets, staring straight at the victim as if trying to recognise it.

"So, this poor arsehole watched while his wife was fucked and murdered at the same time. He must have gone mad knowing he couldn't do anything to help her. He probably even knew and saw the murder face."

"Yeah, probably," River replied.

"Why would you do something as bizarre as this? I mean, this just seems sick."

"But look on the bright side, Mac, you might find your murderer on one of those cameras." She indicated to four cameras now on the floor among the shattered mirror glass. They were small, but powerful, with 4K transmission capability and fitted with infra-red lights, and they could well provide what Mac needed, even though the power was off, and they were inevitably dead. Hope still came through.

He looked back into the chamber. It was completely black inside, the walls lined with a soft absorbent black material. In the ceiling there were small LED light fittings, again not working. He took a step into the blackness. One step was almost as far as he could go, the depth of the area was minimal, no more than necessary to fit the chair in and to be able to walk round the back of it.

"Careful, Mac, please." River said.

"Okay," He stood still to inspect this small and complicated room. To one side, a couple of feet away from the throne, was a black dark shelving unit. Sitting on a shelf Mac could see that there was undoubtedly a computer hard drive, and looking more closely, he saw a monitor with speakers. So not only did Charles watch the horror unfold before him, but he could also hear every word that was said. He would have also seen the murderer walk up to the bed while his wife and lover were fucking, the sounds of their passion blaring out of the speakers set into the chamber walls, only feet away from the encased figure.

"Where's the door?" Mac said out loud. "How did he manage to get into this room in the first place? Then tie himself up and then not be able to release himself either, stopping the murderer?"

"One thing at a time, Mac," River replied.

The other forensic medics now joined River and were going through their tasks, the glass being examined and bagged where required, the surrounding oak frame had also been dusted again. The young apprentice carpenter who uncovered the gruesome room left prints all over the frame and some of the broken glass. He was lucky not to have received far heavier cuts from the shards now laying over the floor.

Mac carefully left the chamber and walked round into the bathroom again. Still trying to find the secret entrance that went into the dark and eerie dungeon, that really was what it had become for the occupant. A dungeon. At the back of the chair was the complete bathroom wall, three full-length mirrors directly opposite the shower. How could there be an entrance? There seemed no way into the cave and no way out either.

Mac took his phone out of his pocket, bringing up Hunter's number. The phone had barely rung before he heard his voice.

"Think you'd better get down here."

"Already in my car, guv, Zodiac is with me," came the reply.

Mac wasn't surprised. His entire team had found this case complicated and frustrating from the beginning. Today Hunter had been with Zodiac the entire morning, drinking coffee and eagerly waiting the call from Mac. When it came they were already winding their way through the traffic as fast as they could. Traffic was heavy as Easter approached.

He'd always known somehow that something had been missing from the initial search, something that puzzled him throughout, but couldn't put the pieces completely together. Now, there would be a chance for him and Zodiac to help solve the puzzle of these gruesome murders.

Mac had been standing watching River's team work for several minutes. They were clearing glass fragments from around the chair when River came across a mobile phone buried among the shards, covered over entirely on the carpet inside the chamber. Carefully she dusted the device, then continued snapping away with her 5D Canon camera every few seconds. It was a larger than average mobile lying face down on the carpet. Long ago the battery would have lost power and died. River carefully picked it up, placed it into a plastic bag and then into her evidence case. The large screened phone had cracked in several places when it hit the floor. As she was doing so, Hunter and Zodiac entered the bedroom, both had already in their statutory white hazmat suits.

"Be great if we could get that working, Doctor." Hunter said as he walked in. He'd just caught a glimpse of the mobile as she placed it into her case. "I think that could hold lots of secrets, do you mind?" He was standing behind her now, hand out, expectantly. "Promise I'll be extremely careful, and it could also explain what went on here." He gave River a smile that was almost like a child begging for chocolate or a sweet.

"Okay, but it needs a charger." As she turned to face Hunter, she saw he'd taken a portable charger from his pocket and was waving it at her.

"Sorted," he grinned, moving towards her. Zodiac was only a couple of steps behind him.

"Why is it you're always so prepared?" River didn't sound surprised at his efficiency.

Retrieving the phone from River's evidence case, he connected it to his portable charger, placing the Huawei AI onto one of the covered bedside tables. He carefully placed it on the port. Its response was almost immediate with the screen bursting into life, starting to load apps and programmes for what seemed a long time but wasn't, really.

Password. Hunter had to bypass the security. Picking up the phone gently, he entered data that accessed his other devices that Hunter distinctively remembered, and lo and behold it accepted the code. Within seconds the phone was going mad, messages, emails and updates flooding in for several minutes, but the buzzing and pinging eventually stopped. Hunter carefully exposed the apps that were last running and didn't have to look too hard for the first one that appeared. It was an app that was specially made and loaded, simply named, Dungeon.

"Guv, I think we know how to open the dungeon." With those words, he'd already touched the screen. Nothing happened. "Wait, there's no wi-fi connection power is down on the hub." Hunter realised what the problem was at once, so turning on the roaming data wouldn't help either. The victim's account would have been disconnected months ago.

Turning towards Zodiac he hoped she'd remembered the power pack and sure enough she stood there with it in her hand, grinning at him. Mac could only remember a few times he'd ever seen her smile, but this was one of those occasions, and he felt pleased that at last she was fitting into the team.

"On it," She announced, leaving the room to connect the router in the main lounge. She ran downstairs into the main sitting area and pulled down the sheeting covering the alcove where the router was still sitting. Plugging it into the power pack, it rebooted the Hub and it sprang into life. Then the waiting and hoping that the supplier still had connectivity in the house, she went back upstairs.

Sure enough, the connection came through on the Huawei. It was a good job someone had forgotten to cancel the internet. Hunter watched in anticipation. With no sound, a small panel behind the chair slid sideways, slowly exposing a doorway into the bathroom. The door was only small, approximately two feet wide, and it moved effectively and silently. The silver restraints round the chair also unlocked and released the decaying body's hands and ankles.

Mac almost ran through into the bathroom. The full-length mirror in the centre section had gone, a panel had opened, sliding back and then behind one of the other mirrors, and disappeared completely. Mac could now see straight through to where Hunter stood, looking back at him.

"Close it," he rapped out.

Hunter did so. The mirror reappeared as quietly as it had disappeared, Mac could only just hear the door click tightly closed.

"Okay, so why didn't he just open it up when he saw what was going on? Surely that would be the natural reaction. He even could have prevented the murder." He was talking out loud to anyone who was listening.

"The door needs power, so perhaps the power was disconnected. Or it also needs the wi-fi connected, as we've just witnessed. Or even the phone itself wasn't functioning properly." Zodiac was back in the room and now fully studying the scene properly for the first time, also thinking out loud.

"Was the phone upside down or the right way up? He could have simply dropped it. Or even knocked it off the chair by accident when panicking." Zodiac spoke directly to River.

"Face down, which means it could well have been dropped and then turned itself off when it hit the floor. A lot of devices have a quiet mode when placed face down."

"We need to see what time it went off, or the last time it responded to any incoming data. Alright, if we take it to our lab?" Zodiac looked as though she'd take it anyway, no matter what the reply was.

"I'll get Victor to take the prints off it now. Soon enough for you?" River looked and sounded surprised that Zodiac was becoming just like Mac.

"Brilliant, thank you, Doctor," Zodiac replied, with a sense of impenitent sarcasm.

Hunter had noticed the computer now after the hard drive and started walking carefully over to where it was on the shelf.

"Please don't touch that just yet," River instructed, "I'll be on it soon enough and yes, I know you want to get onto it as soon as possible!" Hunter had expected that from River.

Mac had returned from the bathroom and was standing staring at the scene before him. He wondered how with the technology around today did they miss this? "How much time do you need?" Mac asked, without even looking at River as she photographed and dusted the small black box on the shelf.

"Mac, you know better than that. But since you ask, and I know you want the rest of the team in here before we remove the body for tests, then I'd say a couple of hours."

"Thanks," He replied, walking towards the door. "Please let me know, River, I want to get the bastard who did this." He was glad to get out the room for some fresh air.

Taking his phone from his jacket pocket, he'd found Jim's contact; it only rang twice before Jim had answered.

"Guv."

"Tell the team they're working late. The corpse is Charles Stone, going by the evidence here."

Mac managed to get a cup of coffee from the builders still left on site. They looked frustrated, ready to lock up and leave for the foreseeable future after giving statements to Kara and Eli. Kara instructed one of the plain-clothed officers to take the young carpenter home and make sure he was with someone he knew for the rest of the day. He was still in shock and looked almost as white as the corpse sitting in the chair upstairs.

Mac and the team spent the next three hours discussing the how's and why's and what the consequences would be for this discovery. Their prime suspect had disappeared, the only one that the evidence pointed too, yet here he was as dead as his wife and her lover. The only major positives about this scenario were the computer and the hard drive. How much had been recorded? Mac was starting to get impatient, wanting to see the footage, but although Hunter and Zodiac had spent three hours trying to get into the files on the hard drive, they'd had no luck. The files were encrypted with a high-level security password, and none of Charles previously used combinations worked. Four hours later Mac was getting irritated by the situation and sent the rest of the team to the station to carry on with their work.

"Yes! Fucking got it, guv," Hunter announced suddenly. "I've got it,"

"At last. Get it back to the station and get set up we'll meet back there in three hours. Oh, by the way, excellent work, well done."

Charles, having been impotent for some time and had eventually agreed to his wife having some fun. Although he hadn't had intercourse with Caroline for the past few years, he regularly pleasured her by other means of gratification. They had discussed the situation several times and tried the various tablets, creams, and natural products, but nothing really worked. Charles, as a younger man had, been very ill with testicular cancer, which had affected him far worse than it should have, despite the attention of specialist doctors. Just six months after marrying Caroline, he'd received the prognosis that he'd never father children, and over the next two years they tried everything that they could. Money wasn't a problem, but money wasn't something that couldn't influence the outcome. Time and time again, the results were the same from every consultant. Even with the breakthrough of Viagra and similar products, nothing helped his predicament. Charles was reluctant at first to allow Caroline to meet other people, but slowly he realised that if he didn't, he could lose her altogether. A situation that he never wanted as he was completely in love with her and she was unreplaceable.

So he gave Caroline his blessing to take lovers if she wanted to. She had always been honest with him and told him when she was meeting other men, and she'd been very diligent about the men she'd chosen to entertain as well. Yet on this occasion things seemed quite different; Reece had only been working for the firm for a couple of weeks before Caroline let him take her to bed. He'd been so charming and so polite, smiling and making her laugh whenever their paths crossed, but the drink that night probably had a lot to do with it.

Eventually Charles asked if he could become more involved and watch or listen to her while she was entertaining her gentlemen friends. So consequently he'd had this special chamber built to allow him that pleasure, without distraction to her or her lovers. He was so close to them, yet so far away, and he always was the one to cuddle her and fall asleep with her at the end of each day, and he was reluctantly happy with that.

This time, though, things backfired badly. Charles must have suffered beyond belief as he was forced to watch his wife murdered, yelling and screaming as his soul mate was killed. Caroline understood him and helped him through some awful and frustrating times over the past few years, going along with him visiting doctors and specialists in Harley Street and other medical organisations all over the world. Now his beautiful, sexy was wife lying dead on top of her lover before his very eyes. The sight must have destroyed him mentally before time did so physically.

Back at the incident room. Mac called Cara explaining the situation, wishing her a goodnight, and saying that he loved her very much, and thoroughly meaning it. Over the years she'd been used to the late-night calls and accepted the devotion he gave his work. It was who he was and always would be. She loved him for that too.

Amid the coffee cups and pizza containers spread over all the desks, the large screened monitor was set up for everyone to see, as Mac made it back into the incident room. Zodiac connected the computer up; it showed the primary interface on the screen. Down the left-hand side were files, all dated and in order. Hunter had organised them into a play list, but hadn't watched or opened any as yet. He had managed however to categorise them into the time periods from each of the four cameras, all four had been fully working during the time period of the murders, each of them having a different angle and focal length of the footage. With luck just one frame would be enough for them.

"Okay, people, listen up." Mac wanted to move on quickly. "I know it's late, but let's push on, is everyone is ok with that? This will not be pretty. This isn't one of your computer games or something you might watch in the cinema or on your phones. This is a more snuff movie, and real. It's rare that we actually get footage of a murder taking place, and especially this close to. But let's hope this time we can find evidence that we need."

Kara turned off the lights. Hunter opened the first file onto the screen. It went black momentarily as the computer loaded the first clip. The crystal clear HD image burst into life, the time and date was displayed in the top right-hand corner. The empty bedroom was dimly lit, only two lamps on the long oak sideboard opposite, and two LED ceiling lights either side of the bed lit the room. The cameras were excellent quality, and it looked as though it was the middle of the day in the room.

Entering, Caroline appeared wearing her elegant red dress from the party and carrying the cut glass flute. Still half full of what looked like champagne. She put it down on the dressing table beside her chest of drawers. Slowly and carefully she unzipped her dress, letting it fall elegantly onto the plush cream carpet. Stepping out from the dress, she turned towards the bed and spoke gently and directly towards the cameras, now zooming in on her scantily dressed body. Dressed now in only a red bra, barely covering her breasts, and matching thong just covering her recent waxing, she continued to pose and flaunt her body in front of the mirror.

"Well, I hope you like what you see, sweetheart. After all, it's your birthday and I know you like to watch first. You can have some pleasure afterwards." Caroline seemed to talk to no one in particular, but looked straight at the mirror, blowing a kiss towards it for good measure. The detectives were left in no doubt and convinced she was fully aware of Charles strapped in the chamber. Was she the one who put him there? Mac thought to himself, but they'd discuss that later.

As she approached the mirror, the lighting increased, the image on screen became clearer and more detailed, with the more focused cameras being fully activated. A black figure emerged in the background.

"Think we have a different camera angle to watch what happened in the background on another file." Hunter said as they continued watching.

"Pause it there, Hunter," Mac interrupted. "We must have four angles to look at recorded from these cameras, the ones we found on the floor."

" Well, at present we've come across four cameras within the mirror and two in the ceiling." Hunter explained. "After finding the mirror units, we checked the ceiling spotlights as well and found two 4k micro cameras with zoom facilities hidden in the specially adapted bulbs. I'm expecting to access those later on today. The combination of the cameras would also produce a 3D image. I'm at present locating a software programme we can use along with the screens to combine the images and play them in that format, but until then, gov, this is it."

"Okay, good, let's move on," Mac motioned to Hunter to continue.

The dark figure came up behind Caroline and was now putting his arms around her, caressing her breasts and kissing her neck passionately. Slowly she raised her right hand, stroking his hair as he continued to caress her. He moved his hands and effortlessly undid her bra with the clip between the two cups. It fell to the floor, revealing her breasts for the first time. She now turned her head towards him, they kissed deeply and passionately. Caroline began undoing the buttons on Reece's trousers, sliding her hand inside to taking him in her hand, gently caressing him as she did.

She broke the kiss, slowly moving her head down as she lowered herself onto her knees, all the while looking directly at him, pulling his trousers down and caressing him as she did so. Her mouth was now at his erection, gently kissing the head first with a brief kiss, then gradually taking him into her mouth. He signed and took a deep breath. Reece then put his hands on her head, gently stroking her black hair and encouraging her to go down further. She did so, slowly taking the remaining few inches into her throat. She withdrew, gasping for air. Her saliva had given her the natural lubrication and was covering him.

"Lay on the bed," he gently instructed her.

"Yes. Master." she replied, playfully playing the submissive role.

As Reece lay her across the silk sheets, she lifted her bottom from the bed as he removed her thong and threw it onto the bed. Caressing her inner thighs, he lowered his mouth over her hot; wet exposed mound. His tongue entered her outer lips and worked up onto her throbbing clitoris. A heavy sigh of enjoyment came from Caroline as Reece continued to lick and kiss her passionately, with every movement, she became more and more aroused, her orgasm building deep in her womb. Reece then slid two fingers into her, he continued massaging her gently. They could see that she started to feel her muscles tightening and gripping around his fingers again as her juices squirted into his open mouth.

Moving her further up the bed and putting her head onto the soft quilted pillows, Reece manoeuvred her so that he could enter her. Gently, he eased into her. His cock was hard as a rock and so large it made her gasp as he gently pushed deeper into her with every thrust. Caroline felt an orgasm approaching as she crossed her legs behind his back, her trembling finally subsided, and her panting slowed. Now she encouraged him vocally to fuck her harder and deeper.

"I want to be on top now."

Changing positions, Reece lay on his back as Caroline mounted him, she lowered herself onto him, taking him fully into her again with ease. She now took control of the tempo and rhythm, she could even control when she would let Reece release his sperm inside her.

"Hope you're enjoying watching this lovely man slide into your wife, sweetheart." Caroline was now looking straight at the camera, directing her words to the mirror, knowing full well that Charles was behind it, enjoying his wife's performance as she slid up and down on Reece. He however had never looked at the mirror, he just continued. The video continued running as they fucked more slowly, he was now meeting her with every thrust. Her breasts swung gently, her nipples brushing across his hairy chest as she rocked back and forth.

Now another shadow had now appeared from nowhere in the background, dressed in a black all-in-one suit, a full head mask, long gloves, and boots to match. Standing watching in the shadows as they were in the full passion of their love making. Standing, watching, waiting, hands behind their back.

Caroline could sense that Reece was almost there, he'd now become more forceful in his thrusting, she felt him filling her. As their climaxes subsided, Caroline leaned forward, kissing Reece deeply and passionately, his hands embracing her as she did so.

 Then the figure behind them slowly and quietly walked up, pulled out the gun then without hesitation pulled the trigger straight into the back of her head.

There was nothing more than a short, sharp bang, more like a small firework misfired than a bullet being fired at such short range. Blood began to appear on the sheets and pillows, splatters across the bodies began to turn into drips of crimson blood. Slowly the gun moved away. As it did the gun, covered in recoiled blood, it shone in the lights and a reflection materialised for a split second. But, despite that, you couldn't see the figure's face, it was completely covered, a full black face mask covered the mouth and most of the eyes.

The figure started slowly to move away, seeming in no great rush to leave, just admiring their work, but instead of going out the bedroom door, the silhouette walked to the end of the bed, bent down, and looked directly at the bodies on the blood stained silk sheets. The assailant walked away but then stopped and retraced their steps to where Caroline's silk thong had been thrown. Bending down, the figure picked it up, brought it to their face as if checking that it was what Caroline had just removed, stuffing them in a pocket and then left. Walking over towards the lift and stairs that led straight down to the garage.

The video carried on recording, but no one was on-screen, just the image of two bodies lying there, Caroline on top of Reece, the blood stain growing ever wider and deeper.

Four times they watched the same scenario from each of the cameras, each from a different angle and perspective. All the same, but original images in the concepts of the murder. Mac got up, telling Hunter to stop the video for a time being.

Looking at the faces of the young people sitting before him, he wondered what they were thinking. Jim was the first to break the silence within the room. "Thong," was his only word. "The killer picked up the thong, but until now we thought she didn't have any on. Looks as if they took a souvenir or trophy with them. We should be able to get an estimate of the height of the murderer and build."

"Let's see that again last bit again and where she took it off, please, Hunter."

Hunter rewound the video to the beginning then frame by frame they went through to where Reece removed her thong throwing it towards the end of the bed. The screen showed it remained there until the couple were fucking hard, when it slid to the floor and where they were picked up by the murderer.

"Okay, so we have this now, but it doesn't really help us that much at the moment, does it. It does mean that we should be looking for someone that would have kept them hidden away." Mac was wondering how to proceed.

"Hunter and Zodiac, can you give me an estimate as soon as you can as to the height, build and their fucking shoe size, if possible. Once we have let's re-interview everyone with those statistics, get warrants to research their homes and places of work where necessary. We can get this arsehole, guy's, so let's make this top priority for a couple of days." Suddenly he had new hope now that things had swung in their favour.

"But in the morning, guys. Get some sleep now."

Chapter 16.

Black Ledgers.

Mac had just returned from the Stones house along with Eli, where they'd been going through a more detailed description with River that afternoon to make a shortlist of possible suspects now that Charles Stone had turned up. They concluded that the assailant had been between 5-8ft to 5-10ft in height, with short hair, and slim. Eli was now making up a list of everyone present at the party who fitted that description, but as he did, he also reminded Mac that there could well have been someone else that used the event and got in unnoticed. Mac hadn't ruled that out either, believing that this was pre-planned revenge killing, not a spur-of-the-moment reaction. But how could someone slip past the security in place that night without being spotted to them?

As soon as Mac had sat down and taken a gulp of his coffee, his mobile rang. It was the sergeant from the front desk.

"Mac, I've a parcel for you, it's just been delivered by a courier on a motorbike. He literally walked in, said good morning, and dumped this rather large package on my desk. It has your name on it and nothing else. I've done scanner checks on it and it looks like books. Shall I send it up to you?"

"I'll send someone down." Mac thanked the sergeant and went back to his emails.

The parcel arrived only moments later; Jim having picked it up on his way back from lunch, it was heavy and the size of a large box file. Mac told Jim to carry on and open it as he was busy responding to Superintendent Willis's email. Willis was now semi-retired but still inquiring about the Stone murders. He'd heard from a colleague that several other bodies had been found in unusual circumstances and wondered if he could help.

"Shit," Jim said, while Mac was trying to concentrate. "These are files from Rose Manor, you know, the old house that burnt down a couple of days ago. They're pages and pages of names, dates, and some other references. There's this letter as well." Jim started to pull out documents in small wallets, each dated by month and year, the first of these going back to January 1980, right up to the day before the fire.

"That isn't our case, they must have sent it to the wrong department." Mac looked at Jim, who now had Kara and Zodiac standing alongside him looking at the files. They'd started sorting the papers out on the table, putting them into piles they used when they had incident meetings.

"There's a letter addressed to you personally, guv." That got Mac off his chair and made his way across to the others. "What does it say?" taking the paper form Zodiac.

Detective Savage,

Please use this information herein to its utmost benefits.

It will help you understand and bring those to justice.

Those who you thought were beyond punishment.

May God be with you, my son.

Mac read it twice before passing it over to the others, who each in turn read it. On the table now were piles of files. All placed in month and year order; Marked on the top of every page was a day of the week along with the actual date. Under each register there was a column with an eight-digit number followed by a dash and then another number containing up to sixteen digits, some of them much shorter than others. Further across the page, in a different column under the title, "Room," was yet another number. These ran from 1 to 12 and also had a colour square alongside each one, red, orange, or green. Under every month there seemed to be two to four dates entered. Within each date there was a maximum of sixteen entries, or was that sixteen names?

Zodiac was the first to spot that the first eight numbers would, if read right make up a date of birth. Following the numbers, she then translated the next sixteen numbers to letters from the alphabet. As she was explaining her idea, Eli started coming up with full names of actual people from the last book from the package. "Fuck, I think this might explain a lot." Turning to show the page to the others, they saw a list of names and addresses of influential people, their occupation and current status. Several were now dead, indicated on the pages next to each of their names. One MP was killed in a hit and run. One high-profile judge had retired and was now in a mental home, but most members of the list had in some way or another disappeared or died.

Hunter had now returned from a late lunch and immediately picked up a file to start a search on each of the names on the list. There were five cases of mysterious deaths and two that disappeared without trace, all over the past six months. Mac thought Detective Cardell should be involved in this, picking up his phone and called him direct.

"Hi, Andy, it's Mac Savage here. I've had some interesting files fall on my desk today regarding Rose Manor and possibly what went on before the fire. Do you know anything about them?"

"Hi, Mac. No, I've no ideas about any files, what do they consist of?"

"Lists of names, dates and presumed activities that went on in Rose Manor," Mac replied.

"Well, you know that the Manor burnt down a couple of days ago. There were two bodies in the fire, an old couple who we've established had lived there for most of their lives. Debbie and Frank Conway, they looked after the running of the manor for a consortium of businessmen. It was a bizarre setup, and more disturbingly we found in the basement rooms, that would have made mediaeval times seem normal. There were two dungeons with chains and shackles fixed to the walls, along with wooden burnt-out benches. Plus other devices that would have been used for restraining someone. Another room looked like it was a complete wet room, a drain was fitted in the centre and a couple of showers in the walls. But then we found a simulated schoolroom completely kitted out with desks and blackboard. Fixed to shelves were whips, crops and various other devices used punishment. When we eventually got upstairs, we found six bedrooms, all large with broken mirrors, and melted glass everywhere."

"Yes, I actually read your report yesterday." Mac had listened with interest to everything Andy said all the time wondering why he'd been sent these files. "Do you have any idea who started the fire, or any suspects?"

"No, we haven't. The only suspect we have is a person on a motorbike the patrol cars passed on the way to the fire. Also, a note from someone we assume is a priest or some religious nutter, which we found in a tin box. We have found out, though, that there was a cult or lodge type organisation using the place. They paid for its upkeep and used it fairly regularly. The only other information we have so far is that there was a registered birth submitted by Debbie Conway, way back in 1988. Now we believe that she registered the birth for someone else. Debbie Conway would have been in her early fifties then. But we do have a girl we believe was raped and was also under age when she gave birth, but that's as far as the records go. No records of where the child ended up. We thought everything else post 1988 was destroyed in the fire."

"We also have a note attached to these the files, also possibly written by a priest." Mac turned to Jim. "What date do we have on that separate file?"

"August, September 1987, guv. We have a name here, Mary, and six other names. All male and get this, guv, believe it or not, one, of them is Theobald John Thorburn. Zodiac, believes, Theobald John Thorburn, was Henry's father. He died in a car accident in 1990, hitting a tree after brake failure close to his home." Hunter was now reading from his computer screen.

"Think we need to get together, Andy. Can we meet at Rose Manor? What's the situation there?" Mac was convinced that it was no coincidence that he'd been sent these files and needed to get to grips with this additional information quickly.

"In an hour? Great." Mac hung up the phone.

"Hunter and Zodiac, you're going to go through the list of those people. I want to know where they are now, who's dead and how, along with anything suspicious you might think went on with their deaths. Cardell's team are sending over the files they have on the Rose Manor fire. The rest of you, you're with me." Mac grabbed his jacket and was out the door.

Zodiac took the first three suspects of the list, which included: -

Theobald Thorburn QC, deceased. Car accident age fifty-four.

Matthew Edwards, senior lawyer, deceased. Age eighty-two.

Clifford Parker, barrister, Crown prosecutor. Died in a home with Alzheimer's, age eighty-one.

She started with Thorburn, getting up on her computer the details from the car accident. According to reports, he had lost control and hit a tree on a dark lane in the Berkshire countryside. He wasn't found until the following morning, by a cyclist. By that time he'd died from excessive blood loss. The post-mortem concluded accidental death at that time, but further investigation it was revealed by the crash examination team showed that the car had no brake fluid in the reservoir. A small hole had been drilled into the reserve tank, so it would have seeped away over a couple of days or so. Zodiac managed to find the crash scene photos on a police file that had been archived after two years following the crash. They showed the car on its side, the bonnet completely smashed up and covering the windscreen, its broken glass everywhere. They had estimated his speed had been around 50mph at impact, and without the technology of today's modern cars, the driver hadn't stood a chance. She delved back into Theobald Thorburn's past and his family. Henry's name came up, as she expected, and by chance a photo of him with Mary Ann Thomas, along with a written article in the school newsletter saying how they wanted to change the world when they left college together in a couple of years.

Zodiac then went onto the other two people on her list, finding out that both had died, but both had a letter sent to each of their families, causing them great distress, yet no police record of those existed.

Zodiac made some calls to the families, asking if any notes or anything suspicious had been found on them or sent to them at the time of death, she wasn't surprised at the answers she got. Edwards had allegedly committed suicide on the London underground, note in his briefcase; Parker, on the other hand, was found slumped in his lounge chair with what coroners recorded as a heart attack, a note left in a pocket. Neither notes were taken seriously by the families, so the notes weren't sent to the police, but both the notes sent read the same: -

The gates of heaven are for those who deserve the righteousness of our Lord. God will judge us all by what we've done.

Forgive me for I have two faces.

One for the world and one for God, who will save me.

I'm ready to be absorbed into the light,

Or thrown into the depths of Hell for eternal damnation. Are you ready?

Hunter was investigating three other men he had written down on his list, each one an important member of the legal system. Each one dead, all having died in accidents, and each one having been left the same note. Six dead men, all having been lodge members at Rose Manor, each mentioned in the files that Hunter and Zodiac were now sifting through, each one rich and influential within the legal system.

Hunter called Mac while he was at Rose Manor with Andy Cardell, familiarising himself and the rest of the team with the burnt out manor house. It now had been boarded up and a set of temporary gates with massive chains prevented entry to the now derelict property. Detective Cardell had contacted the security firm and met the guard on-site before Mac arrived at the burnout house. Having spent a long time walking round the shell, taking pictures, and getting a good feel for what Andy Cardell had explained in detail to them on the phone earlier. Mac felt sickened by the stories he was being told. Cardell explained the finding of the two charcoaled bodies in the bed. Still seemingly asleep on the third floor and how they were identified through the dental records. Also, a few letters that had turned up confirming that after the fire.

Cardell explained that his detectives had discovered from various sources that young girls and boys were brought to the house and used by the fraternity, specially when their parents couldn't afford fees, or if they were disobedient in school.

He went on to say that they had heard the rumours of Mary from past students, as well as her friends at the time. But didn't believe her and weren't aware that she'd been raped as Mac was implying. The more they explored, the more they became convinced that the house had been used for immoral and illegal activities; the layout, design and content of the bedrooms and dungeons told their own story. The more they walked round, the more distressed and saddened they became. It was partly to stop things like this that they had become police officers for in the first place.

Mac answered his phone to Hunter.

"Guv, we think we might have a surname for Reece. Faulkner. There are several references in the ledgers and files that came with them. Zodiac is working on that now."

"That's great, well done. Look into the possibility that he went to the same school as Mary and Henry. Going by Reece's age, it would have been between twenty and fifteen years ago. Also check where he might have gone to uni, photos especially, as we don't know if Reece is his actual name. We also need to check any other instances of pupils being given, 'extra special treatment,' who were also in that photo with Mary. Get the names of all the pupils, double-check each one and get Eli and Danny to start contacting everyone who was connected to Reece at school and uni. Also, go through those files again and see if there are any initials or other ways of identifying the children who were taken to Rose Manor."

"The school is now just a school for girls. They went through a major revamping a couple years go after a fire there, and the head teacher was sacked shortly after, along with most of the staff. Only a couple of the younger staff members were asked to stay on. It's now a comprehensive school for under-privileged girls. But get this guv. It was bought by none other than Rose construction, and their CEO is none other than our Mr Henry Thorburn." Hunter was now bringing up information quicker than he could relay it to Mac.

"We need a connection between Reece and Thorburn, other than that he was working at the office. Find out why he was taken on at Stone's so quickly and possibly without the right qualifications. Thorburn's father came to Rose Manor, so we may be able to prove that Henry did too. There's something we missed before, dig deeper." Mac could begin now to see how the investigation fitted together, one piece at a time.

Chapter 17.

Confrontation.

Henry sat at his office desk at home, the rain pelting down against the window, as it had been for the past few hours. It was the beginning of November and it was now dark and cold outside. The glass of Macallan Rare Cask whisky in his hand was again empty, as was most of the bottle. Reaching across to the bottle, he refilled the glass again for the umpteenth time. He was now getting progressively more drunk and angrier as time went by.

Emma had been due home before now from the shopping trip to Lakeside, no doubt having bought several new outfits. She still hadn't returned home much later when she said that she would, so she texted Henry to say that she was stopping off to get a meal. He waited, getting more drunk and agitated as he did so, but she still hadn't returned, and it was now eight. He was extremely frustrated while he waited, the whisky now taking its toll.

Her bump had started to show, and her clothes were feeling tight round her ever-swelling belly. Emma enjoyed being pregnant; she'd become much more in control within her thoughts and temperament. She'd managed to take back control her life mentally.

Slouching back in his large green leather chair with the Game of Thrones classical piece by Ramin Djawadi playing loudly in the background, in all its different versions, he reflected on the situation he found himself in. Could he once again be king on his own throne? Had there been too much mistrust and deception between him and Emma?

She hadn't wanted sex since being pregnant and he'd put that down to her hormones, but was it? On reflection that was possible, but the more he thought about it, the less likely that was. She remained pleasant and polite to him, but never had the passion and lust she once shown.

Henry had found out that Emma was well aware of his past indiscretions, especially while he was lecturing at university, and his continuing of misdemeanours, and he felt sure that she would use them against him when she felt it necessary. He sat sipping his whisky slowly, deliberating. How he could resolve the situation; it had been constantly on his mind for the past few hours. Could he persuade Emma that for the sake of the baby they should try to sort out the mess? Having a father to look up to, but one locked up for years to come wouldn't help. He needed to be better than his father had been to him.

He also realised that the police must have made a connection between him and Reece. He feared it wouldn't be long before they suspected what was behind it. This was now every increasing worry for him. His sense of guilt was consuming him, and the doubts now returning. Fortunately, his only comfort was that he knew some very good and specialist legal people through his connections at the manor.

Emma drove silently up the recently laid driveway. The shingle was gone, replaced with tarmac recently stopping the noise and disturbing the dogs late at night; whenever they heard something coming up the drive, they would go wild and bark, waking Emma regularly. Henry often worked late at the office and came home at all hours, so she had insisted that must change when she became pregnant, and it had been a godsend ever since it was done.

She knew full well the child wasn't Henry's, but she didn't want him to get suspicious and ask about it. That would be awkward and complicate things even further.

Entering the house as quietly as she could, Emma went to the kitchen, getting herself a glass of water before she went up to bed. But, just when she was going upstairs, she heard a noise that made her turn round. A very drunk Henry was propped up against the kitchen doorway, glass in one hand and doing his best not to fall over.

"Drunk again," Emma sarcastically said, as the shock of seeing him standing there subsided.

"Where have you been?" Henry slurred.

"Why? You getting concerned about me? A bit late for that, surely? Are you sure, you don't want to go have some fun at Rose Manor again? I'm almost certain you could order a dirty little slut who looks like Caroline to fuck. Let's face it, you've done that a few times, haven't you?" Emma's tone turned hostile now as Henry tried to stand upright. "Or would you prefer some nice little boy or girl to play with? Which rooms did you like going to best? Come on, fucking tell me! You piece of shit," Emma was growling at Henry by now.

"Did you like the boys better or the young girls? Come on, what's her name again, you know the girl who looks almost the spitting image of Caroline, but much younger, so much younger. Oh yes, that's it, Alexandra aged fourteen, According to the black leather book, you visited her often, and after spending time in with a young boy named Reginald Faulkner, too. Or shall we call him by the name Reece? Having seen the details in black and white on those pages, I know the number you used while you were there. You know the one you wear on your little gold badge, that of course matches your lodge registration number and Hospital Patient Number. I checked your computer. Or rather Reece did it for me." Emma had picked up a knife they used to open letters with and stood with it discreetly behind her back. Unsure of Henry and how he was going to react.

"What the fuck did you say?" Henry mumbled.

"Oh. You don't think I haven't been suspicious for some time, the dumb blonde wifey, she'll not know, she's just pleased to have me, the complete innocent wife." Emma was getting hysterical, lashed such bitterness and resentment. "You go away to conferences more and more frequently, yet you don't, do you. You know exactly what I mean. You lied and pretended to go to lectures and seminars, talks so very important and so life changing to students. Or so you kept saying. But only a small handful of them were real, weren't they? The rest, or should I say most of the time, you are getting your perverted kicks out of fucking and playing underage boys and girls. What else did you do with these innocent and helpless children?"

Henry was now cowering on the kitchen floor with Emma was shouting and screaming at him.

"How do you know about the manor and the black books?," Henry was trying to counter her accusations but sounded weak and pathetic as he did so.

"You're nothing but a fucking paedophile and a fucking creep."

"How do you know all this? Where did you get your information from? It's bullshit. That's nothing but rumours and lies. I never went to anything like that. Why would I? I'm with you and I love you!" he sounded desperate.

"I've all the evidence I need to put you away for life along with your friends," Emma yelled back at him.

Now clutching at straws, Henry tried his best to sound sincere and honest, yet pathetic, but Emma felt no empathy for him anymore, she knew he was up against the ropes clinging on for all he was worth.

"I've got those black books locked away where no one at all will ever find them or get hold of them unless I say so. Oh, and if you even think about hurting me or getting 'rid' of me, they will be published on the internet across the world, completely in the public domain. Just imagine the scandal and humiliation that would cause. Politicians, lords, baronesses, so many people that have connections and influence throughout the government will all be exposed. This country would be in political meltdown. Far worse than even when those pathetic arseholes who tried to stop Brexit. It'll be fucked."

Henry was now motionless, as Emma still had the knife in her hand, but Henry was seemingly too drunk to fight.

He was curled up on the floor, tears rolling down his face, weeping uncontrollably, slowly he managed to crawl up onto a chair.

"I'm so sorry, I don't know what's wrong. I get these uncontrollable urges to do these things. I can't help it." Henry was at an all-time low, a whimpering, pathetic person.

Emma put the knife down, thinking he was too weak and feeble to even get off the chair, but the moment she turned to walk out Henry got up and made a dash to get it. He'd made it. Emma turned and saw him, just in time, grabbing his wrist, as he tried to slash at her. Henry pushed her away, still holding the blade. The anger in his eyes was clear to see, drunk no longer.

For the first time since she'd met Henry, Emma felt afraid of him. Would he kill her, even though she was pregnant? He was dangerously full of anger and hate, he seemed to have lost his mind as he stood there. Shouting and lashing out at her, she managed to smack his wrist on the worktop, he dropped the knife, but he still caught her across her face with a random elbow. Emma was thrown to the floor, but managing to pick herself up quickly, she pushed him away hard, as he tried to grad her, slipping as she did so. Emma lashed out, kicking and screaming for all she was worth, her foot fortunately landing a blow directly in his groin, and he went down in agony. The hours spent at the gym were holding her in really good stead, she was stronger than the drunk and feeble man rolling on the floor in front of her. Henry looked pitiful now, practically lying on his back, unable to move and sobbing. Emma looked at him with complete contempt and yet despair as she stood over him.

"You know, I thought we were made for each other. But you, you've thrown that all away. What for? A fantasy over a dirty tart who can't keep her fucking legs closed, well, that is for, everyone except you. You're a pathetic piece of shit. Your life, Henry, is over once and for all after all this comes out. You do realise that, don't you? How the hell do you think you'll be able to run the business and get any contracts now?" Emma was now very confident, Henry was in no position to question anything she said to him.

"So, let's recap, shall we? Where we are then, oh yeah, on one hand, you are a paedophile and then on other we have all the other fucking perverts in your Lodge or 'secret society'. That's a major problem because I know all about them, along with other people you can't trust. What's going to be worse? Going to prison for child abuse or ruining the country's political establishment?" Emma paused at this point, as she stood over Henry. The knife in her hand again now. Henry went numb. He didn't respond at all, but just sat there thinking this was all a complete nightmare. Eventually when he spoke he was mumbling and stammering.

"Why are you doing this? We can work this out, surely?" His eyes looked at Emma with some sadness and yet hope deep within them.

"You want to see your child grow up?" Emma looked at him with no empathy, waiting for the obvious reply to her question.

"Yes, of course I do."

"We will divorce and go our own ways. I expect you to sell the house and give me half of the profits as well as £15 million in monies from your offshore account and assets. Please don't try to deny them, I've done my homework. You will be kept informed of how Thomas is doing. That's what I'm going to name him. I will allow access only as and when it is convenient for me." Emma knew this was going to annoy the hell out of a frustrated Henry. But fuck him, she also knew that he'd be in prison for a long time, so that promise meant nothing now.

"The divorce papers will be served to you in a couple of days, don't refuse them or else. The estate agents have been booked for Monday, so don't be here. That will give you time to remove your stuff from the house until it's sold." Emma turned and walked away. Stopping as she got to the door. She turned back to look at Henry as he was trying to fathom what had just been said. She hesitated for a moment, wondering if this was a good time to tell him she was actually expecting twins. Fuck it. She decided as that was no longer any of his concern.

Chapter 18.

Arrest.

The next day Mac had the search warrant in his procession and the team set up ready to go; a minibus of eight officers followed Mac to the Thorburn house. It was still very early, the sun was only just getting over the horizon. Fortunately, the main entrance gates were open when they pulled up outside the house. Jim rang the doorbell shouting "Open up, police" for almost a minute before Henry started hollering on the other side that he was coming. Jim yelled once again. "Police, open up", finally the door opened. Henry stood there, still wearing the clothes he'd worn the night before, having slept downstairs. He'd got too drunk to get upstairs after his confrontation with Emma. His head was pounding and he looked like a tramp who had slept on the streets for a long while.

"What's going on?"

"Henry Thorburn, I'm arresting you on suspicion of the murders of Caroline Stone and Reece Faulkner. You do not have to say anything, but it may harm your defence if you do not mention when questioned something which you later rely on in court. Anything you do say may be given in evidence." Jim took great pride in being the arresting officer. He put the handcuffs on Henry without any resistance from him and escorted Henry out to the squad car along with Kara. After making sure that he was safely placed in the car, she went around the other side and she got in next to him.

Mac let the search team enter the house, they knew what they were looking for. Hunter stopped to speak to Henry before he entered the house, he needed the pass code for the safe and the location, he'd explained to Henry that he didn't want to have to force his way into it, but it would be appreciated if he gave him it. Henry was reluctant to give this information, but after a few moments thought better of it, and he gave the information to Hunter.

The safe was in Henry's study. Behind a book shelf along the far wall was a section of encyclopaedias and looked like the original first edition prints. The books were crammed in tight on the shelf, Hunter went straight to a book in the S section, when he pulled it out the book automatically released the entire section. True to his word. Henry's safe was where he'd said it was, and now Hunter pressed the pass code into the digital locking mechanism. The lock drew back the bolts and the door sprung open.

Mac stood alongside Hunter a photographer videoed the process, along with taking individual pictures. The safe contained a pile of papers that referred to Henry's will and the ownership of the property. It showed that Henry and Emma Thorburn had joint ownership of the house, and that if he was to die the full ownership would pass to Emma and vice versa, then to any offspring they had produced together. He'd obviously decided that it didn't need to be sealed as no one but him had access to the safe. Alongside the papers was an envelope containing five thousand pounds of cash in the form of fifty-pound notes, all bundled together in thousand pound lots. At the back of the safe was another smaller metal compartment this was secured to the back of the main volt, it was still firmly locked. Mac called Kara still outside in the car with Henry, Kara spoke to Henry, he remained silent, insisting that there wasn't anything in that particular compartment.

Zodiac had come into the study and had been going through the desk draws and cupboards. "Try his phone number," she suggested. It didn't work, but after Hunter had tried it a second time, Zodiac interrupted again. "Try it backwards." Mac looked at her as if she was a major safe cracker as the door clicked and sprung open. Zodiac just shrugged.

"Bingo," Hunter gently opened the eight-inch-square door to find a black cloth wrapped round an object. He carefully removed the bundle and placed it on the desk. Using a pair of pliers, he gently pulled back the folds of cloth, the camera constantly clicking as the procedure was recorded. Three folds later, a pistol was clearly visible. Underneath the gun lay a red silk thong.

"Is that a gun?" River now appeared from the hallway behind them, having just arrived with her team, and were setting about their task.

"Looks like a 45mm, Mac, may I?" River already had her gloves on, and picking up the pistol, carefully looked closer.

"Yes, it certainly is a 45mm Mac. I think we might have our murder weapon, along with a soiled red thong.

Caroline's? I'm on it, Mac." She knew exactly what he was going to say.

"Make it priority, doctor. Jim, you're in charge here now, you know what we need." Mac felt positive at this point as he made his way out and made it back to the station just as Kara was booking Henry in at the front desk. He'd already made a phone call to his solicitor and was now waiting for him to arrive and consult with him. Henry had pleaded his innocence of murder all the way to the station, in fact Kara got stressed by his incessant talking. She just hoped he was like that when the solicitor arrived. Mac hadn't mentioned the gun or thong to Kara before she'd left, he wanted to see Henry's reaction for himself during the interview.

Mac went to inform the commissioner of Henry Thorburn's arrest, along with the evidence in the safe, the gun by now was with forensics and DNA from the thong was being cross-referenced with that on file for Caroline Stone. The commissioner was pleased and as enthusiastic as Mac. Saying would prepare the CPS, to allow them to charge Henry formally as soon as the DNA came back.

There wasn't long to wait long before he heard from River, she called him as soon as she'd done her tests, confirming the DNA was 100% that of Caroline Stone. There was matching samples on the gusset of the thong, along with semen DNA, that of Henry. The gun was taking longer, River hadn't completed her test but had fired the gun and was now testing the bullet for the same markings as that of the one removed from the Stones bedroom floor. Henry's lawyer had now arrived, so Mac allowed him the time he'd requested to speak to his client in private, but soon Mac decided it was time to interview Henry so interrupted their meeting, much to the lawyer's annoyance.

The interview room was small and square area with a table situated in the centre, along with four chairs. It had two-way mirrors, as did all the interview rooms in the station, along with cameras. Mac had been firing questions at Henry for the past forty-five minutes, but with every question the same response was given, "No Comment." Mac was getting frustrated with Henry so decided that a break would help. Mac spoke to Henry's solicitor, advising him that Henry really needed to cooperate; the evidence was stacking up and quite overwhelming, and he was going to be charged with two counts of first degree murder, unless he could prove otherwise, so he really did need to cooperate.

Mac ordered a takeaway as the troops returned from the Thorburn's house shortly after lunch, it was very much appreciated by one and all. They looked the happiest he'd seen them for some time, and that pleased him.

"So what other evidence did you find guys?"

"We picked up a couple of pairs of trainers that looked as if they could well have carpet fibres on them. They were stashed right at the back of the garage in a cupboard, nice pair of expensive Nikes, though." Jude replied between mouthfuls of pizza. "Dr Banks has them at present. We also found pictures and some porn clips of someone very similar to Caroline Stone, probably a few years younger, but certainly very similar in appearance."

"Okay, enjoy lunch guys." Mac left them to it and went to his office to call the CPS, to find out if he could charge Henry Thorburn with murder. It was good news; they agreed that they now had enough hard evidence to get a first degree murder conviction in court.

Recalling Mr Higgins, Henry's solicitor, to inform him that the CPS could now charge Henry. Also that he would send Jude and Jim to collect him and take him back to the interview room immediately. Mac and Jim went back into the interview room, Jim had been the arresting officer, Mac knew it was fair for him to see things through, especially as Mac had already put him forward for his own position when he retired.

Mr Higgins entered the room first. Henry stood and waited outside, hands cuffed, and head hung down, dejected, and broken. Higgins sat and spoke to Mac.

"Detective Savage, my client is willing to make a full statement for the manslaughter of Caroline Stone and that of Reece Faulkner. He insists that there are mitigating circumstances and consequently would plead guilty to the lesser charge."

"We'll see what he has to say before we agree with your proposal, but will bear that in mind."

Henry now entered, still dressed in grey overalls supplied by the cell warden when he had arrived, still looking down to the floor until he'd sat on the chair. Then he slowly looked up at Mac with no emotion at all on his face.

"Okay, I believe from your solicitor that you wish to make a statement?" Mac said.

"Yes," Henry replied in an almost inaudible voice, before repeating it louder and firmer. Jim began writing his statement as well as recording it as Henry began.

"When I was sixteen for my birthday, Mum and Dad organised a birthday party for me and a few of my friends. Some family came, but not that many. We had fun. The adults stayed out of the way, me and my friends played music, had a bit of drink. Nothing to heavy, just a bit of shandy and stuff like that. We chatted a lot, and it was fun. It finished around eight. The other kids all left and went home. But Dad said he had a pleasant surprise for me, so while Mum was tiding up and talking to her friends. He drove us down the road to a place called Rose Manor. He said to me on the way he'd hired a room for me to use. He told me he went there two or three times a month to meet his friends for a laugh. Assuring me it was innocent fun, and that Mum knew he visited there. But all the same he made me swear not to tell Mum because it would upset her, and she'd be furious with him for taking me there.

Anyway, we arrived at this rather old house and went inside. Six of Dad's mates were there drinking and having a laugh. They gave me a drink of lager and we all drank for a time, where they all ribbed me for still being a virgin and all that. Then they led me to this room, and they told me that my real birthday present was inside. I of course at this point was getting excited and wondering what I was getting, I entered with Dad behind me. Inside stood a girl,

Mary, from school, who I'd fancied for some time. She was dressed in sexy lingerie, the full works, and made her look amazing, but thought she looked very frightened, I'd fancied her at school, and had talked with her frequently. Here's your birthday present," Dad said, laughing. "She's a cracker and a virgin too, so we thought you should have first pickings."

"I told Dad she was only fifteen and underage and there was no way I was going to do anything like that with her. His response, his fucking, response was if you don't, me and my friends will! Mary was now starting to cry. She looked so beautiful and innocent. Her long black hair, her body was amazingly mature and if you'd seen her you'd think she was older." Henry's face and expression told Mac how much he was fighting his emotions, the anger and disgust he had shown at sixteen showed. Henry went on.

"I thought he was joking to start with, but it soon became clear that he wasn't. The others from the bar had now followed and came into the room. All these perverts were Dad's age in their fifties or more. They got hold of me, sat me on a chair, tried to persuade me it was natural, and that she'd asked to see me. All fucking bullshit. I was made to watch as they all took it in turns to rape her. She screamed and cried, and lashed out, but no-one took any notice. I shouted and begged them to stop time and time again. For the next two hours they did everything they wanted to her. I just sat there like a fucking pathetic idiot, having to watch. I felt sick to my stomach every time someone else got on top of her and used her. I was just made to watch."

Henry had tears were rolling down his cheeks now, as he stopped to take a moment to gather his thoughts.

"After they finished, I tried to talk to her, but this other older woman came into the room and took her away. I never did see her again. She left school. It wasn't until three, maybe four months later that I found out she was pregnant; she was only fifteen, for fuck's sake. Anyway, I made a vow to myself that I would find her and look after her as soon as I could, give her the life that I truly wanted to. It was then I found out that two months after giving birth she threw herself in front of a train. She'd had the baby by then, and it had already been adopted. I found out that eventually it was a girl and that the baby was named Emma."

"Your now wife, Emma? But she could be your sister, you do realise that?" Mac looked surprised and interrupted him.

"Yes, I know, but we aren't, I did a DNA test later, after getting to know her. I got a private investigator to find her a few years ago. It took a few months, but I did. So, then I started to make payments into an account for her. When she turned eighteen she'd have a good start in life, pretended it was set up by her mum before she died. I eventually met her when she turned up, out of the blue at Charles's house. You see, I'd met Caroline a few weeks before that at a business meeting and fell in love with her the moment I saw her. Caroline was the exact image of

Mary, when Mary was alive and younger, the way I still see her in my mind, all these years later."

"What about Emma?"

"Emma is a lovely woman. But unfortunately she got the genes from her father and looks nothing like her mother. Yes, she has her smile and her manner, but not her attractive features, if you know what I mean, not what I really like. I love Emma for who she is rather than what she is. It's a different love, more of a sister type of relationship as far as I'm concerned."

"How did you feel when your Dad was killed in the car accident?" Jim asked.

"What accident was that, then? I drilled a hole in his brake fluid pipe one day after I'd begged him not to go to that place again. But did he listen? No, he fucking didn't. He kept going, doing things I knew Mum didn't know about. I kept asking him to stop, but he just laughed, so I sorted it for all our sakes. I never told Mum about Rose Manor and what went on there, it would have destroyed her. But yes, you could say that I took care of him. Unfortunately, though, Rose Manor had a reputation by then and was more popular by those posh, rich arseholes." Henry seemed proud that he'd said that.

"So why shoot Caroline and Reece?"

"Please understand that despite being in love with Mary, I also fell head over heels for Caroline. But I have these maddening desirers, the things Dad did and to other boys and girls, I couldn't get them out of my head. So when I started lecturing, I got to know Reginald and some of his friends. Some were struggling with the course work, so I offered extra lessons. Before I knew it, I really enjoyed the extra time I spent with them. I explained to them that tutor wanted to give them better results, I said they had to try harder or I'd have to punish them. I started with a leather belt and progressed to the cane. After a while one boy said that instead of my canning him, could he please me another way. Before long I was out of control and battled immense, overwhelming, and uncontrollable feelings. I went to see a councillor and I quit my job. Thought It was the only way to stop the thoughts and anguish going round in my head.

It wasn't long before the urges returned though and the powerful thoughts exploding in my mind. I decided that I'd go to a masonic lodge meeting, something that I'd learned through work and teaching, and it turned out to be at Rose Manor. It wasn't the house that I'd remembered though, it had been completely changed and revamped with such a unique style. I started seeing young boys there and that switched off those awful thoughts. I tried to compensate for what I did. I gave regular money to charities to help unfortunate families and children. Trying to ease my guilt and trying to give myself redemption, even that I know wasn't enough.

"Reginald, or should I say Reece, turned up at my home one day demanding I give him money and a job. I did, but he then wanted more. I found out that he was fucking most of the girls at work, even the married ones, He didn't care as long as they dropped their knickers. He kept saying to me that Emma was next unless I paid him to leave her alone. I paid him of course, I had too. I put it down as bonuses going through the company because I didn't have the cash, but then Caroline got to know about it. I figured out that he'd been bragging to the other staff about how much he was earning. I also realised that by that time he was shagging Caroline too. I almost caught them one day in Charles' office." Henry was getting thirsty now and asked for a drink. Mac offered him a glass of water as he continued.

"The shooting, tell us about that."

"I don't remember the shooting, to be honest. We had been at the party and the last thing I remember was getting into a car to come home. I woke up the next day with this almighty headache. I found blood spots on my face, but I just assumed I'd had one of my nose bleeds. I often get them when I've been drinking or experience a sleepwalking episode. I remember there was dried mud on the carpet, just a bit, but I've no idea how that got there. Emma wasn't in bed, she'd got up early to take the dogs for a walk. But other than that, I recall nothing." Henry sounded very sure.

Danny entered the room at this point with a note and gestured to Mac that it was important. Mac took the note. It was from Dr Banks, confirming that the bullet of the murders was from the gun they had found in Henry's safe.

"How come, Mr Thorburn we found a 45mm gun in your safe with a red silk thong?, we know these belonged to Caroline Stone, and that they were the one's she wore on the night of the murder, we have video footage of her removing it minutes before being shot. Also, we'd like to know how your DNA is on it? And also why the gun used to kill Caroline and Reece was in your personal safe along with the thong." Mac knew he had all the evidence to put this man away for the rest of his life and was very confident about convicting him.

Henry stared as if he'd no idea what Mac was talking about. He remembered nothing about the thong either, nor how he could have got possession of it. He remembered Caroline in her red dress and had commented to her about it, saying how gorgeous it looked on her, but that was all.

"I've no recollection of the thong whatsoever. The gun I've had in my safe for a few years. It was given to me when we had some trouble with rats, an American client sent it to me as a deterrent against them, he didn't seem to understand that guns aren't legal in the UK, so he just sent it. It's been in my safe, inside a sealed case, for the past four years. I've never even fired it."

"The gun has traces of your DNA on it, and the bullets have the same markings of those we extracted from the bedroom after the murders. Why's that?"

"I've no idea. I'm the only one who even knows the combination to the internal lock."

"Our team opened that lock quickly. Detective Kostopoulos cracked it within minutes. Could anyone else have done the same? Your wife may be?" Mac waited a while before Henry managed to reply.

"My wife, detective, wouldn't have a clue. I've always done her accounts and anything to do with numbers.

Emma couldn't remember a simple phone number, let alone a complicated set of digital numbers. She was diagnosed with dyscalculia at school. So certainly not."

Mac was now debating in his mind what they could charge Henry Thorburn with, first degree murder or diminished responsibility. He thought they had enough evidence to charge him with first degree murder, and now the unlawful murder of his father some thirty years before. He brought the interview to a close and the officer outside the room took Henry back to the cells in the detention area. Mr Higgins stopped Mac in the corridor outside the interview room as Henry was taken away.

"Detective, I'm going to ask for a full mental assessment of my client. He's psychotic, and his admission would suggest to me his is not stable, and therefore not responsible for his actions. As you're probably aware, with the statement he's just given you, he'll be locked away in an institution for some considerable time, without parole, but getting the counselling he needs. He's a broken man, detective. Let's put this to bed as soon as we can. A murder trial will mean a long process, whereas my offer would be justice and far more painless for all concerned."

Mac knew that Mr Higgins was right, but he needed to talk to the CPS and his bosses, ultimately. It wasn't his decision to make, and he told Higgins he'd let him know.

When they left the interview room for a break after Henry's confession, Mac watched the room that Emma was being questioned in. Emma had arrived an hour ago after Jim had called her. Jude and Eli sat opposite her and a lawyer who seemed to appear from nowhere. He worked at a top city law firm in Mayfair, Goldman and Co, and dressed in an expensive obviously tailor made suit that could only have been made on Savile Row. Alex Goldman was the firm's main partner and was in his late sixties. A grey-haired small man ~~of medium height~~, he wore a platinum Swiss watch that Mac estimated would cost a year's salary for him, his shoes personally designed and handmade. A briefcase rested by his chair, which only seemed to be there for show. No papers, no notes, and every question Eli was asked Emma came back with the same response; no comment. She wore a flowery patterned full-length dress with a cardigan over the top, looking immaculate and unconcerned, as if expecting this to happen.

This was starting to worry Mac. Jim was beginning to have the same thoughts though as Mac. Emma sat very still and looking confident and smug as she repeated the same answer time and time again, and Mac decided that it was time he went into the interview room. He had a few questions to verify about Henry's confession, especially the fact that Henry didn't recall the murder, but had assumed that he'd done them, mainly because of the sleep disorder he suffered from. It didn't make sense to Mac so, grabbing a coffee from the machine, he stepped into the room.

"For the purpose of the interview recording, Chief Inspector Savage has now entered the room," Eli announced.

"Ah, Inspector Savage, at last. I was hoping you'd be here. I would like to be allowed time with my client. When

I arrived, although Mrs Thorburn had been cautioned, she was already being interviewed by your officers. I therefore request immediately that I am given time with her. I do believe that she is willing to make a statement but refuses to do so, until I have spoken to her."

Mac looked across at Jude and Eli as if he expected a response from them. "I'm sure my officers followed proper procedure, Mr Goldman. If you need time with your client, then I'll give you an hour." Mac wasn't pleased to see Alex Goldman, who he heard had a reputation for being ruthless on other cases. His presence did however bring to mind why Emma had wanted him in the first place. What did she know, that could worry her about her own situation in all of this. As far as Mac was concerned, she was only there to help get a better picture of Henry. But did she know about Henry and her mother? That could well be the situation, after all, they still had no-one in the frame for the fire at Rose Manor. Could she have started that? More and more questions started to go round in his mind.

One hour later Alex Goldman re-entered the interview room with Emma. In the meantime, Mac had brought Zodiac would be helpful in this discussion, along with Jim.

"Before you start, Inspector, after speaking to my client over the past hour and a former colleague who is representing Mr Thorburn, I believe that Henry Thorburn has made a statement regarding the matter you're interviewing him for, admitting responsibility for the murders of Caroline Stone and Reece, sorry, Reginald Faulkner. Therefore, I think that this interview is over. I kindly ask you to release her." Goldman had already shut his now open briefcase and preparing to leave.

"Sorry, but we have a problem. Henry can't remember anything about the night of the murders other than being put to bed by Mrs Thorburn. So, as you, might guest, I'm struggling with that, because surely even if he was in a state of unconsciousness where you don't know what you're doing exactly, there would be something to tell you that something is wrong. And then there's the gun and thong. They were found in his safe, but again, he has no knowledge or recognition of putting them there at all. So you see my problem; I'm not sure he's responsible at all. I think he could be a fall guy. Now the fact your client is refusing to answer questions me more suspicious." Mac looked and sounded implacable.

"Please, Inspector," Goldman said in an authoritative tone. "I've told you that my client will make a full statement when we have spoken further. I also think that you will need to have the Commissioner present, and the Minister of Justice and the Foreign Secretary. I will post bail of two million pounds in a bond for her immediate release and I guarantee that tomorrow at eleven you will have answers."

Mac knew he couldn't hold Emma. He had a full confession from Henry, as well as substantial evidence, which would put him away for a long time. So he put in a call to Superintendent Willis, to get confirmation that they could accept Mr Goldman's proposal from and set the bail as offered. Willis then had to ring the Justice department to ask the Secretary of State could attend the interview in the morning. Almost laughing at that the idea, he told Willis that he couldn't be there and that it probably not that important anyway, but he'd send an assistant along as a gesture of good will. Willis had to accept what he said but was put out by his attitude. He had a bad feeling something really serious was going to surface, or why else had Goldman asked for their attendance?

Once away from the station Emma and Jason spent the next few hours briefing Mr Goldman again about the entire Rose Manor situation, every last detail, every video and every member who attended the Manor. Mr Goldman sat and listened, asking the odd question here and there, but continually taking notes and looking at the footage on Emma's laptop. After going through all the evidence and putting together a watertight case for Emma and Jason, he left them to get some sleep. Tomorrow would be a day of reckoning.

The meeting room that Emma and Alex Goldman were led into was the station boardroom. A large oval table with ten plush chairs sat central in the room, a coffee and refreshment cabinet stood against the wall to the left as they sat down facing five men and Zodiac. Directly opposite Mr Goldman sat Superintendent Willis, to his right sat the Commissioner, and next to her the minister who had been sent from the Justice department. To his left were Mac, Hunter, and Zodiac. They all had laptops set up in front of them, and acknowledged Both Emma and Goldman as they took theirs seats.

"Good morning, ladies and gentlemen. Thank you for permitting this meeting to take place. I believe that you have formally charged Mr Thorburn with the murders and other offences that he confessed to you yesterday. His lawyer and my colleague contacted me this morning to also confirm the charges."

"Yes. He has been cautioned," Mac replied.

"That's good. Before we get into the reasons and the purpose of Mrs Thorburn's request, I reiterate that she at no time knew of nor conversed with Mr Henry Thorburn at any point about the crimes that he committed. However, Mrs Thorburn would like to present to you the following information and documents regarding her findings concerning Mr Thorburn's activities. These include the atrocities that took place at Rose Manor and at institutions in several major cities throughout the world." Goldman started a slide show presentation on the large television at the far end of the room. Pictures of various buildings were shown one by one on screen along with the building's, names, and locations. All of them in their own language translated as Rose Manor. Twenty-six pictures in total.

"Ladies and gentlemen, these buildings are all connected to Rose Construction and Rose subsidiaries. The board of directors for all these companies are the same people. Here's the list of those who run them and benefit from their profits. As you can see, on that list, there are six very powerful and rich people who have contributed to the formation of this empire of institutions. Of the twenty -six, nine have been destroyed over the past two years and no longer function. Each of the manors was used for the abuse of children, as well as for other extreme, perverse sexual activities, and for murder."

The six people opposite Goldman looked dumbfounded.

"How did you come across this information and how can we tell if it's the genuine article?" Commissioner Jordon Cobbe spoke before anyone else had chance.

Zodiac and Hunter now had the footage and pictures of the various fires on their laptops as they scoured the internet for information, both nodded to Mac and Willis to confirm what Goldman said. No deaths had been recorded, but the fires had completely destroyed the buildings and everything in them.

Goldman spoke. "We have the black ledgers and videos from each of the buildings that have been destroyed by fire, all dated and all safely stored. Each and every person who attended each manor is named, with time's, dates and activities logged. These ledgers are in our possession and stored away for safe keeping. They will only be released as and when required. All this information is within the computer file. Some of the buildings are historic properties, so we are giving you and each country's government time to disband the activities that take place in them. There will be a timescale for you to do this. Failure to do so will cause the release of all this data to the internet and the dark web." Alex Goldman now saw before him the faces of six very concerned people. Brian Shepard, the minister the Secretary of State had sent down, was on his phone to his boss, who was now making his way to join the meeting as quickly as he could.

"Let move on. How we have these documents is irrelevant to the situation. As you can now see on the screen, there is a full list of prominent and influential individuals who are not only in the current administration but past ones too. If these names were in the public domain, I'm sure you would realise the effect that would have on the country, from government to the financial sector. Companies would collapse, and when their trading partners realised why, and who released the information, imagine the fallout to the economy around the world, and the detrimental outcome of that." Goldman took a sip of water, then continued. "As you might now realise, after the finding of Mr Stone's body the assets from Stone's PLC will shift to Mr Thorburn. Who has now confessed to the murders of Caroline Stone, Reginald Faulkner and of Charles Stone, albeit an unforeseen and tragic contribution. The main control of Stone's PLC will pass into Emma Thorburn's hands. We expect that to happen ladies, and gentlemen, as a formality, and part of our proposal for you. Now for the nitty gritty, if you'll pardon my speech."

"My client's requests are as follows:-"

"Every listed building on the list will be shut down. You will be given one year to complete this, along with the appropriate authorities from associated countries.

"Every existing minister on that list will resign forthwith.

"Efforts will be made to find and compensate the abused children and their familiar. My client will reimburse the compensation paid out from the Thorburn estate and Stone's annual profits.

"Any attempt to find and destroy the original copies of the ledgers will automatically trigger release of the information to the internet as stated.

"Any attempt to dispose of my client's or commit harm to her or her family, will automatically trigger release.

"Any investigation into how my clients acquired this information triggers release.

"If her husband gets to know any of this, it triggers release.

"My client has copies of all information in several places and protected by encrypted algorithms, that change continually. Any attempt at breaking these will be known. If my client doesn't verify the codes with her part of each part. In that event, the process of release will begin after ten minutes. Last thing, ladies, and gentlemen, you have four hours to prepare documentation signalling your agreement to all of this and the clock is ticking."

"I think my client would like a private word with Detective Savage before we go to lunch." Goldman put his laptop into his briefcase and followed the others out. Leaving Mac and Emma seated at the table.

"Detective Savage, I've asked to see you because I think I can help you with Mick Jones's murder. My friend came across a site while he set up my insurance policies on line, a site that upset him and reminded him of something in his past. I don't know what, but I hasten to say that it was on the dark web and he recognised one of your, victims. So here is that site's IP address. Everyone has two faces detective, you of all people know that." Emma passed Mac a piece of paper and smiled at him.

She moved to leave. But Mac, sitting back in his chair, asked, "Why did you kill those innocent people?"

Emma looked back at him and said, "Did I, detective?" and walked out to her lawyer.

Mac stood by the window and watched as Emma left the building. She went down the steps and walked up to a figure, dressed in all black and hugged them, before she got into a silver BMW and driving off. The lone figure turned mounted his motorbike and driving off after the car.

Henry's trial was quick. He was taken away from court, his ordeal was over for now. Judge Kennedy gave him the least sentence that applied for the crimes, knowing that had he not done so, Henry could well have put him and a lot of his friends in a very serious situation. Kennedy therefore recommended that Henry was to serve a minimum of twenty-five years in a mental institution, to be continually monitored for psychoses, and knowing full well that he could be released within ten years with the right help and guidance.

Chapter 19.

Visit a year later.

Henry sat in his cell waiting for visiting time to come round. The four walls he'd occupied for the past twelve months had driven him into further depths of depression, and the thought of seeing his son was the only thing left. The dark grey walls closed in around him, making him wonder if he'd ever last the term of his sentence. Twenty-five years for the murders of Caroline, Reece, and his father. He still couldn't believe that he'd had no choice. Either he went to prison as the paedophile he was or the murders, which he knew he didn't commit. But put in such a position, what could he do? As a paedophile he wouldn't have lasted in confinement, he'd have been tortured and murdered for such crimes: Even hardened criminals wouldn't stand for that. So he'd had no option, as far as he was concerned. If he kept his head down, he could get out in less time. His lawyer was still working on his case, trying to reduce the sentence, but seemingly not holding out too much hope.

Deep down, he still loved Emma in his own way, but now she'd given birth to his son, he thought he still had a life to look forward to, albeit a few years away. She'd told him she'd named him Thomas, and that he was just like his father.

A son was what he'd dreamt, someone to whom he could pass on the knowledge and money he'd accrued, someone he could love. Unlike his father, he was going to make sure his son would be well looked after and want for nothing. He knew that he had to put his own past behind him to become a father. He'd chosen, that day when he was confronted by Emma telling him that if he didn't tell full disgusting truth, it would be made public across all the social media networks, times and dates, the full story. He'd even been sent pictures and voice recordings, but how Emma got those he'd not as yet managed to work out. Somehow or someone must have infiltrated the parties regularly.

He still was unsure of what she had hidden away and thought continually about the injustice he felt. Why was he in prison for murders he never committed? Yet the evidence that convicted him had been overwhelming, and he had admitted to virtually killing his father.

He wondered if he really had had an experience he couldn't control that night when Caroline and Reece had died.

Henry was so looking forward to the visit of Emma and his son, he'd not been able to see him since he was a babe in arms and wondered what he was like now. Looking forward was all that he could manage if he was to keep his mind focused and not go completely insane.

The time came. Henry stood outside the visiting room, excited and in a happier mood than he could remember. He'd even thought about ending it all at one point, his depression had grown deeper as time went on.

Emma arrived with Thomas, slowly toddling alongside her, his thick black hair bobbing as he walked with his mummy. Jason followed behind carrying Luna. Emma become a loving mother and cared so much for her children, something she thought she would never do, thank God she thought frequently. Her mothering instinct became second nature to her since the birth of Thomas and Luna. She'd become so protective of her children, and now her brother Jason, too.

Entering the prison with its grey walls and concrete floors, was scary for Emma, as she hadn't been before. She'd not visited Henry since his conviction. She was led into a small room and politely directed to sit at a glass cubical by the female guard who escorted them, she helpfully pulled out the chair for Emma to sit on before showing Thomas the small table where Luna had already sat down. Toys had been placed for him and Luna, along with colouring books and crayons. The table had been especially put there at Emma's request with various toys to play with so the children wouldn't be overwhelmed and scared. Jason, waited outside for Emma, knowing she'd need him to comfort her later. The sides of the booth were made from dark grey composite board, as was the countertop at which she sat waiting. A thick glass partition separated her from where Henry was going to be sitting very shortly. Her chair wasn't that comfortable, but it was practical. Two guards stood ten feet away either side of a door which started opening a minute or two later, and Henry appeared on the other side, walking slowly looking frail. Dressed in the prisoner standard uniform of light grey overalls and white tee shirt, he'd grown a beard and was almost completely grey now, unrecognisable to Emma as the man she'd fallen in love with a few short years before.

He approached his side of the booth, his hands and ankles in shackles; he sat directly looking at Emma the entire time, staring directly at her. Emma was dressed in a black dress, her hair tied up neatly at the back of her head.

"So nice to see you, thank you for coming. It's been far too long." Henry mumbled and with a hint of a relief that she had even come to see him, eventually, despite having asked her consistently since the trial and his conviction. "I've been counting the days for this visit. Where's Thomas?"

Emma turned and looked towards the small table where he was sat playing. The colouring pens and paper had been a hit and he'd just finished doing a scribbled drawing and was looking proud of his achievement.

Emma beckoned the twins over with a wave and a smile. Without hesitation, Thomas toddled across and jumped on his Mummy's lap.

"Wow, haven't you grown?" Henry was now smiling and put his hand up to the glass partition, hoping to get a response from the young boy. Thomas waved his small hand and gave a grin which made Henry smile back.

"Who's this man?" A quiet child's voice asked.

"This is Henry, you know the man we discussed before we came. Mummy was still married to him when she was pregnant with you and Luna."

"Who is Luna? You didn't tell me about a girl, did we have twins?" Henry was confused by what Emma said.

"Why would I tell you about that?"

"But you had twins?" Henry looked as though he was struggling to understand.

"Are you their father? Is that what you think?" Emma's expression became one of sarcasm. "You think that I'd have your children after what you did? My god, you are one fucking selfish arsehole, aren't you?" Emma held her hands across Thomas's ears so that he couldn't really hear her swearing. She then whispered to the boy that he should go and sit down and play with his sister. Immediately he did as he was told.

"You honestly think that finding all that fucking shit out, I would let you get me pregnant? When were you going to tell me I could be your fucking sister?"

Emma was remorseless with Henry, she hated him so much for his lies and deceit. She couldn't help herself.

"You're nothing, just a fucking perverted old bastard, along with all those other old perverts. All you, pathetic arseholes playing with people's lives and destroying their families and futures for the sake of what?, Self-gratification and depravity. I only ever let you fuck me when I felt I had to. It made me cringe every time I looked at you. I felt sick to my stomach when you even touched me, let alone when I fucked you. What you did to those boys and girls was fucking unforgiveable. How they must have suffered. The torment you put them through was horrendous, unforgivable and immoral." Emma now shifted forwards on the chair and was close to the glass divider.

"Since now I got the black books from Rose Manor, I know every boy you abused, every girl you forced yourself on. Everything is written down by date, who was present, which rooms everyone visited, which boys or girls were in each room. You name it, I know it all, thanks to Jason."

"Those books were destroyed in the fire, I was told. And who the fuck is Jason?" Henry was bewildered and shocked at Emma's revelation, jumping up from his chair. His chains tightening around his wrists and ankles as he did so, then only to be shouted at by the guards in the far corner to sit down again immediately. He had no choice.

"Oh, the books, you believe they were destroyed, Well believe me when I say they weren't," Emma snarled back at Henry, despite the promise she'd made to herself that she'd remain calm.

"I've got those books, and with others dating back thirty years, all safely locked away. So if you breathe a word to anyone in your circle of dirty, depraved friends they will all go to prison for one hell of a time. Oh, and as you know, many of them are now running this country. Members of this and past governments all feature in these books, some far more than others. So, large corporations would collapse overnight. Making life so fucking difficult for many families. I bet they'd all want to know how and where that information came from, right? Your life in here would be nothing but hell on earth. Oh, and by the way, Jason is my twin brother, something if you really loved our mother you would have known."

Henry was sitting there in silence now, he was in complete shock. When he'd pleaded guilty to the murder charges with diminished responsibilities, it was so that he could at least be part of his son's life when he'd done his time. Let alone a daughter he now knew about. He was beginning to realise that none of that would happen. He'd been duped all along by this scheming, devious, revengeful bitch. Emma was determined to make sure that he suffered, at least for the next twenty-odd years.

"I read those books and thought about the way you treated those poor kids, and some were, weren't they, just kids?. So I decided, I needed to give these poor helpless boys a chance to get some compensation for their mental and physical torture. I contacted as many as I could, it wasn't easy. But I have a couple of very good friends who helped me find them. Then I invited them individually to a reunion. I pretended to be the college co-ordinator and that this party was a special one just for them. I sent out ten invites, got six replies. Did you know two of the boys you abused committed suicide last year? Never got over the trauma and humiliation. Another two are okay and married and have managed to move on." Emma waited to see his reaction at this point.

"When each of them turned up, we sat drinking and chatting. I listened to them talking about their present lives and I was slowly getting drunk as they were. I asked then, why they said little about their school life and how they coped with the way they were treated by you. The looks they gave me, the horror in their eyes, trying to make excuses for that. I stopped of course them, comforting each of them when I could. At this point, I explained that I was your wife, that I'd found out about your past with them. So they could do whatever they wanted to me as retribution. Do as you did to them. Let's face it, you didn't give them that much choice, did you?

To say they enjoyed doing just that is an understatement. They took turns fucking me in every way possible, slapping and whipping me, calling me names. You name it, they did it to your wife. I have whip marks across my bum and another baby in my belly. But the marks faded eventually, and I'll have a beautiful baby girl as well as the twins to cherish and love."

Emma lent back in her chair, showing her now swollen baby, she was four months gone. She watched cold-heartedly as Henry began to shed tears. The sadness across his face was a picture Emma had waited to see for months. Now she was now enjoying watching this man being demolished from within.

"Oh, and before each of them left, I rewarded each of them with one of your fucking dreadful paintings off the wall in the hallway. And a couple of those vintage vases you liked so much. God, I was glad to see the fucking back of that shit."

Smiling now at Henry, she knew he was livid and getting more so every second that went by. His face was red with rage, his eyes fixed on her. She could almost feel the raging contempt coming through the partition, and yet still with the perplexity showing on his face as to why she'd done this to him. Eventually he seemed to regain some composure.

"Who is Thomas's and Luna's father?" Henry shouted at the top of his voice.

"Reece."

"What the fuck! Not that fucking blackmailing bastard."

"What, you think I didn't find out?" Emma felt in total control as she continued to torment him. "Oh yes. Reece fucked me every chance he could. Even across your desk at work once and in your bed several times. When you were away, he'd stayed over often. I'm surprised you didn't find out one day. He told me he passed you outside just a hundred yards down the road. I know he only wanted me because I was your wife and because of the way you treated him, the fact he could fuck your wife was revenge for him too. Oh, just so you know, he was a good fuck, so big and thick, and I enjoyed every minute of him inside me in case you were wondering."

"Trouble is, I found out that he was fucking everything in a skirt who opened her legs. That including that bitch Caroline. She knew Reece was fucking me as well, yet she continued to see him. What a fucking friend she turned out to be, nothing but a slut. Poor old Charles, I thought, being made to watch as she fucked my Reece. I'd got pregnant by him before I realised what he was up to. Now that caused me a problem. I mean, I couldn't have everyone knowing and laughing at me, now could I? Ha-ha, here comes the stupid Emma who got knocked up by Reece, the catholic slut. You know the sort of thing, women can be so cruel and judgemental, can't they?" She smiled with contempt at Henry.

"Anyway, it was then I decided that they both had to go. So when the party was announced, I knew Caroline would plan something special for Charles that night. Imagine my delight when she informed me that she was pregnant too, and she was going to tell Charles that night as a birthday gift. Everyone knew of Charles' predicament, you know, the ball and sperm thing. So, I asked her who was the actual father. I'd already guessed, though, and wasn't surprised when she told me the father was Reece. For some reason, she seemed to trust me. Stupid bitch.

"Then she told me she'd also caught him balls deep in Vicky, in the offices late one evening, but that seemed okay by her. She'd never leave Charles, and she'd just used him to get her pregnant. Reece promised me he'd support me and wanted the baby when I told him he was going to be a daddy, he seemed happy and said we could be a nice respectable family, all living together. We even planned how to tell you before leaving to start a new life in a warm and sunny country. What a fucking arsehole he turned out to be, another fucking useless man couldn't keep his cock in his pants. You know I caught him fucking Candice at the party! The black whore, she's married with kids for Christ's sake. I nearly told her husband, but thought better of it, her poor husband and kids stopped me."

Emma was now looking and talking completely unstable. Her voice was sarcastic, yet childish as she spoke, making Henry feel every bit of her wrath and retribution.

"The plan was to kill Caroline and get Reece framed for the murder, which wouldn't have been difficult, as he had a motive, what with her being pregnant and all that. You are keeping up with this?"

Henry had sat motionless throughout since he last spoke. He wondered what had happened to the sweet, innocent girl he'd married a few years before. Here she was telling how she planned to murder not only his best friend but also his worst adversary, the guy he'd abused years before.

"So, the party's nearly over, you're pissed as usual, so I got us dropped off at home. I asked the driver to take you upstairs and help me put you in bed, then he could go back to the party. I told him I was desperate for a pee and was going to wet myself if I didn't go right then, so left him to it,"

He left quickly, and gave him a nice big tip for driving us home, just so he'd remember if the police came knocking. I gave him time to get back to Caroline's before I called an Uber from your phone to collect me from the end of the road; told them I'd been with a friend and needed to get back home. I managed to give you a couple of sleeping tablets, which wasn't as difficult as I thought you didn't even flinch. The clothes you were wearing, I put into a backpack. I slipped into a black all-in-one outfit I'd bought for yoga, and then opened the safe to get the gun. Reece did have his uses. I persuaded him to open it for me after he'd been drinking, said I wanted to make sure you hadn't got money stashed away in offshore banks or bonds. Imagine my surprise to find a gun! It couldn't have been more convenient. So, anyway, I got an Uber and got him to drop me about half a mile down the road, couldn't take the risk of being too close to the house. Then having to jog down the road, what do I see but the Harley going past me like a clap of thunder. So now I'm thinking Charles has gone out, and I thought about turning back, but decided that wasn't what I wanted, and anyway Charles was drunk and wouldn't be able to ride too far.

"I crept round to the side door of the garage I'd unlocked it earlier when I'd gone for a piss. I also moved the CCTV camera ever so slightly there, just enough to allow me to get to the stairs without being seen. I got into your shoes and shirt so any DNA would be yours and not mine, and I put on Caroline's first set of leathers, the ones that went missing were her new ones. I must admit they smelt good, that leather was amazing, got me quite aroused when they were fully on. I was really lucky that the lift was on the ground floor, I didn't want the lights alerting them in the bedroom did I. The lift has a default setting of returning to the basement and locking itself until the right entrance code is entered, a security feature that I'd programmed into it, good yeah? The override was a 4 digit code. Shame the old guy who set that up died with a heart attack not long afterwards. I really did like him, he was always polite and respectful to me. Still, no witnesses meant I wasn't going to be questioned, not as a suspect. Get my drift?

"Anyway, creeping upstairs quietly. As I got nearer to the bedroom, I could hear those two fucking and moaning. Caroline was never a quiet girl, especially with a cock being thrust into her. I'd heard her a couple of times when I went to her house early for meetings. Emma, was now talking as though drifting into her own seedy world, starring into open space.

"I heard her telling Charles about her being pregnant and that she was pleased he would be thought as the baby's father. I naturally assumed that she was fucking her husband on his birthday, as most wives should do. But no. It wasn't until pulling the trigger I fully realised it wasn't. It was Reece.

I knew I'd have an opportunity to do what I needed to do, but I'd not worked out how. But when she'd finished riding him and they started kissing, I knew that was my opportunity. I'd been watching them for a couple of minutes, just fucking. So putting the gun right up behind the fucking bitch's head and just pulled the trigger. No hesitation, no remorse, just sheer release and pleasure.

"What a relief it was when I saw the bullet had gone through her, and Reece as well. He took longer to die, but not by much. I did wonder if I'd have to shoot him again, but I thought that would just complicate things, so I didn't. I looked at them both, waited until I knew the life had gone out of them. The blood seeped onto the silk bed sheets and running down, dripping onto the carpet. I watched for a while, their bodies lying there motionless, two faceless bodies entangled together. Quite poetic justice, I thought."

Emma drew breath with a big inhale and a long exhale of air. "Shame Reece had to die. Thought he could have been a wonderful Dad to his children, but he was now lying under that slut. And even though I loved him, he got what he deserved in the end. I thought that I'd better take something from there to use as backup evidence against you. So I looked around, found her dirty, soiled thong and made sure they were the ones she'd been wearing, so stuffed them into my pocket.

"When I got home, you were still out for the count, snoring away, so I showered in the spare room, threw away my underwear, just in case it had any of that fucking idiot's DNA on them. I put the shoes back in the cupboard where they were in before." That was it really, job done. Bye, bye slut and dickhead.

"How did the police suspect you? Well, that wasn't easy until they found Charles dead. I had to rethink everything a bit. You see, all the time Charles was missing he was the prime suspect. Jealous hubby murders wife and lover. You know the sort of thing. But then he turned up as he did, real shame. I had to work out a new backup plan. Those trainers were yours, I was really glad I kept them, as well as the socks, so I returned one day before the police had finished for the second time around, and planted a few fibres from the socks and some of your DNA, just enough evidence for them to want to question you again and search our house. I still had the red thong stashed away, so I got some of your sperm after I let you fuck me and put it in the gusset, simple really. Then I put them with the gun, along with a couple of spare bullets for good measure. The rest, well, the rest just fell into place. I knew you went up to her room that night. You went through her underwear. But what also got me was that you relieved yourself, while sitting on her bed with a pair of her soiled pants didn't you?"

"I think you don't really need to know any more, do you?," Emma got up from her seat, pushing the chair back as she did so, rubbing her stomach as she adjusted the dress which had ridden up a bit. Emma smirked as she turned and started to walk away. She turned round just as she got to the children, "Oh, don't bother talking to the police again, they're not going to entertain anything you say. I've seen to that." she said, smiling.

"Come on, kids, we need to go now, sweethearts." She picked up Luna and held Thomas's hand. They walked out the room into the corridor and out to the carpark. Jason had already gone back to the car but came to meet her as he saw her approaching, giving her a big hug.

"You okay?" Jason asked as he put his arm round her.
"Yes, that's me done. Let's go live our lives. The dogs will be okay, won't they?"

"Yes, they're with the dog walker at the moment, we'll get them passports and send for them very soon," Jason replied.

Emma smiled as Jason opened the car door to put the kids in. Driving away into the distance and their future life.

Mac will investigate the death of Mick Jones and the other corpses that are turning up regularly in the River Thames. Find out more in the sequel to Triangle

Hoped you enjoyed this and want to carry on the story with

Trophies.

Emma and Jason's journey will continue in:-

The Princess and The Panther.

Any person named within this novel is factious and not representing anyone in real life.

I would very much appreciate any reviews you wish to submit.